Egg Drop Homicide

MICHELLE BUSBY

Patent Print Books
Panama City Beach, Florida

EGG HIDE HOMICIDE

Published by PATENT PRINT BOOKS
www.patentprintbooks.com
PATENT PRINT BOOKS and the fingerprint colophon are registered trademarks of PATENT PRINT BOOKS

First Edition: 2021
Printed in the United States of America

ISBN 978-0-578-83077-3
Library of Congress Control Number: 2020925886

10   9   8   7   6   5   4   3   2   1

Dedicated to my children,
Who were the most difficult mysteries
I ever tried to solve.

In Appreciation

I want to express my appreciation for those who had a part in the inspiration and completion of this book: my publisher, my editor, my proofreaders, my fellow sleuths, my friends, and especially my family.

Introduction

Peppermint Patty: "These eggs have to be boiled. You boil them, then I'll show you how to paint them."

Marcie: "What do we do with the Easter eggs now that we have them, sir?"

Peppermint Patty: "We eat them. We put a little salt on them, and we eat them."

Marcie: (eating her egg with the shell still on) "Tastes terrible, sir!"

~ Charles Schultz,
It's the Easter Beagle, Charlie Brown!

HAVE YOU EVER WONDERED why we hide and hunt Easter eggs and get Easter baskets from the Easter Bunny?

Contrary to popular opinion, the most important Christian "holiday" is not Christmas, but Easter. It's the time in which to celebrate the resurrection of Jesus Christ.

But how did eggs and bunnies and baskets come to be entangled in a religious celebration?

In old English and Germanic cultures, the origin of the word "Easter" is thought to reference the pagan fertility goddess of Spring named *Eostre*. Among Spanish and French Basques, the word is derived from the Greek and Latin *Pascha* or *Pasch*, and the Hebrew *Pesach*, which mean Passover.

The practice of hard-boiling eggs and painting

them came about long before Christianity. Around the world, many cultures have considered the egg as a symbol of fertility, new life, rebirth, and the completion of the circle of life. There are many legends and customs that speak to these beliefs.

On the Vernal Equinox, ancient Persians commemorated *Nowrooz*—the first day of Spring—by painting eggs and sharing them. During Passover, Jews place a hard-boiled egg among the items on their ceremonial *Seder* plate and perform a ritual of praise and thanksgiving by eating the egg dipped in salt water to symbolize the tears of the Israelites in bondage.

One Eastern Orthodox legend claims that Mary Magdalene brought eggs to the crucifixion of Jesus. Blood from his wounds fell on the eggs, coloring them red. Another speaks of her bringing a basket of cooked eggs to share with the other women three days after the crucifixion. When the tomb was found empty, the eggs turned red. Yet another tells that Mary was holding an egg in her hand when she proclaimed of the resurrection. Emperor Tiberius Caesar announced, *"Christ has no more risen than that egg is red."* Immediately, the egg became scarlet.

In other Christian traditions, early Orthodox Catholic churches dyed eggs crimson to represent the blood of Christ that was shed on the cross. The eggs were blessed by the priest following the Passover vigil and given to the congregation to enjoy with specific correlations: the hard shell represented the sealed tomb; rolling the eggs on the ground represented the stone that was rolled away to allow the Savior to ascend; and cracking the shell was symbolic of the release of Jesus from the bonds of death.

During *Lent*, the 40-day period of reflection observed to replicate Christ's sacrifice and journey into the desert to begin his ministry, many religious leaders forbade the consumption of eggs, as well as meat and milk. Any eggs laid during that Holy Week were set aside and decorated with vegetable dyes and ribbons to be given to the children as special treats on Easter when the families feasted on meat, milk, and eggs.

The Spring Equinox was celebrated by European pagans as the time in which the sun god returned to drive away winter. According to legend, the fertility goddess *Eostre* found a little bird frozen almost to death. In pity, she turned the bird into a rabbit so its fur could keep it warm. Though it was a mammal, it continued to lay eggs like a bird and decorated the eggs to show its thanks to the goddess for her mercy. It is the first appearance of the Easter bunny.

In the 1700s, German immigrants brought their annual tradition of the egg-laying rabbit called *Osterhase* (*Eostre's* hare) to America, and the Easter Bunny rapidly grew in popularity. Because rabbits have large litters of kittens (that's what baby bunnies are called) in the spring, they were seen as symbols of new life. Legends surfaced that the Easter Bunny laid and hid its decorated eggs in the fields and grass. To lure the bunny to their houses to lay its colored eggs, children fashioned nests and placed them on the front doorstep. Easter baskets grew out of this *Osterhase* tradition.

To bring the legends in line with religious beliefs, people declared that the Easter Bunny represented the renewal of life—much like the resurrection of Jesus—and the pagan customs were assimilated into religious traditions throughout the world.

What's all that have to do with tea and potions? According to Tommie Watson, there's no better excuse for a Sunday afternoon Easter tea!

~ *Michelle Busby*

Chapter One

"*... In the neatest sandiest hole of all, lived Benjamin's aunt and his cousins—Flopsy, Mopsy, Cotton-tail and Peter.*"

"*Old Mrs. Rabbit was a widow; She also sold herbs, and rosemary tea, and rabbit-tobacco (which is what we call lavender).*

"*I am sorry to say that Peter was not very well during the evening. His mother put him to bed, and made some chamomile tea; and she gave a dose of it to Peter!*

'*One table-spoonful to be taken at bedtime.*'

~ Beatrix Potter,
The Tale of Benjamin Bunny
The Tale of Peter Rabbit

THREE DAYS. WHAT CAN HAPPEN IN THREE DAYS?

On Easter Sunday, Christians around the world

celebrated the resurrection of Jesus after three days dead in the tomb. In Floribunda, Florida, when Mrs. Veranell Collins collapsed during the annual Easter Egg Hide and Charity Raffle, Thomasina "Tommie" Watson and Finbar Holmes took one look at her sightless eyes staring at the ceiling of the Confederate Memorial Park Gazebo and knew: Veranell Collins would not rise from the dead.

What can happen in three days? Homicide.

Chapter Two

THOMASINA "TOMMIE" WATSON unsuccessfully tried to rest with her feet up on the chaise lounge in her small living room, gazing into her oversized mug as though she could read her future in the tea leaves. There were no prophetic messages in her *Blues Reme-Tea*, however; she always carefully strained her herbs after steeping. *What customer wants to take a sip of a delicious brewed herbal tea blend and end up spitting out a mouthful of dregs?* she mused.

Nonetheless, Tommie wished at that moment she believed in tasseomancy, just for the sake of being able to know what was going to happen. Had she been gifted with the ability to divine tea leaves, maybe she would have understood how to avoid ending up in her current predicament—sitting home alone in the middle of the day with no business at her shop, Watson's Reme-Teas.

The dreadful events of Easter Sunday had given way to what she dubbed "Morbid Monday." The front door of her herbal teas and natural potions store was mercifully uncrossed with yellow police tape denoting a crime scene, but her business was shut down nonetheless, pending an investigation and further testing of her snacks and herbal tea blends ... again!

She sniffled—the runny nose having nothing to do with the temperature of the tea—and took a tentative sip as her mind wandered to a day just six weeks earlier when her shop was closed for several days. Ms. Coral Beadwell, a regular patron, had been poisoned with a combination of deadly pharmaceuticals that tainted her favorite special teacup. Tommie and her products were cleared, but she still experienced PTSD-like symptoms from the memory of seeing Coral's cherry-red face as she took a nose-dive onto the floor and died. Tommie had tried CPR, but her efforts had been in vain.

Tommie Watson had been the prime suspect for a while, and her shop suffered a devastating setback, due to gossip around the town of Floribunda. She could vividly imagine their raised eyebrows and hushed whispers. Fortunately, her faithful friends and customers continued to patronize her shop, and business had taken a decided upswing ... that is, until yesterday's incident. She sighed, fighting more tears.

Setting her steaming teacup on the end table, Tommie dropped her right foot down to the smooth, cool floor and pushed, leveraging herself farther back on the cushions of her chaise. She leaned against the nubby grey fabric and rested her cheek against the plush backrest, smelling the new upholstery. She adjusted the position of her left leg on the overstuffed extension, flexing her toes to ease the discomfort of the swelling in her ankle.

"Thanks a lot, Hurricane Adam," she muttered as she recollected that day, six months earlier in October 2018, when Hurricane Adam had come ashore as a monstrous category five storm and descended directly on Bay City, catastrophically destroying downtown and many of the outlying inland areas before it moved off to the northeast. Tommie's beloved cottage in Beavercreek woods had survived the storm's seven-hour wrath, but her herbal remedies workshop had not been so fortunate. Indeed, there was no trace of it in the piles of wreckage in the vicinity.

Tommie remembered stepping out to survey the damage. All the surrounding trees had either blown over or snapped off, leaving the area desolate and broken, as though a massive bomb had exploded. She jerked, clearly recalling the gunshot-like cracking sounds as the towering pines had splintered and crashed to the ground.

The fenced-in enclosure which her small dogs Zed and Red so enjoyed had been mangled beyond repair, and Tommie had to venture outside to walk them on leashes several times a day, picking her way through the fallen limbs and loads of debris that littered the ground. Prior to one of these walks, Tommie had stepped out of her cottage and slipped, shattering her left ankle in the process. She winced at the sense memory of the searing pain and regarded the puckered six-inch red line that traced up the side of her leg.

Though the pins, screws, and metal plate had stabilized the fractured bones, the injury had been severe, and the ongoing recuperation continued to be long and arduous. Her doctor had warned her she may never regain the full flexibility of the ankle, due to her age (64), her weight (200 pounds), and the severity of the damage to her nerves. He was right. She glanced at the teal-colored aluminum cane leaning against the end table and sighed.

In the subsequent months since the accident, she had gone from a wheelchair to a frame walker to hobbling around with a heavy immobilizing boot to finally being able to walk with a cane, but she would never again run or jump. The swelling always returned with a vengeance when she stood or walked too long and even if she sat with her feet flat on the floor, so she kept her leg elevated as much as possible. Thankful she had the overstuffed loveseat and chaise on which to recline, she stroked the soft upholstery and turned her head toward the dining room wall, smiling as though it were a window into the unit next door.

The new furniture had been graciously gifted by her neighbor and current landlord, Finbar Holmes, the Irishman from Dublin who had bought the duplex and who now inhabited the B-unit. Upon their first meeting when he arrived in February, he had consented to lease the A-unit to her for the outrageous rental fee of $10 a month. The two of them had grown to be great friends since that day.

Though they were close enough in age (he was 71), they were most definitely not a romantic duo. Finbar's wife Mary had succumbed to cancer years earlier, and he was yet faithful to her, preferring to remain a widower in honor of her memory. Tommie, on the other hand, was three times divorced and had resolved to stay a divorcee after the dismal outcomes of her marriages. She was content to live a single life in Floribunda and work as a certified herbalist.

Though on the surface they seemed different as day and night, the two of them shared some common interests, including independence, plain speaking, solving mysteries, and total devotion to their pet dogs. Their personal quirks and lifestyles seemed to complement one another well.

Tommie blew on her hot tea as her mind's eye surveyed the living spaces on both sides of the duplex. She could clearly visualize them without having to move from her spot on the chaise.

Finbar himself had redecorated the old, outdated building to make each unit cozy and livable. While his space featured warm honey-blond oak paneling throughout with brown furnishings, he had redone her side to match her eclectic taste, with soft grey paint, pops of bright red and cool aqua, wood plank flooring, and industrial chic fixtures. He bought the comfortable living room seating to match and in consideration for her mobility issues. By far, the most appreciated of the refurbishments were the locking doggie doors in the kitchen and bedroom which led out to the privacy fenced backyard. Through these portals, Zed and Red could spend the day with their new best friend Sherlock, Finbar's Jack Russell terrier.

Tommie took a sip of her herbal blend tea and stared into the reddish-brown liquid. Her shop came to mind immediately, and she slowly shook her head.

Finbar also owned the building where she conducted her herbal remedies business. It housed two adjoining spaces: the right half was Watson's Reme-Teas; the left half was named Caife Caife Holmes, Irish Gaelic for Holmes Coffee Café. Formerly a thriving morning establishment called Brewster's Coffee Shoppe, the space was now the site of Holmes's afternoon Irish coffee bar during the week, and his intimate 20-seat restaurant on Fridays and Saturdays where Chef Finbar Holmes himself delivered a cooking demonstration, followed by dinner for the reservations-only guests. Tommie worked with him as his assistant/waitress/table busser/dishwasher.

Tommie set her empty cup on the end table and looked fondly at a picture in a lacquered teal frame—two smiling women in their 40s and a younger man, all three with dark hair and black eyes. A smaller frame held the picture of a pale boy with dull green eyes ringed by dark shadows. Tommie frowned and looked back at the first picture. Her two married daughters now lived about an hour's drive away in Tallahassee. Her 33-year-old son, Kevin, lived a bit farther in Sugar Sand Beach, which had been mercifully unharmed by the hurricane. She and Kevin usually got together each Sunday for a movie, followed by lunch at the beachside restaurant he managed.

Often, they looked in on Barry Brewster, the troubled young man in the second photo, who was a resident in a mental health rehabilitation facility on the beach. She had grown to care for Barry, despite the actions of his unhinged mother, who had killed two people in Floribunda. Had Tommie and Finbar not uncovered Sarah Beth Brewster's misdeeds, Tommie herself would have been the third victim. She wiped away more tears.

Now, another suspicious death had occurred, and Tommie was once again a suspect. Earlier that morning, she had officially been interrogated by her unofficial boyfriend, newly promoted Detective Earl Petry. Tommie shifted her position on the chaise and closed her eyes, bringing to mind their recent conversation in her shop. She frowned. It had not gone so well.

*　*　*

"Tommie, how is it you're involved again in a potential murder investigation? Darlin', I swear you're like a death magnet," Earl had said, running his hand through his short mostly salt and some pepper hair.

Tommie stared unblinking into the depths of his steely blue-grey eyes.

"Oh, I get it. Somebody drops dead, look for Tommie Watson. Is that it?" she said.

"You know that's not what I mean, Tommie."

"Earl, you were there, too. We were *both* in the

gazebo. And so were Finbar, Father Duncan, Amos Mosby, Levi Muller, and Aubrey Rush. We were *all* standing there when she died."

"Yes, but whatever happened to Veranell Collins probably happened *before* we were gathered there to give out the prizes. You know that. If she had just collapsed from a heart attack or an illness, we wouldn't be having this conversation at all."

"Interrogation, you mean." Her espresso eyes narrowed to slits.

"No, no. I'm calling it an interview." Earl leaned back and chose his words carefully. Tommie was the most interesting woman he had ever been involved with, but he had learned she was a feisty gal with a hair-trigger temper. She kept Earl on his toes, that was for sure. As an added precaution, he called out orders to the forensic technicians dusting surfaces and bagging herbal ingredients.

"Hey! Be careful with that, Chuck. No need to get powder everywhere. Phil, only take as much sample material as Sanderson needs for testing. And please, don't leave those refrigerator doors open. Y'all know better than that. Be professional. This ain't some redneck dive, you know. It's a respectable establishment."

Tommie smiled, despite the intrusion into her personal workspace, as she took in the full measure of the man sitting before her. Earl was quite a catch, and there were plenty of females interested in him.

He was a tall, burly, twice-divorced man, just

slightly past the prime of his life at 59 and enjoying bachelorhood. His handsome face was angular and chiseled, with a snowy white manicured beard that set off his square jaw. His khaki shirt was snug across muscled biceps, and a few white hairs curled above the top button at his neck, hinting at the firm, barreled chest beneath.

Tommie's breath caught, and she continued to be amazed she was the one with whom he chose to spend his time. They had been a "thing" now for eight weeks, going out every Saturday night in March until he passed the detective's exam. The Floribunda Police Department changed him to a weekend shift beginning in April, and since then, he took her out every Wednesday night, with frequent drop-ins at her shop during the week.

"I apologize, Earl," she said with a shrug. "You understand how I am about my stuff."

"I certainly do, darlin'. Let's just get some facts collected, OK? I know you've thought about it, and I have no doubt you and Holmes will put your devious little heads together and do your own investigation, no matter how strenuously I object. Right?"

"Well … yeah, that's right." She hated to admit it.

"All right, then. Think, now."

How can I think when you're so close and looking so delicious? she thought. "All right," she said instead.

"What do you remember about everything that happened yesterday? Start at the beginning of the day when you first got to the shop. Be thorough, Tommie."

"Let me see. I got here about 8:00 yesterday morning. I unloaded the food I prepared for the Easter Sunday brunch and put the cold things in the big cooler in the storeroom." She looked toward the direction of the large supply storage room by the back door.

"Tell me what food you brought."

"You were there, Earl. You ate the food."

"Tommie, I realize that. I need to know for the record and so Phil can check things off his samples list."

"Oh. OK. Here's the menu and the ingredients you asked me to write down." She held out a paper and paused, but Earl kept his steely gaze on her. "All right, I'll go ahead and say it out loud." She flashed a quick grin at Phil, who was standing behind Earl holding a clipboard. Earl passed him the list in a manilla folder.

"Tommie?" Earl raised his eyebrows and cocked his head to the side waiting for her to continue.

"All right. The first thing in the cooler was *Mr. MacGregor's Garden Veggie Salad.* It was an assortment of fresh raw vegetables in individual zipper lock bags." She consulted her copy of the list. "I had bib lettuce, yellow squash, celery, cucumbers, carrots, zucchini, French beans, radishes, and cherry tomatoes. *Flopsy's Favorite Dressings* were in plastic containers in the cooler. I'd fixed one creamy dressing, which was made with yogurt, white vinegar, mustard, and sugar. I had a honey mustard dressing made with apple cider vinegar, mustard, olive oil, honey, lemon juice, salt, and pepper. I also made a strawberry vinaigrette dressing with fresh strawberries, red wine vinegar, olive oil, honey, salt, and pepper. Got all that?"

"Got 'em, Ms. Watson. Go on to the next," Phil said with an encouraging wink.

"*Mother Josephine's Jam,* in a glass jar, was put in there toward the back. It was made with fresh blackberries, cane sugar, lemon juice, and lemon zest."

"Check. Next?"

"*Peter Rabbit's Eggstra Devilish Eggs.* I used fresh eggs from the farmer's market. They were boiled, halved, and piped with three different fillings. The ingredients I used were mayonnaise, yogurt, mustard, white vinegar, blue cheese, cheddar cheese, chicken, ham, cream cheese, sour cream, chickpeas, olive oil, and sweet pickle juice. All separately, of course. And they were garnished with smoked paprika, walnuts, chives, celery, mustard, parsley, dill, pimentos, and sesame seeds."

"OK. Got all of those checked. Were these things kept cold in the cooler prior to the brunch, Ms. Watson?"

"Yes, Phil, the whole time."

While Tommie listed the ingredients for Phil, Earl moved his muscular thigh against hers for encouragement. She acknowledged with a slight nudge of her own.

"What about those fancy streaky colored eggs, Ms. Watson?" Phil asked.

"Oh, yeah. They were in the cooler, too. I call them *Mopsy's Marble Tea Eggs.* I boiled and dyed the fresh eggs with teas and other natural ingredients."

"I'm ready for that list, please."

Tommie sighed and recited the ingredients, which included eight types of teas, along with herbs and spices used to dye the eggs different colors. When she finished, she gave him the ingredients used in her *Cotton-tail's Criss-Cross Buns*, which were also served at the brunch. The entire meal corresponded to the Beatrix Potter's *Peter Rabbit* theme she had arranged in her two display windows.

"Why so many kinds of dressings and deviled egg fillings, Tommie?" Earl asked, knowing the answer, but needing her to confirm the reason.

"Oh, I did that because there are people who can't tolerate some ingredients. I made plenty of substitute choices for them," she said.

"Can you elaborate?" Earl prompted with a nod.

"Sure. Veranell Collins had a number of issues, like lactose intolerance, IBS, and celiac disease, and she couldn't eat the dressing or the deviled eggs made with whole milk yogurt, so I made some with hummus and some with minced meats. She couldn't digest the buns made with regular flour, so I made half of them with almond flour and used minimal butter. All the marbled eggs were fine for her except the ones made with black or green tea because of the caffeine. The Alvarez brothers are Mormon, so they could only eat the eggs dyed with herbal red Rooibos tea. Bettina Taylor has diverticulitis, so I strained the seeds from the berries in the jam and the vinaigrette dressing. I also avoided peanuts because Elly James can't eat them. Several of the other luncheon guests are allergic to shellfish … Father Duncan, Melinda Layton, Eva Edgerton, and me included … so no shrimp or crab or lobster."

"I'm impressed, Ms. Watson," Phil said. "You really seem to know your stuff."

"It's my business to know, Phil. Being an herbalist is no different from being a doctor in many ways, except I don't have a medical license, and I use herbs and natural ingredients to promote wellness instead of prescribing pharmaceuticals."

Earl nodded and gently laid his large hand on her knee, impressed with her extensive knowledge of herbs and remedies, her sensitivity to her customers' needs, and her ability to stand up under pressure.

"Is that all you need, Phil?" she asked.

"Um, I need the tea blend ingredients," Phil said, consulting his list. "That'd be *Easter Sunrise, Bouncing Bunny Blend, Passover Peppermint Patchouli,* and the one you gave Mrs. Collins called *Tender Tummy.*"

"Oh, forgot about those. My cousin Sanderson shouldn't find anything harmful in them. My customers and I have been drinking the first three for weeks without issue. I've written them all down, along with their warnings and contraindications for existing conditions and medicinal interactions. Do you really need me to recite them?"

"No, Ma'am. I don't guess so. Like you said, the County Coroner will test them. I think that's enough." Phil closed his folder and smiled. "Anything else, Earl?"

"Nope, that should do it. Thanks, Phil. So, darlin', how about you and me getting some fresh air for a few minutes? Feel like walking over to the gazebo?" Earl rose to his feet and extended his hand to help her from the chair.

"Great idea. I could use a break." She grabbed a couple of bottled waters from the small cooler near the door on her way out. "Besides, I think sitting out there where Veranell collapsed might help bring some of the details into focus."

"My thoughts exactly." Earl put his strong hand beneath her elbow and escorted her out the door for more "conversation."

Chapter Three

FINBAR HOLMES reclined against the cushions on the wrought iron lounge chair in the backyard and listened to the sounds of Floribunda around him. He was stripped to the waist and wore only short jean pants. Already, his slight, wiry body was deeply tanned from daily sunbathing, and a rosy flush shone on his head beneath his thinning, light brown hair and along the tops of his large, half-moon shaped ears. In his hand he gripped a 14.9-ounce can of Guinness beer, from which he took several deep swigs. This activity (or lack of activity) was what had prompted Finbar to buy the duplex and settle in America. He was a sun worshipper, the backyard was his temple, and Guinness was his sacrament, as evidenced by the two empty cans on the ground by his side.

"Ah, Dublin," he said, raising his beer in a toast. "If yer weather had been like this, I'd never have left ye. But, sure, with the children grown and m'sweet Mary up in Heaven, 'tis a happier place I'm living now. Dear auld Ireland, they call you 'the Emerald Isle' for yer lush swaths of emerald green fields. But I know yer lovely verdant color occurs because the sun is a fickle creature who only appears for short periods of time betwixt long episodes of rain. She teases with her presence and then disappears to make way for clouds and gloom and precipitation. Here's to Florida." He took a deep swig.

Beautiful as Ireland was, Holmes made a habit of spending month-long holidays throughout the year in places like Portugal, Spain, and the Canary Islands so he could bask in the warmth and perfect his perpetual tan. A septuagenarian pensioner, with his children living their own lives and his wife long in the grave, he had decided to chase the sun and take up residence in America. He scoured internet websites until he happened upon a duplex on Camelia Street in a hamlet with the charming name of Floribunda in which all the streets were named after flowering flora. He bought it, sight unseen, and wired cash to the agent at Floral Real Estate. Several weeks later, he arrived at the airport, took an Uber to the realtor's office, collected his keys, and became a Floridian.

Holmes's first order of business had been to completely redecorate his unit to make it more like his townhouse in Dublin. Over the course of a week, and without the knowledge of the neighboring unit's occupant, he had transformed the shabby interior into a cozy recreation of home. He had worked only when the woman was away, and he had rested when her two small dogs announced she was home. He lay back and admired the tall wooden privacy fence he had constructed that enclosed the back yard, kept the dogs safe, and allowed him to sunbathe seminude.

He picked up his watch and checked the time.

"Yer Missus should be coming home soon. 'Tis nearly time for lunch," he said to Zed and Red, who were sunning themselves with Sherlock. Finbar thought about his first meeting with Thomasina Watson.

He had wondered at the time what to do about the other occupant. Holmes had originally intended to utilize the entire duplex for himself and his canine companion. He debated on the best way to inform the lady who lived next door. In the end, he elected to let the animals drive his decision. He reached down and patted the little Jack Russel Terrier's head.

"What d'you think of our home here, Sherlock? I think you chose yer neighbors well, lad," he said.

The dog looked into his master's face as though he understood every word the man said, which was usually considerable. Having no one else with which to converse, Sherlock was often Holmes's sounding board.

"'Tis my opinion that pets—especially pet dogs—are honest and generally without connivance. You blindly love and are loyal to yer owners, provided they treat ye kindly and humanely. I can tell the character of the owner from the behavior of the pooch. D'you know?"

Sherlock wagged his two-inch tail rapidly. Red, thinking he was part of the conversation, wagged as well. Zed lay snoring in the grass.

"Sure, 'tis true," Finbar told the dogs. "Violent people create aggressive canines, whilst caring people foster warm and devoted pups, like you lads. And d'you realize personal habits rub off on the animals living within the domicile? Shaggy, unkempt animals reflect a lack of care in the home. Growling, yipping, or whimpering animals are unhappy with their surroundings. Now, before ye take offense, I'm not saying happy pups don't bark a warning when the post is delivered or the doorbell rings or when they hear strange noises from the other side of the wall. But we both know the difference, don't we, lads?"

When Thomasina Watson had opened her back door on that sunny day in February, her two dogs bounded outside on their leashes and finally made the acquaintance of the strange dog they had been smelling for a week. A merry-go-round ensued as the three fellows—Boston Terrier, Portuguese *Podengo Pequeño,* and Jack Russel Terrier—circled nose to butt and greeted one another. Thomasina was greeted by the man who had bought her duplex and might possibly evict her. He was dressed then exactly as he was today.

"Halloo! How're ye doin', Missus?" he had called. "I'm yer neighbor. 'Tis nice to meet you at last."

"I'm ... I'm Thomasina Watson, but people call me Tommie. Please, don't evict me," she had blurted.

Noticing the congenial behavior of the pooches and the obvious care taken by their mistress, Finbar Holmes had made his decision on the spot.

"I'll not do it, Missus. I'll be glad to have ye here," he responded, much to her relief.

Thus, Finbar and Tommie had forged an immediate friendship with one another. Over the course of just a few weeks, they developed a relationship that morphed into a professional partnership, as well. Their similar interests in dogs, puzzles, and mysteries contributed to their close personal bond, which was cemented in their love of food.

Finbar raised his can and sat up. "Here's to a retired Food Safety Authority of Ireland Inspector turned chef and a retired classroom teacher turned certified herbalist. Cheers to Holmes and Watson, Investigators," he said, draining the last of the ale.

Chapter Four

ON THE MONDAY after Easter, at the very same time Tommie sat outside relating her account of the Easter Sunday events to Earl Petry, Finbar sat in his garden and reflected on what had occurred the same day when a woman named Veranell Collins dropped dead in the Confederate Memorial Park Gazebo during the annual Easter Egg Hide and Charity Raffle. He and Tommie remembered the events of the day almost identically.

Every year on Easter Sunday, St. Mary's Catholic Church sponsored the Easter Egg Hide and Charity Raffle. The activities took place in three locations around the center of town.

The Floribunda Garden Club was the site of the 2:00 p.m. egg hide and hunt. It was a beautiful and safe place in which to conceal the 500 candy- and toy-filled

plastic eggs for the children to find. The grounds featured
a well-manicured Bermuda grass lawn with flowering
shrubs and a wrought iron fence making a squared-off
perimeter around the building and the central seating area
of red brick pavers. Scores of children would run here and
there within the fenced garden, squealing, and hunting the
brightly colored eggs to fill their baskets, while parents
meandered around talking and watching the melee.

The garden covered an entire city block and was
bordered on the four sides of the compass points with
oakleaf hydrangeas along Coreopsis Road, loropetalums
along Oleander Street, firebushes along Dogwood Drive,
and dwarf Walter's viburnums along Nandina Street.
Pineapple guava shrubs surrounded the building and the
paved seating area and were a fitting decoration to the
hunt because of their egg-shaped silver-colored leaves and
white and burgundy flowers which bloomed in the spring.
They also produced edible egg-shaped fruits from August
through October, making the gardens a popular school
field trip.

To the east of the Floribunda Garden Club was
the Farmer's Fresh Food Market. Oleander Street was
always blocked off for the day, allowing pedestrians
access to the covered pavilion for egg-in-spoon relay
races, as well as the open field to the south for the egg
toss and egg roll events which took place at 3:00 p.m.
Parents tended to hover around the various lemonade and
snack stands while their children tossed and rolled eggs

to their hearts' delights.

At 4:00 p.m., the crowds typically made their way to the Confederate Memorial Park and Gazebo, a grassy, triangular gathering area along the main street—right across from Watson's Reme-Teas and Caife Caife Holmes on Bottlebrush Boulevard—where small tables had been set up for local vendors to sell snacks and other items. Facing the grounds, directly inside the front of the gazebo, sat a long table on which the more expensive raffle items were displayed. Proceeds from the raffle were used to fund charities, organizations, and sometimes needy individuals throughout the Floral County communities.

The organizer of the Easter Egg Hide and Charity Raffle was a woman named Veranell Collins. She had taken charge of the event successfully for eight years. Sunday, April 21, 2019 marked the final event of her life.

On that day, Finbar recalled he and Tommie had manned the raffle ticket table on the lawn in front of the gazebo, along with some of the other prize donators. While Veranell called out the winning ticket numbers into the microphone of the portable karaoke machine set up in the gazebo, they checked the winners' stubs. There were four categories of prizes which had been graciously donated by different community businesses.

The first category of prizes had been $25 gift certificates for goods or services. There were six chances at the prizes, which were awarded by different members of the community, beginning with Detective Earl Petry representing the Floribunda Police Department. He gave out certificates for treats from I Scream for Ice Cream and Sweetie's Sweet Shoppe. Finbar Holmes of Caife Caife Holmes had given away two free dinners. Tommie Watson of Watson's Reme-Teas, Amos Mosby of The Barber Shop, Elly James of Elly's Jelly Jar, and Jo Clay of The Clay Pigeon, had each donated merchandise equivalent to $25 from their respective establishments to lucky ticket holders.

Veranell had devised clever ways to create suspense when announcing the winners. Six small beribboned baskets had been lined up on the table inside the gazebo for all to see. Nestled in each basket was a huge hollow ostrich egg, donated by Levi Muller of Muller's Animal Farm and hand dyed and decorated by Veranell. Beneath each egg was a raffle ticket. As she lifted the egg for the crowd to admire and called the number, the prize winner presented a matching stub at the raffle table to collect the gift certificate. The eggs and baskets themselves were usually offered up for sale (at $35 each) at the conclusion of the raffle.

The second group had featured prizes valued at $50. Those were white wicker hampers adorned with colored bows, and they were filled with actual merchandise. The winning ticket holders collected the prizes at the gazebo from the persons who had assembled the baskets.

One basket had contained an assortment of clothing, books, and toys from Kids' Klothes, Read-a-Lot Books, Five & Dime, and Toys 4 U. It was presented by Mrs. Melinda Layton, president of Trinity Episcopal Church Ladies' Charity Organization.

Another basket had held bingo cards, ink daubers, cookies, and hard candies. That prize was given by Father Horace Duncan of St. Mary's Catholic Church.

Game tokens and comic books from Galactic Games Arcade and Boox & Comix had filled a basket decorated with a bright yellow bow. It was donated by siblings Don Lareby, Ms. Susan Clay, and Ms. Elaine Frank and their best friend Henry Erving.

Paul and Louanne Weller of Weller's Wine & Spirits offered a basket which held two bottles of wine and 12 miniature bottles of top-shelf quality liquors. Theirs had been a much-desired prize, to say the least.

Leo and Santino Alvarez of Leo's Leather Goods and Santino's Shoe Shop had donated a basket with items from their stores, including a hand tooled calfskin belt, a suede-billed baseball cap, and a pair of leather sandals.

The final beribboned basket, filled with an assortment of baked goods and a gift certificate for two free meals with dessert, had been given by Jeanette and Sid Spock of The Lunch Pad, a popular space-themed restaurant on the main street.

The $75 third prizes were cleverly symbolized by an open-topped wire cage containing three fluffy, lop-eared, brown and white bunny rabbits with large colored bows around their necks. Tied up in each bow was a raffle ticket. Levi Muller, who owned the rabbits, had stood next to Veranell and lifted them out one at a time for the crowd to see (and ooh and ahh over) while she read the ticket on the bow. The three winners received either merchandise from Audrey's Antiques, clothing from Eva's Divas Boutique, or jewelry from Bettina's Baubles.

The final tickets called had been the five grand prizes. Each award was represented by a hand painted ceramic rabbit embracing a large cup. Inside each cup sat a hollow emu egg which had been gilded and covered with tiny imitation jewels. Beneath each egg rested the winning ticket, and the prize was a crisp $100 bill. Jo Clay had crafted and painted the rabbit holders in her ceramics store, and Veranell had decorated each of the emu eggs, which were donated by Levi Muller. Earl Petry had custody of the $500 during the event, but the person who donated the prize money traditionally remained anonymous.

Earl had taken his place behind Veranell in the gazebo, along with Finbar, Amos Mosby, Father Duncan, Aubrey Rush, and Santino Alvarez as representatives of the different ethnic, religious, or cultural factions within the community. Earl had handed each of them a $100 bill to present to the prize winners, and they held them aloft while the crowd buzzed excitedly.

Father Duncan had taken the microphone at that

time to commend the crowd for its generosity in support of the charity event that benefitted so many in the community. During his talk, Finbar had scrutinized the Collins woman. She was pale and sweaty, despite the coolness of the afternoon. She frequently wiped her mouth and nose with a handkerchief, and he realized she had become sicklier as the raffle prize presentations progressed. When the time came for the grand prize awards, he noticed her swaying, and she had to grip the table to stay on her feet.

Tommie had caught a look at Veranell's face and was visibly alarmed. She quickly grabbed a bottle of water from her portable cooler and ascended the steps to the gazebo. Finbar had watched her move up beside Veranell and whisper in her ear.

Veranell had tried to get something from her pocket, but her arm flopped back onto the table. Tommie had then reached into Veranell's side jacket pocket to remove a tiny, stoppered glass vial. She withdrew the stopper, poured the contents into the water bottle, and handed the bottle to the sick woman. After a couple of sips, Veranell had given Tommie a wan smile.

Tommie had then moved over to stand with Earl as Veranell took possession of the microphone and called the five lucky winners in succession. The excited winners had come forward to claim their figurines, jeweled emu eggs, and cash.

The next events had occurred rather quickly.

Veranell Collins took another swig of water and cleared her throat. She looked out over the crowd of people and tried to thank them, but the words never fully formed. She dropped the bottle, uttered a gurgling moan, and collapsed in a heap to the floor.

The crowd had been aghast, and some of the women closest to the gazebo had screamed. Earl rushed forward and, finding no breath sounds, had started to perform CPR.

Tommie and Finbar had stared at Veranell's open eyes. The whites were glazed, and the black pupils were enormous. They both knew what that meant.

Father Horace Duncan had knelt beside Veranell to hold her hand, and he had begun to murmur. The last words Finbar Holmes and Tommie Watson had heard were his.

"... and thus do I commend thee into the arms of our Lord of earth, our Lord Jesus Christ, preserver of all mercy and reality, and the Father Creator. We give Him glory as we give you into His arms in everlasting peace, to be prepared to return into the denser reality of God the Father, Creator of all. Amen, Amen, Amen."

Chapter Five

EARL PETRY had listened quietly as Tommie recounted her memory of the death of Veranell Collins, not daring to interrupt her to ask the questions which were uppermost in his mind. When she finally finished speaking, he leaned back against the bench inside the gazebo and stared at the domed ceiling. He draped his arm casually around her shoulders, and he felt her body tremble as she struggled to maintain her composure. She turned slightly to face him.

"And that's how I remember it, Earl. One minute she was talking, and the next minute she was dead."

"I know, I know."

"And I'm a suspect, right?"

"Afraid so, Tommie."

"Dangitall! Do you …?"

"Nope. Nope. Nope. I don't believe you had anything to do with it."

"How do you know what I was going to say?"

"Because … because I know you, I think. But I'm sorry to make that assumption. Were you about to tell me something else?"

"No. Yes. Why *am* I a suspect? It's not because of the food I served at the brunch, is it?"

Earl shook his head slowly and pressed his lips together. "You tell me, darlin'. Why do you think?"

"The herbal tonic. Right?"

"Yep. Unfortunately, there are lots of witnesses who saw you pouring something into that water bottle just before Mrs. Collins keeled over. This is a small town. Tongues are a'wagging."

"I *gave* you the preparation vial *immediately*. I wrote down everything that was in it and how it was made. Sandy'll tell you …"

"Sanderson will analyze it and get back to me, but officially, I need *you* to tell me. OK? You know how this works. What you say is on the record. Hell, I'm not really even supposed to be interviewing you because of our relationship, but we're shorthanded, and I'm the lead investigator. So, for the record, Tommie. What was in the medicine vial you poured into the water bottle?"

Tommie threw her head back in exasperation and closed her eyes as she took deep breaths to control herself.

"It was not medicine. It was *Tender Tummy Tonic*. I sell it in the shop quite often. It's made with the crushed seeds of dill, fennel, and coriander, mixed with dried and crushed lemon peel and organic sourwood honey. That's all. And they're macerated in vodka."

"It's not a tea, then?"

"No. It's a tincture. Different process. The ingredients are covered with the vodka, sealed in a glass jar, and left to soak in a sunny spot for about six weeks. Then, the strained liquid is poured into a glass medicine vial and stored in the refrigerator. It's good for about a year. Dosage is one teaspoon after meals or as needed."

"Why'd you pour the whole thing into her water if dosage is only one teaspoon?"

"She was in *acute abdominal distress*, Earl. I couldn't just take a spoon and stick it in her mouth out there in public! Pouring it into the full bottle of water ensured it was the correct dilution of the concentrated liquid. She could sip it and get the same relief in the correct dosage. Even if she had downed the entire bottle, it wouldn't have harmed her because the water diluted it. Dangitall, I *know* what I'm doing!"

"Easy, easy. I'm not disputing your expertise. Damnit, woman! I am not your enemy here. I am doing this for you, to protect your reputation and keep you safe from arrest or prosecution. Stop fighting me!"

Earl slid forward on the bench and rubbed his beard with both hands in frustration. The pleasant day had devolved into an impasse of wills, and all his attempts to remain professional and keep Tommie Watson calm had failed miserably. He heard her sniffle and turned slowly to face her.

Huge tears rolled down her face and spilled onto her pale pink scrub top, creating a polka dot effect across her chest. She turned her head away and stared resolutely at her closed shop across the street.

Earl gently wrapped her in his arms and let her cry it out on his shoulder. His shirt quickly became damp, but thankfully, Tommie kept a few folded paper towels in the pockets of her scrubs and was thoughtful enough to wipe her nose with those instead of his shirt. As he sat holding her, he heard her repeating soft words.

"Can't win for losing. Can't win for losing," she whispered between sobs.

You won't lose me, Tommy Watson, he longed to say, but the words did not leave his lips. His arms, however, remained tightly around her until her breathing returned to normal and all the fight had left her. It had been an emotional morning for them, and Earl was afraid there was much more unpleasantness in store. He hoped their relationship would survive the ordeal.

Chapter Six

FINBAR HOLMES knew when Tommie came home because Zed and Red raced back inside through the doggie door. He waited for her to come outside, but she stayed in the house. Normally, after waiting a reasonable length of time, he would knock once and walk on in with a shout of "Halloo," but he knew she had been questioned by Earl that morning. *Must've been a bad meeting with the police*, he decided, remaining in his chair, and giving her the space she needed to decompress.

After an hour, when neither she nor the dogs came out, Finbar slipped on his sandals and walked to the back window. He glanced into the kitchen. Finding it dark, and hearing no sounds of the television, he surmised she was nursing an herbal reme-tea and reclining on the loveseat.

He stood awkwardly at the window for a few moments until his stomach told him it was past midday, and then he turned, entered his own unit, and began to prepare lunch for the both of them. Sharing meals together had become customary for Finbar and Tommie, and he was usually the designated cook.

Half an hour later, Finbar wrote out a note, tied it to Sherlock's collar, and carried the small dog to the door.

"Go find Zed and Red, Sherlock. Ah, that's a good lad. Hurry now," he cooed.

Sherlock shot out the door and onto the porch on his short little legs, scrambled around, and then burst through Tommie's kitchen doggie door. Finbar returned to the stove and waited for his guests.

Tommie's dogs happily announced the arrival of their visitor. Sherlock hopped up on the chaise beside their mistress and wagged his stub of a tail. Tommie shook her head as she read the note attached to his collar: *Bangers & mash with onion gravy being served. Come now!*

"We have been summoned, boys. Let's not keep the chef waiting," she said with a half-hearted smirk. As though they understood, the canine pals took off. She heard the *slam, slam, slam* of three projectiles sailing through the dog flap and limped along behind them. Finbar was waiting at the open door of his unit with a smile.

"Halloo, Missus. It's about time ye made yer way over. I've lunch on the cooker and a suppa tea in the pot. Yer *Honey-Honey* is on the table, and the afghan is already on the sofa for afterwards."

"Bangers and mash with onion gravy, huh? I'm game, Finbar, and suddenly very hungry. Let's eat."

Taking her usual seat at the table, Tommie watched as her friend served up a plate of steaming mashed potatoes covered with a thick brown gravy which was teaming with sliced onions, alongside what appeared to be sausage links. He set the plate before her and dished himself up a serving. While he did so, Tommie poured herself a cup of Irish tea from a cozy-covered teapot and added two spoonfuls of the honeysuckle-infused honey blend. She poured a cup for Finbar, who took his with a dash of milk and no sweetener, due to his diabetes.

Finbar sat and raised his cup. "And here we go again, Thomasina. Another mystery to puzzle out. I know yer probably not up to it, but let's get some food in our bellies to fuel our crime-solving minds. Eh?"

Tommy raised her cup, her mouth downturned. "Yay," she said with no trace of enthusiasm.

"Ah, now lad. 'Tis not that bad." Finbar called everyone *lad*, both male and female. "You've lots of people behind you. 'Twas not like Ms. Beadwell who died in yer shop. This was in a very public place."

"True. But I'm still a suspect. Earl told me so."

"Bah. We'll get to the bottom of it directly. For now, let's eat. D'you know what yer eating?"

"Yep. I can guess this one pretty easily. Potatoes, onions, and sausage. Right?"

"Right. Bangers is pork sausage links, mash is spuds with butter and milk, and the gravy is made with onions and red wine. I likes the mash lumpy. Takes the gravy better. What d'you think?"

"Mmm. Delicious. Didn't realize I was so hungry until now. All right. No talking about death until we finish eating. Deal?"

"Deal," Finbar agreed. He used his knife to load up the back of his fork and stuffed the food into his mouth.

I'll never understand why Europeans don't use a fork and knife as they're intended, Tommy thought with amusement. Her own efforts to mimic the technique had been a disaster, so she continued to cut with her knife, change hands, and scoop with her fork.

Why can't Americans be civilised and use their cutlery properly? Finbar thought with a puzzled frown.

When the meal was finished, Finbar set the dishes in the sink to soak while he refilled the teapot. Tommie took up her place reclining on the sofa with her leg elevated on a crocheted afghan, and Finbar sat in a facing armchair. The dogs, having been allowed to feast on scraps of sausage and potatoes (though not the gravy because onions are not good for dogs), took their own places on the cool wood paneled floor and fell instantly to sleep.

"Shall we talk first or begin our outlines?" Finbar asked, patting two yellow legal pads on the end table.

"Let's talk. I'm a little too full to think clearly."

"All right, then, Missus." He crossed his legs and

sat patiently.

"They went through my shop today. It was better than last time. They were much more careful and only took small samples and left less fingerprint dust."

"Good. Officer ... I mean *Detective* Petry must have taken them to task for the mess they made before."

"He did. He did. It was still unnerving, though."

"Yes, I'm aware of how fastidious ye are with yer products and yer workspace, having had to help ye clean yer shop a couple of times already."

"Yep," she agreed. Finbar had helped her restore order to her shop once after Coral's death and again after Sarah Beth Brewster had tried to kill Tommie ... twice.

"Yer interview?"

"Interrogation. Yes, it was upsetting. Earl was sweet, but the fact remains that tons of people saw me put something in a water bottle that Veranell Collins drank from just before she collapsed and died. That's pretty compelling evidence of my guilt, no matter what Sanderson finds when he tests it. *You* know, and *I* know, and even *Earl* knows I didn't poison that woman, but other people believe what they want, and it looks like I killed her."

"Thomasina, did ye mention to Earl that Mrs. Collins was unwell before the Easter event? She was ill even during the luncheon yesterday."

"I did tell him. The problem is, she had been having stomach issues for several days. She came in on Monday and got the *Tender Tummy Tonic* from me. That makes it look like I could have been systematically poisoning her for a week."

"She ate at my café a weekend ago, but she cancelled for both this Friday and Saturday nights past. She said it was because I wouldn't change the menu for her."

"Yeah, I heard her telling Louanne Weller some crap on the phone about that when she came in my shop. She said your food caused her stomach distress flareup."

"Rubbish. She just didn't want to eat fish. Fine Catholic she was. Most of us refrain from eating meat for Passover and eat fish instead. That's why I've served pescatarian dishes for the past month."

"She was a complainer, Finbar. Fish is not my favorite, but I can handle it once or twice a week. Supposed to be better for you, they say. Regardless, she told Louanne, who probably told Bettina and who knows who else? Anyway, I gave her a tonic I had already made up. I didn't make a new one just for her. It was from an existing batch, and nobody else has gotten sick from it."

"And that will come out in Detective Petry's reports, so never you worry, lad. It'll work out."

Finbar reached over to the table and pulled open a small drawer. He grasped a wooden pipe with a deep bowl and fitted the curved stem into his mouth. He did not light it. The pipe hung on his lower lip while he sucked air through the hole. Tommie smiled. Once a smoker, he had given the habit up long ago when his wife Mary came down with cancer. Now, the pipe was merely a prop that served to focus his mind when he sought to solve a puzzle. *All he needs is that double-billed hat to look like Scotland Yard's finest detective,* she thought.

"Well, now, lad. Let's get down to business. The game's afoot. It's time for us to assemble the clues," he said.

Chapter Seven

EARLE PETRY was feeling more than a little disquieted after his conversations with Tommie Watson. He knew she was innocent, but he would have to work hard to convince just about anyone else in his department and probably most of the town of her innocence. After the disaster with Coral Beadwell's murder in Tommie's shop, followed by Beverly Cantrell's murder in Sarah Beth Brewster's shop, all eyes were suspiciously on the relative newcomer to Floribunda.

   Not helping Tommie's case was the word about town that she and Earl were considered a couple. The rumor itself didn't bother him because they *were* a couple. However, he and Tommie both had similar views on what that meant. He was resolved to remain a bachelor, and she was resolved to stay single. Neither of them wanted to embark on the road to matrimony yet again at their age, *so rumors be damned,* as far as Earl Petry was concerned.

Tommie Watson was a fiercely independent woman, and Earl liked that about her. Her age and weight were not factored into what made her attractive. In fact, he found her tremendously sexy. She was smart and funny and an excellent companion in all the right ways. Tommie definitely cocked his trigger, but he was content for things to continue like a slow, steady creek through a lush meadow, and she was okay with that.

The problem was Earl Petry was actively pursued by women all over town, regardless of marital status. He was a big, well-built man with a gentle, yet strong presence and a ruggedly handsome face. That he was off the market in a town where eligible men were in short supply chagrined more than a few unmarried ladies. That he had taken up with a newcomer made them downright infuriated, especially after they had competed so vigorously for his attentions over the years. Many a spinster, divorcee, and widow secretly hoped Thomasina Watson was found guilty of murder this time around.

Earl wasn't yet ready to admit the L-word, but he was dancing dangerously close to it. What troubled him was he felt Tommie was also playing on the edge of it, and the admission might tip the balance on the delicate scales they had carefully constructed.

Even more bothersome were the red flags. Along with her independence came a stubbornness that matched his own. She was a spitfire. She was opinionated. She was her own woman and had survived many years without the help or influence of a man. And that terrified Earl Petry.

These were the thoughts that raced through his mind as he entered the medical examiner's office. Taking the stairs down to the basement level, he opened the door and found Sanderson Harper, the Floral County Coroner, kicked back in his chair perusing the contents of a manilla folder. Sandy peered at Earl over his black framed glasses when the burly officer entered.

Sandy was a jovial man, somewhat shorter and heavier than Earl, with salt and pepper hair, dark brown eyes, and an olive complexion. His shirt buttons strained and gapped across his middle age spread. At 63, he was a year younger than Tommie, but the resemblance to his herbalist cousin was clearly evident.

"Hey, Earl. Wondered when you'd be in. Have a seat. Ready for some preliminaries?"

Earl perched on the edge of the desk. "Yeah. Just got finished talking with Tommie. What can you tell me?"

Sandy snickered. "She's in the clear, so far. Tommie's potion is benign. Nothing harmful in it. Just a preparation of crushed fennel and coriander seeds, fresh dill, lemon peel, and honey in a suspension of vodka. Even if there were something contributory, the full bottle of water would've diluted it."

"Yeah. That's what she told me," Earl confirmed. "Anything else?"

"Lots. Veranell Collins was one sick woman. She

had a serious case of celiac disease. That's an autoimmune condition that wreaks havoc on digestion and the small intestine. She would have been intolerant to a number of things. Gluten, wheat, barley, pasta, oats. She had bowel abscesses from acute diarrhea, which also caused her to become dehydrated. The stuff in Tommie's potion would have helped her by replenishing those fluids and easing the bloating that comes with gas buildup in the intestines. There were fermented sugars in her colon. Must have been extremely painful. The potion would've helped with that, too. Her esophageal sphincter was burned from acid reflux, and she had a rash on her knees and elbows called *dermatitis herpetiformis,* consistent with the serious nature of her disease. She wore false teeth, most likely the result of tooth loss due to decay associated with her condition and persistent vomiting."

Earl grimaced. "Sounds terrible. Would that condition make her pass out? Would it have killed her?"

"Not by itself. She passed out because the disease impaired the absorption of vital food nutrients and vitamins in her system. Made her weak. Plus, the constant loose bowels just sucked her dry. But it wasn't the disease that killed her. It was what exacerbated the disease."

"Elaborate, please."

"I checked her stomach contents, and it appears she ingested some things that made her condition much worse."

"Really? Tell you what, here's the list of the ingredients from Tommie's luncheon yesterday. How about check it over while I get us some fresh coffee? I've put an X by the things Tommie said Mrs. Collins ate. Be back in a couple of minutes."

Sanderson Harper took the list and pushed his glasses back up on his nose as Earl disappeared out the door. By the time he returned, Sandy had finished reading.

"Well?" Earl set a mug down before the coroner.

"Yeah, as far as I can tell, Veranell Collins ingested exactly what Tommie said, including the herbal potion. However, from my examination of the stomach contents, I found traces of the makings of a chicken salad, a potato salad, and a coleslaw, prepared with dairy and a commercial type mayonnaise. All consumed within the last 48 hours. And an oatmeal raisin cookie."

"Are those bad to eat along with celiac disease?"

"They can be if she was also lactose intolerant."

"Tommie said that, too. She told me she knew Veranell had celiac, IBS, and lactose intolerance."

"Tommie knows her stuff, Earl. She's one smart woman, if I say so myself."

"I agree." *Smart enough to heal and smart enough to kill,* he thought, *and somebody else will eventually come to that conclusion.*

"I see your mind working, Earl. No. I absolutely do *not* think Tommie Watson hurt this woman, so get that out of your head right now. Besides, those foods weren't even on Tommie's menu." Sandy's eyes burned into Earl's.

"I have every bit of faith that she's innocent, Sandy.

I've just got to be able to prove it if it's suspected down the road." Earl gave the coroner his own direct stare.

"I understand. I did find evidence of malt vinegar, brewer's yeast, oats, and barley. There was quite a bit of barley, actually. None of that on this list. And, come to think of it, Tommie usually uses yogurt, or she makes her own mayonnaise from eggs, olive oil, and lemon juice, but I didn't find evidence of that, either. Nope. Nothing came from Tommie's kitchen that would have hurt Mrs. Collins. In fact, I would say the opposite. Tommie took great pains to prepare foods and an herbal tonic to provide relief to the poor woman."

"What else can you tell me?"

"Here's the big kicker, Earl. The thing that pushed Veranell Collins right over the edge was *salmonellosis*. Somewhere, somehow, she got ahold of something that contained salmonella. People can get it from raw milk or contaminated water or even alligator in this part of the country, but mostly raw chicken or eggs."

"Tommie served eggs at the brunch ..."

"... and not you or anybody else who ate at Tommie's has turned up sick. I'll be testing all her eggs and other foods. We'll know if there was anything tainted, but don't worry, my friend. I have every confidence in my cousin's innocence. She did not cause this woman's death."

"What's your take, Sandy? Natural or suspicious?"

"Given her history and underlying conditions, my first instinct would have been to say natural causes."

"Would have been?"

"Yeah, at first pass, it seemed that way." Sandy ran his hand through his short hair as his eyes passed over the folder in his hand. "Seemed that way, but given her stomach contents, I have to say her death is very suspicious."

"Because ...?"

"A woman this age, with a lifelong condition, would know *exactly* what to eat and drink and what to avoid. Why on God's green earth would she have willingly consumed anything to put herself in such agonizing pain, and which would likely cause her to die? Nah-ah. Tommie didn't kill her, but *somebody* did, Earl. Somebody caused this death deliberately. I'm ruling this a suspicious death. My official finding is dehydration, fluid and electrolyte imbalance, and septic shock due to prolonged diarrhea and vomiting directly resulting from exposure to salmonella bacterium and ingestion of substances leading to complications of celiac disease." He snapped the folder shut and dropped it on the desk.

Earl chewed his lower lip. "Well, damn. Have you told Tommie yet?"

Sandy choked on his coffee. "I ... why would I?"

"Don't con me, Sandy. You know as well as I do that Tommie's going to be calling you while she and her friend play detective."

"True. She will. But I haven't talked to her yet. I wanted to wait until I had tested all the evidence from her shop ... even though I'm positive it'll be clean. Want me to ghost her?"

"No. Just don't tell her about the salmonella. Give me a day or so to do my own investigation, so I can stay ahead of them."

Sandy snickered again. "You don't fool me, Earl. You know good and darn well they'll be out and about doing their interviews. But, that's what you want, isn't it?"

Earl's face reddened slightly. "They *are* surprisingly good at it, you know. I think I'd like them to do the legwork and not hit on the salmonella angle just yet. I want to take a run on that before they get their focus clouded."

"Are you sure you won't catch flak from the department for letting them investigate on their own? They're not exactly licensed detectives."

"That's why I want to let them do their thing. They're just two people asking questions."

"Yes, until they get too close to the truth. Then they become liabilities to the real killer," Sanderson said with pursed lips.

"Yes, they do," Earl agreed with a frown.

Chapter Eight

TOMMIE WATSON pressed a button on her cell phone and ended her call. She flipped through the pages of the yellow legal pad, and then handed it back to Finbar.

"All right. I'm ready. You be the scribe while my lunch digests," she said.

"Right, then. Let's begin at the beginning." Finbar turned back to the first page which bore a heading.

CRIME: DEATH IN CONFEDERATE MEMORIAL PARK GAZEBO.

Beneath it was a word, followed by a name.

VICTIM: MRS. VERANELL COLLINS.

The remainder of the page was a list of words.

WEAPON:

METHOD:

DATE/TIME:

DISCOVERED BY:

PRESENT:

DESCRIPTION OF VICTIM:

A linear-thinking man, Finbar Holmes had a propensity for anything puzzle-related, which included sudoku, crosswords, mystery novels, and crime shows on television. He had devised the list as a means to help him unravel the mysteries before the solutions were presented by the TV detectives. He and Tommie had successfully employed the legal-pad method to solve two murders and a drug smuggling operation in the past couple of months.

Although they were rank amateurs in the crime investigation field, their shared intelligence and persistence had born credence to the unofficial title of "Holmes and Watson, Investigators." It was a fitting homage to the legendary Sir Author Conan Doyle crime investigating duo—Inspector Sherlock Holmes and Dr. John Watson. Tommie found the sleuthing process exciting and working with the quirky Finbar Holmes was full of surprises, beginning with the use of the list.

"Before we start, Thomasina, are we certain there is foul play involved in Mrs. Collins's death? Or could it have been a natural demise due to the disorder ye say she suffered from?"

"According to what Sandy told me just now, he's ruling the death suspicious. His words were to the effect of 'dehydration, septic shock, loss of fluids and electrolytes from diarrhea and vomiting after swallowing things that made her celiac disease flare up.' He also told me he didn't believe she would intentionally make herself sicker. Suspicious death is not natural causes or accidental. I'm thinking homicide. What do you think?"

"I'm inclined to agree. So, let's say the weapon is food or drink, for now. The method would be ingestion, most likely."

"I agree. Date and time are Sunday, April 21, 2019 at 4:38 p.m. by my watch."

"And I know yer watch is precisely right, as always. Now, Missus, we've got to list who discovered her. She collapsed on the floor in front of you and Detective Petry."

"Levi Muller was inside the gazebo. He was standing by the rabbits. And you were there with Amos, Father Duncan, Aubrey, and Santino, all holding $100 bills. So, counting me, there were eight people total in the gazebo, excluding Veranell."

Tommie waited while Finbar listed the names: Thomasina Watson, Finbar Holmes, Earl Petry, Levi Muller, Amos Mosby, Father Horace Duncan, Aubrey Rush, and Santino Alvarez.

"Who else was present?"

"Besides scores of people milling about on the grounds? How about we list those who presented prizes?"

"Seems logical. Ready when you are, Missus."

"I don't remember them in order, but here goes. Elly James and Jo Clay. Those two are thick as thieves lately. Eva Edgerton and Bettina Taylor. Those two probably *are* thieves judging from the prices in their stores. Leo Alvarez was there. Sid and Jeanette Spock. Louanne Weller had left, but her husband Paul was there. Melinda Layton. And the 'fab four,' of course … our pals Henry Erving and Don Lareby, and Don's sisters Elaine Frank and Susan Clay. I think that's it. That's a lot of people. Should we count them all as suspects?"

Finbar grimaced. "I don't think so. Too many. Right off, I'm striking you, Earl, and m'self from the list. Also, our gossipy group Henry, Don, Elaine, and Susan. I honestly don't think Father Duncan would be a suspect, but let's list him as a person of interest and a possible resource. I'll bet he can give us some good information."

Tommie held up her fingers and counted as she named the remaining witnesses. "That leaves Levi, Amos, Aubrey, and Santino in direct proximity, with Leo, Elly, Jo, the Spocks, Paul, Eva, Melinda, and Bettina nearby. Sheesh. Thirteen people. That's a lot of interviews, Finbar." She shook her head.

"Hm. Yer right. We can have a meeting at The Lunch Pad and get insight from the Spocks whilst having a meal with our four talkative friends. That's six at once."

"Yeah. And in the morning before that, we can catch most of them at their shops along the strip. If we split up, we can cover more ground. I can see Jo and Elly while you talk to the Alvarez brothers."

"Lovely. I can practice up a bit on my Spanish," he said with a wink.

"And after lunch I can talk with Eva and Bettina while you get some Guinness at Weller's."

"I do likes the way you think, Thomasina. Will ye buy yerself a pretty frock from the boutique?"

"At Eva's prices? I think not."

"Maybe I'll get a haircut from Amos Mosby, and then stop off at the fishmonger's across the street."

Tommie blanched. "Kinda tired of fish."

Finbar laughed at her expression. "The butcher's, then, just for you, Missus."

"We'll have to take a drive to Aubrey's store and to Levi's farm, but I think we can get to all of our suspects and people of interest by Wednesday or Thursday."

"We must set that as a tentative plan, but let's not get ahead of our process. We've got to finish our list. Description of the victim is next."

Tommie took a deep breath and called up the image of Veranell Collins ... before she was lying dead on the gazebo floor.

"Veranell Collins was 70 years old. I know that because she had a birthday bash last January. I wasn't invited, but I heard about it. She was a few inches taller than me, so maybe five feet and four or five inches, and she was a skinny woman, but not exactly frail."

"I put her at 9 stones, roughly 126 pounds."

"OK. What else can you say about her?"

"By my observations, she was Caucasian, with pale papery skin, a wrinkled face, dark brown eyes, and thin grey hair worn in a chignon."

"Is that what you call that little bun on the back of her head? A chignon? I thought it was a snood. I wore my hair that way when I did 'The King and I' at the community theater several years ago."

"No, Missus. A snood is the fabric covering worn over a chignon," Finbar said with a chuckle.

"Oh! Whatever. She didn't wear a snood, but she was always dressed in a fashionable pantsuit with matching pumps. I never saw her in a dress and never without that hairdo. Yesterday she wore a jaunty little pink hat. I guess for Easter." The recollection made Tommie a bit sad.

"I take it she lived on a generous pension, judging from the chic apparel I observed when she attended mass at St. Mary's, and she ate at least once each weekend at Caife Caife Holmes until this weekend past."

"I believe she had been a widow for many years with an ample death benefit. She promoted a lot of charities, I'm told."

"Right, then. Anything else on victim description?"

"I hate to say this, but I found her unpleasant. She was condescending and had this air of superiority I didn't care for. Once, she came in my shop wearing a pair of white gloves and drug her finger around my counters like she was an inspector checking for dust."

"Did she find any?"

"You know she didn't, but it really ticked me off."

Finbar snickered. "No moss on yer rolling stone,

Missus. You've the cleanest countertops in town. But I understand yer affront. When she came to my dinners, she always regarded m'food with a face like one who's just bitten a lemon."

"I know! And, did you ever notice her sniffing her plate? I saw her doing it once. It was just weird. Why make a show of smelling food that's been prepared right in front of you? It was a blatant put down of your cooking."

"Ach. Makes you wonder if she gave St. Peter the once over at the Pearly Gates." He crossed himself quickly, a gesture Tommie had seen him make whenever he spoke of death, dying, saints, or Heaven. "Anything else?"

"No. I don't think so. Leave a couple of extra lines for if we think of something else. Now what?"

Finbar flipped to the next page. It was labeled at the top in bold capital letters.

SUSPECT DESCRIPTIONS.

"Let's sketch out our suspects for now as just the people inside the gazebo. May change later. First will be Mr. Muller," Finbar said as he filled in the name on his list.

I. LEVI MULLER

"OK. I'll do his physical description. Levi Muller is Caucasian, mid-fifties, hovering somewhere around six feet tall and solidly built. I can't tell people's weight, you know," Tommie admitted.

"I would say 185 pounds, give or take a few."

"All righty. He has short brown curly hair. Real curls as opposed to waves. He's a strong, attractive man.

Ruddy complexion from being in the sun a lot. Dark blue smallish eyes. He's a widower with two grown sons. Bob is about twenty-five or twenty-six. Bill and his wife Libby are mid-thirties. All three of them live on the property with Levi and help him on his farm."

"What else?"

"They're Mennonite and attend the Floribunda Fellowship. He owns Levi's Animal Farm and raises ostriches and emus and small livestock like rabbits, goats, sheep, mini-donkeys, and mini-cattle. The school kids go there for field trips a lot. They're kind, likeable people."

"Does he have a woman?" Finbar teased.

"I don't know! Not me, that's for sure," she replied.

Finbar threw his head back and laughed aloud, startling the dogs.

"Sorry, lads. Go back to sleep. I've been to Muller's farm for seasonal vegetables for the café. I find the man to be humble and quite intelligent. He told me he learned all about the proper care for soil and growing things from his late wife, Gayla. The Mennonites are quite grounded in all things regarding nature, y'know. His contribution to their marriage was the animals. D'you know he has a degree in animal husbandry from university? Not the one in the state capitol ... the other one."

"University of Florida. They have a big agriculture program. I didn't know he had a degree."

"Yup. He and Gayla met there. They got married and started the farm. She passed on just a few years ago."

He crossed himself again, and from the sad expression on his face, Tommie wondered if the conversation made him think about his wife Mary.

"Let's move on, Finbar. Amos Mosby, suspect number two."

"My barber." He scribbled on the notepad.

2. AMOS MOSBY

"Yes. Amos is the sweetest man. He's about 60 years old, slightly shorter and smaller than Levi."

"Let's say 5'10" and 175 pounds?"

"OK. He's African American, bald, with large dark brown eyes, a wide nose, a pencil-thin mustache, and perfect white teeth. He's the owner of The Barber Shop. Amos and his wife Sheela have five adult children in Floribunda and a slew of grandchildren of all ages. They go to St. John's Missionary Baptist Church. I'll tell you now, I don't believe he could have hurt Veranell. He's too nice a man."

"One can never tell, Thomasina, but I tend to agree. I likes the way he talks with me when he cuts m'hair. He treats me like I've been a friend forever, even though I've just lately come to the states. Have ye ever considered letting him cut yer hair?"

"No, but that's not to say I wouldn't let him. I've just always gone to the Hair Express since I moved here. They're cheap."

"Cheap is good, but I'll bet Amos could do a fine job with a cut like yers."

Tommie scowled at him. "Because I have a man's

hair style? Is that what you're saying, Finbar?"

Finbar pursed his lips and arched his eyebrows. "No, no, no, Missus. I just mean, yer man's a good barber, and you wearing yer hair in that short do, Amos would be reasonable and give ye good conversation, and . . ."

"Quit while you're ahead. This is not a man's haircut. It's called a pixie and it's a woman's style."

"Righto. I meant no insult to ye. It's just that he told me he likes cutting women's hair, but not many ladies come to him because he's a barber."

"I gotcha. No offence taken. I'm just used to only paying $20 for a cut and style."

"Twenty dollars? That's robbery. Amos said he'd only charge ye $10."

"You've talked with him about cutting my hair? Are you kidding me?" Tommie was aghast.

"Maybe," Finbar muttered, quickly looking down at his legal pad and writing. "Let's crack on, shall we? What d'you know about Aubrey Rush, suspect number three?"

3. AUBREY RUSH

Tommie was still self-conscious about her hair, and it showed in her tone of voice. "I don't know her all that well, but physically she's about your height and weight. Five foot seven and 135 to 140 pounds, maybe. She's Caucasian and has a sturdy build. Every time I've seen her, she's wearing her wavy dark brown hair to her shoulders or in a ponytail. Probably doesn't need to go to the barber to get it styled."

Finbar avoided her direct stare. "Her eyes are a medium brown. I think she's quite an attractive woman, with full lips and an olive complexion. She's probably in her mid-forties, divorced, with no children that I know of. She owns Aubrey's Antiques and attends the Beth-el Jewish Synagogue. Have ye met her?"

"I have. I bought a really pretty padded three-legged footstool from her antique store when I moved back and first opened my shop. I use it behind the counter to prop up my ankle when I'm sitting there prepping my remedies. She gave me a nice discount because I brought her some of my house blend teas. She said she loves to barter goods for goods. I like her."

"Lovely. I'll do the last one." Finbar filled in the name on his list.

4. SANTINO ALVAREZ

"I'm listening," Tommie said.

"Righto. Santino Alvarez is a single Hispanic gentleman, forty years old, 5'8" tall and 175 pounds. He has a muscular build, strong hands, brown skin tone, very dark brown eyes, slightly wavy black hair cut above his ears. He's handsome and good humored, with a perpetual broad smile. He co-owns Santino's Shoe Shop and Leo's Leather Goods with his brother, Leo Alvarez. They are both legal Mexican immigrants who are working towards American citizenship. They attend the Church of Jesus Christ of Latter-day Saints, commonly called the Mormons. He and Leo speak fluent Spanish and English." He set the pen and the legal pad on the table.

"How do you know him in such detail?" Tommie stared at Finbar with a surprised expression.

He lifted his feet. "Santino custom made these sandals for me. Quite smart looking, don't ye think? I had a grand conversation with him while he was measuring m'feet. And he's tutoring me in the Spanish language. I could use it if I take another holiday to Spain or Portugal. Anyhow, shall we take a break, lad? I have a throat."

Tommie knew that was Irish-speak for "I'm thirsty," so she freshened up her tea while he popped open another cold can of Guinness.

Chapter Nine

EARL PETRY beat Finbar to The Barber Shop. At 3:00 p.m., he sat in the chair and chatted with Amos Mosby while the man trimmed Earl's hair and beard. They had been friends since high school where, because of their strength and size, they were both stars on the football team and had the nicknames of Freight Train and Tank.

"Terrible shock that happened yesterday about Miz Collins," Amos said.

"Yeah, it was. Hate that she died right there in front of all those people," Earl said.

"Mmm-hmm. Sheela said it was the horriblest thing she'd ever seen when that woman's eyes rolled up in her head like that."

"Did you see it?"

"Naw. I was like you, behind her at the time. Just

saw her drop to the floor. Kind of crumpled down, you know? Like a wadded-up piece of paper."

"Uh-huh. What else do you remember, Amos?"

"I remember your lady trying to help her. She pulled that tonic outta Miz Collins's pocket when the old woman couldn't hold on to it and put it in the water bottle. I saw that."

"How did you know it was a tonic?"

"Oh, I reconnized the label and the bottle. Sheela been taking the same stuff for her sensitive stomach. I think it's called *Tender Tummy Tonic*. Something clever like that. Miz Watson sure has a way with words … and with making folks feel better. Sheela got me some foot soak from her. Called it *Rosemary Rabbit-Tobacco Tootsie Soak*. Works real good on my achy feet from standing up all day long. You know what rabbit-tobacco is? It's lavender."

"Huh? I thought rabbit-tobacco was that red weed we used to pick in the field and chew."

"Naw, that's bitter-weed. Chews good, though." He chuckled. "Miz Watson's a good woman, Earl. My wife says she's a keeper. I'm inclined to agree with her."

"Yeah, she is at that. Say, Amos. You were at the luncheon yesterday. Do you remember Mrs. Collins looking or acting sick?"

"Sicker than normal? Mmm. Not really. She been sick as long as I been knowing her. Some kind of intestine disease. 'Course, my Momma used to say when people act ugly, that ugliness gets to growing and eats up your insides.

I hate to speak ill of the dead, but Miz Collins was eat up with it. Mean. Ugly. Woman." He snipped so close to Earl's ear with the scissors on the last three words, the *snaps* made the detective flinch.

"Whoa, pump the brakes, Train," Earl warned.

"I'm sorry, Earl. Did I cut you?" Amos asked.

"No, but you like to have. You seem pretty upset. Was Mrs. Collins a problem for you?"

Amos stepped back from the chair and dropped his hands to his sides. He hung his head and breathed deeply.

"She was a mean, ugly woman, Tank. The meanest. She'da been a sticker in Christ's crown of thorns if she coulda. Are we off the record here?"

"Um ... well, no ... not really," Earl stammered.

"Figured you'd get around to questioning me. I understand." Amos walked over to the door and turned his sign from OPEN to CLOSED. He laid his comb and scissors on the counter and sat in the chair adjacent Earl.

"Amos? Before you say anything, I have to tell you that you are a person of interest and a material witness in the suspicious death of Veranell Collins. You are not, and I repeat, *not* an official suspect, you understand."

"I get it. Let me go on record by saying I had nothing to do with whatever happened to Miz Collins. I'm not sorry she's dead 'cause she was a hateful old lady who'd done harm to me and mine. But I didn't kill her, if that's what you're saying by it being a suspicious death."

"Good. That's what I wanted to hear. Can you tell

me what harm she did to you?"

"Oh, yes. She near about caused me to lose my business and my home. That's what she did."

"How so, Amos?"

Amos leaned back in the softened leather barber chair, the springs creaking from years of use. "You remember about six years ago when I was struggling to keep my doors open? There was a rumor went 'round."

"I remember. Something about head lice."

"Yes, that was it. Somebody spread 'round that I gave some of my customers head lice. Nobody ever proved it, but I had to close shop and do a fumigation in here. I sterilized all my equipment. Sheela and the kids come in and we cleaned the place top to bottom. Threw away all my towels and got brand new ones. Had a health inspector check everything and got cleared to open up."

"I remember that, Amos."

"By then, I'd lost all my customers from St. Mary's Catholic Church, except Father Horace. Lost a lot of the other men in town, too. They started getting their haircuts at Walmart." He looked at Earl and smiled. "Not you, though. You never stopped coming by, and I appreciate that, Tank. I do."

Earl shrugged but kept silent, so Amos continued.

"Business was so bad, I had to take out a loan against the shop just to get by. This place was passed down from my daddy, see, and I owned it free and clear. Loan come due, and I couldn't pay, so Charles Williams of Floral

Real Estate paid it off and took my property. He said he'd lease the shop to me, but it was for way more than I could afford. I fell behind on the rent, and Charles was gonna kick me out. Well, the shop got bought out, and then somebody else held the lease to my business. That was Miz Veranell Collins. Funny thing was, come to find out, she was the one that started the lice rumor. Mean, ugly, hateful woman."

"Why, Amos? This shop isn't some great piece of property. Why would she want it?"

"Hate to say it, but she don't like black people … or brown people … or poor folk. Nobody that ain't rich upper crust Catholics in her town. She especially don't want them to be successful businesspeople."

Earl sat back as if slapped. "Are you saying she was racist, Amos?"

"That's exactly what I'm saying. Miz Veranell Collins was a hateful racist woman. She tried to ruin me with the head lice story, just like she tried to run off Miz Rush because she's Jewish and the Alvarez brothers because they're Mexican. You do some digging, Earl, and you'll find that Miz Collins had bought up the leases for every business in town that was run by a minority, and she held them over their heads and threatened them, just like she did to me."

"I … I don't know what to say, Amos. I certainly didn't know that. In this day and age, I didn't think it was possible for someone to be that bigoted."

"Prob'ly ninety-nine percent of the people in this town are God-fearing, good people who love their fellow human beings. But Veranell Collins was a real bad apple trying to ruin the rest of the barrel."

"Amos, now that she's dead, who do the liens revert to? Do you know?"

"Hmm. Woulda been Charles Williams, but he's in prison now, and his partner Miz Cantrell is dead. I guess the liens revert to the sisters, Susan Clay and Elaine Frank, and their brother Don Lareby who bought the real estate company and changed the name to Floribunda Real Properties. Gotta nice sound to it, huh?"

"Wow. Listen, Amos. I want to thank you for this information. If you don't mind, please don't tell your story to anybody else."

Amos threw himself against the chair's headrest and belly laughed. "You mean, don't tell your lady and her Irish friend, don't you?"

Earl's face reddened. "I do."

"Don't you worry none, Tank. I got plenty else to tell 'Holmes and Watson, Investigators' that'll satisfy their curiosity. By the way, am I still a person of interest?"

"Yep. But you're also my barber, so how about finish my haircut? And be sure to leave my ears intact."

Chapter Ten

TOMMIE WATSON sat in her usual place on Finbar's sofa on Camelia Street as, across town, Earl Petry sat in Amos Mosby's barber chair. Though their methods differed, each meticulously investigated the death of Veranell Collins. Tommie set her teacup on the folding tray table beside her, picked up the legal pad, flipped to the next empty page, and wrote a title on the top line.

PERSONS OF INTEREST DESCRIPTIONS:

She began the list with her first entry.

POI I: LEO ALVAREZ

"You did so well with Santino. Do you want to describe Leo?" She asked Finbar.

"Sure, sure. Leo Alvarez. He's 38 years old, 5'8" tall, 155 pounds. He's a single Hispanic man with a muscular build like his brother. He's quite strong, has a brown skin tone, and dark brown eyes. He wears his straight black hair cut above his ears with no sideburns. He's good looking and good humored like Santino but with a shyer smile. He co-owns Leo's Leather Goods and Santino's Shoe Shop. Leo's also working towards American citizenship, attends the Mormon church, and speaks both Spanish and English but with less of the Mexican accent."

"Excellent. He's basically a younger version of Santino, but with straighter hair and a smaller smile. Got it. Want to do the Spocks?" She wrote on her list and filled in the description as he spoke.

POI 2: JEANETTE SPOCK

Finbar took a big gulp of his Guinness. "Yup. Jeanette Spock is 50 years old, about 5'9" tall, and weighs 180 pounds, I'd say. She's Caucasian, stocky build, medium brown hair worn in a straight, squared-off bob. Her eyes are a light blue, and she has thin lips and large teeth. Her complexion is rather pale. She and her husband Sid own The Lunch Pad and attend First United Methodist Church. Same place yer Earl Petry goes," he said with a smile.

"That's true. How about Sid?" She added his name.

POI 3: SID SPOCK

"Sidney Spock is 54, just under six feet tall, and is about 200 pounds or so. He's also Caucasian, with a stocky build like his wife. Have ye noticed, Thomasina, that if they stand side by side, they appear to be two rectangles?"

Tommie laughed. "Not really, but now that you mention it, they're like two Sponge Bobs."

"Forgive me, but what's a Sponge Bob?"

"Cartoon character. He's a sponge that lives in a pineapple on the ocean floor. Sponge Bob Square Pants. He's a yellow square with stick legs and arms."

"That must be an American telly show. Sounds idiotic, but children probably like it. Nevertheless, back to Sid Spock. He has dark hazel eyes. His hair is thin and light brown, worn in a crew cut. He has a ruddy complexion, a wide mouth, and small teeth. Almost the exact opposite of his spouse."

"Weird," Tommie said. "You never know what attracts people to one another."

"As you say." Finbar attempted to suppress a smile.

"They're a bit peculiar, I guess, but I have to say I'm intrigued by the way they name their food dishes. Remember the first time we ever ate there?"

"I do. You had the *Satellite Salad* with *Crater Croutons*, and I had the *Orbit Omelet* with *Hubble Ham*."

Tommie laughed. "That's right. I didn't know what to expect, but my food was really tasty."

"Mine was, as well. As I recall Elaine Frank had a *Rocket Rueben* with *Meteor Mustard*, Susan Clay had the *Full Moon Swiss Cheese Melt* and *Venus Vegetables*, and Don Clay ate the *French Big Dipper* with *Sputnik Spuds*."

Tommie's mouth dropped open. "I can't believe you remembered all that! Your memory amazes me."

"Elementary, my dear Watson."

"Hmph. I'll do the next one. Paul Weller. Hey, do

you think we should do him *and* his wife, Louanne Weller? She was there until the prize presentation."

"Might as well. Start with her—number four."

POI 4: LOUANNE WELLER

"All right. I think she's about 45. She's close to my height, so five feet and two or three inches tall. She weighs about half of me, so maybe 100 or so."

"I put her more at 110 pounds."

"OK. That'll work. She's Caucasian, petite, and stylishly thin. She has light blond hair, and she wears it in that trendy wavy bob that's not quite straight and not quite curled. It's more like bent here and there. Her eyes are like upturned cat's eyes and a medium blue. She owns Weller's Wine & Spirits with her husband Paul. She's snooty, like Veranell was. I believe she goes to your church, St. Mary's."

"Yes, she does, along with her husband and their two grown sons. The daughter attends university in South Florida. The family seems to be well off, money-wise."

"OK. Number five?" She listed the next person.

POI 5: PAUL WELLER.

"Right. As for Paul, he's 50, 5'11", a fit 180 pounds, Caucasian with a medium dark complexion. His eyes are a light brown, and his hair is dark blond, worn in a close crew cut. I quite like the man. He's very pleasant … more so than his wife."

Tommie nodded and stopped writing. "You know, Finbar, I use 80 proof vodka in most of my medicinal tinctures. The alcohol evaporates enough that a full dropper taken three times a day is only equivalent to eating a piece of overripe fruit. Anyway, I went to Weller's Wine & Spirits and bought several bottles of the Blue Ice brand. It's an American vodka made with potatoes that is gluten free. I overheard Louanne commenting to Paul about how many bottles I got and speculating that I was a lush. That's ironic because I'm allergic to alcohol and can't drink it."

"Is that right? Cheeky woman."

"Yeah, I thought so, too. Paul shushed her."

"Yes. He wouldn't hold with her condescension. I play poker with him on Tuesdays. Nice fellow."

"I hope she didn't go around telling people I'm a big drinker."

"I think, if she did, we'd have heard about it from Elaine or Susan by now. Never ye worry. Who's our next person of interest?"

"Melinda Layton," she said. "Person of interest number six." She wrote on her pad.

POI 6: MELINDA LAYTON.

Finbar shrugged. "I'm not acquainted with her."

"I know her because she's the president of the Trinity Episcopal Church Ladies' Charity Organization. She's 47 and a bit taller than you, like 5'8" or so. Weight maybe 140, more or less. Pretty woman. Caucasian, mid-length strawberry blond hair in zig zag waves. She's fair-skinned with gorgeous jade green eyes. Her husband's name is Carl, and they have two adult married daughters."

"Oh, yes. I know Carl Layton. He's in our poker

club. Nice lad. Didn't know she was his wife. D'you like her, Missus?"

"I do, Finbar. They have money, and she runs with the ritzy glam crowd, but she's also friends with people outside her church and social circle. She and the ladies in the LCO help keep me in business. Yeah, I like Melinda."

Finbar noticed her expression didn't quite fit her enthusiastic affirmations.

"What is it, Thomasina?"

Tommie gave him a wan smile. "She was one of Sarah Beth Brewster's best friends. I miss Sarah Beth."

"St. Brigid! The woman tried to kill ye!" He sat bolt upright in his chair.

"I know she did. But before that, she was the best friend I had in Floribunda, until you came along."

Two huge tears coursed down Tommie's cheeks. She quickly wiped them away and tried to hide behind her tea mug. Finbar came to the sofa and took the legal pad from her lap.

"Here, lad. Let me finish it. You drink up yer tea. We'll get these last few done, and then I have some leftover scamp and champ from Saturday night we can heat up for supper. Dry yer eyes now. Let's see who's next." He wrote.

POI 7: FATHER HORACE DUNCAN

"Father Horace Duncan," he continued, "the priest at St. Mary's Catholic Church. He's an easy one. Sixty-one years old, six feet tall, 210 pounds. A brawny man. Caucasian, likely of Scottish descent with that name and complexion, with a full head of wavy grey hair and blue-grey eyes. I quite enjoy his sermons at mass. Bit of a jokester, if I say so m'self. Done. Who's number eight?"

"Elly James," Tommie said, attempting to smile.

Finbar wrote her name on the list.

POI 8: ELLY JAMES

"I've got her, too," he said. "She's remarkably similar in looks to the Weller woman, only younger. She must be early- to mid-thirties, same height, maybe ten pounds heavier. Same light blond chin length hair in bent waves. Medium blue eyes and fair skin. She's a single woman, but she's secretly dating Leo Alvarez."

"How do you know who she's dating?" Tommie's eyes widened, and she sat up a little straighter.

"Leo told me. Anyway, she owns Elly's Jelly Jar and goes to the First Baptist Church with her partner in crime, Ms. Jo Clay, who is our person of interest number nine." He scribbled on the legal pad again.

POI 9: JO CLAY

"Jo is about 40, 5'5" inches tall, and about 145 pounds. She's a full-figured Caucasian beauty with long dark auburn hair. She wears it pushed behind her ears.," Tommie said.

"She's divorced from Jimmy Clay. Did ye know that he is our friend Susan Clay's ex-husband's brother?"

"Ha! I never put the names together until you said it. How about that? I'm anxious to hear what Susan has to say about her."

"Yup. Ms. Clay owns The Clay Pigeon, a ceramics shop. She made all the ceramic rabbits that held the emu eggs. D'you know who she dates, Missus?"

"Let me guess. Santino Alvarez?"

"Good guess."

"Elementary, my dear Holmes. It only stands to reason. They're like sisters and are attracted to brothers."

"Quite a fine leap there, Watson. Our next person of interest is Ms. Eva Edgerton of Eva's Divas Boutique." He added her name to the list.

POI 10: EVA EDGERTON

Tommie rolled her eyes. "Eva Edgerton."

"As you say, Thomasina. I put her at 41 or 42, 5'8" tall, and 125 pounds. She's Caucasian, slender, shapely, with honey blond hair worn in a wavy chin bob. Gads. These women must all go to the same stylist, d'you think? Brown eyes. She's a pretty woman, but she wears too much makeup, like Miss Beverly Cantrell, God rest her soul. What's her marital status, d'you know?"

"She's divorced with a daughter in her 20s. She's in the Trinity LCO. Eva was friends with Sarah Beth, too. Super stuck up, if you ask me, and the clothes in her shop are way overpriced. I went in to her boutique once, and she barely acknowledged me. It didn't matter. As soon as I got a look at the price tags, I slipped out. She was big buddies with Veranell, and with Louanne, and Bettina Taylor, who owns Bettina's Baubles ... where Barry Brewster got my teacup stickpin."

"I believe Miss Bettina Taylor is our final person of interest," Finbar said, writing in her name.

POI II: BETTINA TAYLOR

"Hmph. She's not *my* person of interest."

Finbar looked at her in surprise. "Thomasina? Have ye a history with Miss Taylor?"

"*I* don't, but *Earl* does. They used to date."

"Is that a fact? I've not seen evidence of the two of them together, but I've observed her after mass flirting with several men, married and not. She's quite pretty, though."

"I'm aware of that, and she's younger and not fat."

"Ah, lad. I don't think yer Detective Petry is the kind of man to be swayed by a shiny bauble," he said, making a play on the name of Bettina's shop. "Let's finish with her. Forty-ish, 5'2" tall, 100 to 110 pounds. A skinny, bony, runty woman to be sure."

"Oh, stop it. She's nothing of the sort. She's slender, with long dark black hair worn loose to her shoulders or in a low messy bun. Large dark brown eyes."

"Too much makeup, though."

"OK. I agree with that. Anyway, it's over with Earl and her, so I don't have any reason to be jealous. Right?"

"Righto. That's the spirit, lad. He cares for ye because you're you." He yawned and stretched his arms over his head. "Let's be done for this evening and have some dinner. We'll do our legwork tomorrow."

Finbar hopped up and began pulling covered dishes from the refrigerator, preparing to reheat the mashed red potatoes and fry up the extra fish. The dogs planted themselves at the edge of the dining room, knowing there would be plenty of scraps for them.

Tommie moved to the table and watched her friend go into chef-mode. They had laid out the foundation for their new investigation. The next part of the process was Thomasina Watson's favorite part—the interviews.

Chapter Eleven

FINBAR AND TOMMIE met in her carport at 7:00 a.m. the next morning. Since it was much too early for any of the shops in town to open, they decided to take the drive out to Levi's Animal Farm. Finbar provided thick slices of brown Irish soda bread lathered in butter and Wexford cheese for the trip, along with a thermos of hot tea. Half an hour later, they pulled up to the gate of Muller's Animal Farm and were met with a multitude of curious emus. Having never seen them before, Tommie was amazed at what huge creatures they were. In the distance behind them, she saw the larger ostriches from which the giant eggs came.

Since the main gate was open, Tommie drove on through and down the road toward the house in the distance. The road was flanked by fencing on both sides which kept the small herds of miniature donkeys, cows, and goats protected. An avid animal lover, she was anxious to park the car and pet them.

Moments before they arrived at the house, Levi Muller stepped into the drive, legs apart, arms folded across his chest. He did not look like the friendly, happy man Tommie and Finbar knew him to be.

Tommie stopped the car and killed the engine. Levi remained standing as Finbar exited the vehicle and waved his hand in the air.

"Halloo, Levi. How're the rabbits today?"

When the man failed to respond, Tommie joined Finbar, and the two of them approached slowly, smiling despite the defensive posture of the farmer. They stopped when they were two arms' length from him.

"Tag teaming now, are we?" Levi asked, his lips tightly pressed together.

"We … what?" Tommie stammered.

Levi continued in a clipped tone. "I've already told your boyfriend everything I know, Ms. Watson. What were you doing, waiting outside the gate for him to leave?"

"Earl was here? This morning?" she asked.

"Of course, he was here. You know that. Not ten minutes ago. He send you here to see if you could trip me up? Get me to admit I didn't sterilize those eggs?"

"Levi, I don't know what you're talking about." Tommie's eyes were wide. Her hand involuntarily went to her throat as if to protect herself from attack.

Levi scoffed and turned his wrath to Finbar. "I thought you were my friend, Holmes. You're no different from the others. Just because we're simple people don't mean we're stupid or criminals. I had nothing to do with the salmonella that woman got ahold of. Nothing!"

Finbar and Tommie stood stock still in the middle of the drive, staring at Levi Muller. They took a quick look at each other and then back at the man before them.

Finbar took a casual step forward. "Levi, we come to check on ye, to see if the bunnies were all right, and to bring some homemade brown bread and cheese."

Tommie nodded enthusiastically and hurried to the car to retrieve the Tupperware container with the rest of the soda bread and cheddar cheese. She returned, winded from the exertion, and held the container out to him.

Levi looked from one to the other, and seeing the confusion on their faces, hesitantly accepted the offering. Opening the lid slightly, he smelled the aroma of the fresh bread, closed the lid, and hung his head.

"I'm so sorry. I thought, well I thought you were here because … well … I'm a suspect in Veranell's death. Thought maybe you were here to … maybe they thought I'd confess or something …"

"Levi, we're your friends, not your enemies. Earl's your friend, too," Tommie said.

"I believe that. I told him I bleached those eggs just as thoroughly as I always do when I sell them. There's no way they would've left here contaminated. No way."

"Ye mentioned salmonella?" Finbar prompted.

Levi nodded. "He said salmonella killed Veranell Collins. Salmonella on the eggs I donated."

Tommie jumped as surely as she'd been shocked with a taser. Finbar took her arm and moved her forward, his other hand on Levi's shoulder.

"Let's have a bit of bread and talk about all this, shall we?" he said.

"Come on into the kitchen. Nobody's home right now. I've just put on a fresh pot of coffee," Levi said, ushering his guests through the screen door.

His house was exactly as Tommie imagined: white painted clapboard exterior, spotlessly clean kitchen with a large farmhouse style ceramic sink, white appliances, tiled countertops, wood plank flooring, and a huge picnic-style table with benches on the sides and ladderback chairs at either end. On shelves spaced about the white beadboard walls were pictures and memorabilia, interspersed with chicken and rooster figurines, along with eggs from the emus and ostriches Tommie had seen earlier. Looking at the eggs, her mind was immediately drawn back to his comment about salmonella killing Veranell Collins. She desperately wanted to ask but decided to let him broach the subject again himself.

Levi brought the coffeepot and three enameled mugs with matching saucers for the bread and set them on the long table.

"I'll just have water, if you don't mind, Levi,"

Tommie said. "I'm not a coffee drinker."

"Water, it is," he replied, getting up to fill her mug with water from the tap. "Serve yourself, Finbar."

The three of them sat and nursed their drinks for a bit, each taking a slice of the dense, still warm bread.

"Mmm. That's good. Did you make that yourself, Holmes? Maybe you can give me the recipe?" Levi asked.

"'Twill be me pleasure. How're the rabbits? I saw yer face on Sunday, and ye looked concerned. They're not unwell, I hope," Finbar said.

"No, they're OK. Thanks for asking. You know, small creatures like rabbits can contract human diseases if they're mishandled. I could tell Veranell was sick, and I was afraid she had something contagious. I took them to the vet right after ... right after she died. He said they were fine."

"I don't believe Mrs. Collins ever touched yer rabbits, lad. She didn't seem to like them. Father Duncan called me when he found them in the Bingo room and asked me to take them to m'own place for safekeeping."

"Did he? You mean, she was just going to leave them at the church in their hutch without giving them any food or water?" Levi was visibly alarmed at the idea. "What was that woman thinking?"

"I gather Mrs. Collins was not a fan of animals."

"Not her. Bettina Taylor. She was the one who came out and picked them up."

"Bettina?" Tommie said. "Why would Bettina Taylor come get the rabbits?"

Levi scoffed. "She was Veranell's little errand girl. She came here Thursday afternoon and demanded three white bunnies. I told her my white rabbit litter was too young, but the brown and white ones were old enough to be caged and rented for four days. She pitched an awful fit. Said Veranell wanted white bunnies, and she wanted them for free. I usually get $20 a day per rabbit, and I send along feed and fresh bedding."

"That's cheeky of them," Finbar said, "for quibbling with ye about the color *and* the money."

"Now you're telling me she just dropped them at the church and left them? How long?" Levi's face was red.

"Father Duncan called me Thursday evening after the Mass of the Lord's Supper service. I took them to my storage room and fed them and gave them clean water through the weekend. I delivered them to the gazebo after we finished the luncheon at Thomasina's. I took good care of them for ye, Levi. I loves the little ones, too."

"I have no doubt. That eases my mind. If I'd known Bettina would just dump them, I never would've let her take them."

"Did Bettina pick up the ostrich and emu eggs, too?" Tommie asked.

"Yes. Veranell had called and wanted six ostrich eggs and five emu eggs, all of them hollowed out and cleaned. I usually sell them, you know, for my spending money. I get $25 for fresh eggs and $50 for hollowed ones. But seeing as it was for charity, I agreed to donate them."

"That's very generous of ye. What's yer process for hollowing and cleaning these eggs, Levi? Is it difficult?" Finbar asked.

"I already explained it to Earl. Oh, sorry. I didn't mean to imply ... oh, what the heck. First of all, I only take the fresh eggs that are unfertilized. I drill a hole in the top and the bottom of the shell with a quarter-inch bit and blow the contents out with a compressed air canister into a clean pail. I save that and cook it up for the family. You can get a lot of scrambled eggs from one ostrich, you know."

Tommie giggled, and Levi echoed her laugh.

"Next, I submerge the shells in a mixture of bleach and water. You've got to make sure the bleach gets inside and out to sterilize the shell from any contaminants. The process takes a couple of hours because I do it several times. After that, I hang them in the sun to dry. I rigged up a little contraption out back with nylon fishing line and thin stainless-steel pieces of rods. The rods go in the top holes and out the bottoms. I twist them, and they hold the eggs on the taut fishing line while they dry. Works great."

"I'd like to see that," Finbar said.

"Sure, and I bet you want to pet the animals, don't you Tommie?" Levi winked at her, and she blushed. "Come on, then. Let's take a walk behind the house where the littlest critters live."

Levi directed them through the back door of the kitchen into a wire-fenced enclosure that was like a screened porch, but with a chicken wire roof. Tommie was delighted to see rabbits, chickens, turtles in a little pond, squirrels, and even some small potbelly pigs, all moving about freely.

When the three people walked into the area, they were set upon by the creatures, who happily cavorted about their feet. Levi took some broken pieces of carrots, lettuce, peanuts, and corn from boxes mounted on the side of the house and distributed treats. Tommie sat down on a wooden glider and was immediately surrounded by squirrels who crawled onto her lap and crept along her shoulders. While she was engaged in dispensing snacks, Finbar questioned Levi.

"So, what's this about the salmonella Detective Petry was talking about?" he asked.

Levi glowered. "He said they found salmonella when they did Veranell's autopsy. She had some kind of stomach condition, and the salmonella made her sick enough to kill her. I swear to you, those eggs were not contaminated with salmonella when I gave them to Bettina Taylor on Thursday."

"Did he say they actually found traces of salmonella on the eggs?"

"Yes! Sanderson Harper found salmonella on the outside of the shells, and he scraped the dye off a decorated ostrich egg and an emu egg and found contamination beneath the paint on the surface of the shells. I promise you; those eggs were clean when they were picked up!"

"Levi, don't get angry, but did ye have any problems with Veranell Collins that would brand you a suspect for her death?"

"She was a wicked woman, but there's plenty of those around. I didn't have any motive to kill her, even though she finagled free bunnies, eggs, and grand prize money from me. That's not reason to murder someone. Even the rumors she passed around are not reason enough."

"Rumors?"

"Oh, it was before you and Tommie moved here. She and Bettina spread a rumor that I mistreated my farm animals. It was upsetting, but people eventually believed that I would never do such a thing."

"I'm so sorry, Levi. Anyone who knows ye would never believe such rubbish. Yer a kind man. If it weren't so, yer animals wouldn't be so affectionate. D'you think Detective Petry believed you?"

Levi exhaled deeply. "I do, Finbar. He's a decent man who's doing his job. I didn't mean to go off on y'all when y'all first came up. I'm upset is all. Until they get the egg thing cleared up, I'm a suspect. That gets around in a small town. Piggyback that with the story about Bettina's dogs, and people will turn against me. I depend on money from the sale of eggs and animals for my livelihood. And from the school field trips, too. Who wants to bring kids to a place where they might get sick? Yeah, Earl believes me. I only hope everyone else will."

"Never fret, lad. The truth always outs. One last thing before I pull Missus Watson away from her admirers. If yer eggs weren't contaminated, how d'you think the salmonella got on them?"

"Finbar, when those eggs left my farm, they were clean and sanitized, or I would've gotten sick myself. The question Earl Petry needs to be asking is, who had access to them after they left this farm ... besides Bettina Taylor and Veranell Collins? Maybe y'all need to find out if anyone else in town has come down with salmonella."

Chapter Twelve

EARL PETRY was making his inquiries into exactly the idea Levi Muller suggested, but so far, nobody had visited Floribunda Urgent Care or any of the local physician's offices with symptoms suggesting salmonella. At present, Earl was having coffee in the office of Father Horace Duncan, the priest of St. Mary's Catholic Church.

"Cream or sugar for your coffee, Detective?"

Earl shook his head. "I'm good, thanks, Father. And I wish you'd call me Earl."

"All right. I didn't know what to say when you're in your official capacity."

"I'm not that official, right now. We're two men talking, that's all. I'm trying to get some details nailed down about Mrs. Veranell Collins."

"I'm happy to help, unless it involves something disclosed to me in confession. I'm afraid I can't reveal information my parishioners tell me in confidence."

"Oh, no, no, no. I wouldn't ask that. I just need a little insight into the woman who died, what she was involved in, who was in her circle of friends, that type of thing. That doesn't violate your oath, does it?"

Father Duncan's dusky eyes squinted as he broke into a wide grin. "Not at all. Let me see, Veranell Collins." He took a deep breath and held it a moment before continuing. "She was a faithful member for more than 50 years, from long before I came to this church. I'm told she was born and raised here in Floribunda, and her family was held in some esteem. Her husband passed over 20 years ago, and his family was quite well-to-do. Suffice to say, she was financially secure, even without the additional income she collected from a number of investments she made."

"Do you know what kind of investments?"

"Oh, no, no. That was none of my business. She had plenty of money, I'll say that."

"What about her health, Father?"

"Oh, well, I do know that she had a serious issue with her stomach and intestines. She suffered from celiac disease, irritable bowel syndrome, had food allergies. When we held our covered dish suppers, the families always had to list the ingredients on a card beside their casseroles and such so Veranell wouldn't accidently eat something that triggered her condition." He chuckled. "Whenever we got new members, that's the first thing the ladies informed them of. I remember once, when a visiting family attended a supper, and nobody had a chance to tell them to label their food. Veranell went on the warpath accusing them of trying to poison her. Needless to say, those people never visited again. And Finbar Holmes, when he brought food, he flat out refused to list the ingredients, just to spite her."

"Ha! Sounds like him. How did that go over?"

"Veranell snubbed his dishes, and so did her groupies." Father Duncan clapped his hand over his mouth. "Saints forgive me. That was a terrible thing to say."

"Hey, I'm a big proponent of 'if the shoe fits' school of thought. Tell me about the groupies."

"I shouldn't have said that. She had ... followers, I guess you'd say. Women who doted on her and hung on her every word and deed."

"Who were they? Can you give me their names? They may be helpful in this investigation, if they can shed some light on Mrs. Collins and her untimely death."

"Well, if you put it that way, I don't suppose it'd do any harm to name them. Let me see, from St. Mary's there was Bettina Taylor, Louanne Weller, Cynthia Rizzoli, and Linda Beadwell before she moved away. Melinda Layton and Eva Edgerton from Trinity Episcopal were in the group. Katherine Clay and that French lady Simone Lorence from First Baptist were, too, but those four were the only non-Catholics. Did you know Eva was Catholic before she married into the Episcopal church? Lately, though, I have seen her at the suppers, but she never attends mass. Naturally, Veranell didn't have much to do with any of the Protestant churches."

"Naturally. Father, did you notice whether or not Mrs. Collins seemed to be more ill than usual in the past week or so, specifically just before Easter Sunday?"

"Now that you mention it, Earl, she did seem to be paler and shakier ever since Friday."

"What happened on Friday that brought her illness to your attention?"

Father Duncan got up, refilled his coffee cup, added three packets of sugar, and splashed some caramel creamer into it. He nodded at Earl, who refused a refresher. Sitting back at his desk, the priest took a deep swallow, smacked his lips, and grinned sheepishly before continuing.

"Mmm. I confess I've got a bit of a sweet tooth. Let me go back to Thursday because that's when I last saw her feeling well. Bettina Taylor came to the church about noon and brought a bunch of ostrich and emu eggs. Veranell met her in the Bingo hall. You see, Veranell was going to decorate them for the charity raffle. She did it every year. It was kind of 'her thing' for Easter, and it had to be just so. Anyway, Bettina also brought in a cage full of cute furry bunnies. It was those that you saw in the gazebo, little brown and white ones. I was in the hallway when I heard Veranell go off into a rage shouting at poor Bettina about the bunnies."

"What was wrong with the bunnies?"

"They weren't white. Veranell wanted white ones. She called Bettina a 'stupid, good-for-nothing, empty-headed idiot' for getting the wrong color."

"She said exactly that?"

"She did! I was appalled. Bettina started to cry, and Veranell called her a 'sniffling baby' and a 'woman-wannabe.' I tell you; I was rooted to the floor in shock."

"I imagine so." Earl blinked his eyes rapidly.

"Bettina explained that Levi wouldn't let her have the white rabbits, and Veranell said she would see about that. She told Bettina to be sure and deliver her lunch on Friday because she'd have to work the whole afternoon and all-day Saturday to decorate the eggs for the prize raffles. Then she said, 'don't mess it up,' only she used the F-word, and she left the room. They both attended the Mass of the Lord's Supper that evening, but they didn't sit together as they usually did."

Earl was silent as Father Duncan drained his coffee cup. He could see the old priest was shaken.

"I'm sorry, Earl. That was wrong of me to be so talkative about things concerning my flock and to relate such graphic language, but I feel you have good reason to ask, and I want to be helpful. I'm sure there must've been some reason for Veranell to act so cruelly to Bettina. She was likely already sick, don't you think?"

"I don't know, Father. Tell me when you knew she was getting sicker. When did you first realize it?"

"Oh, that would've been early Friday evening. I had

been in the office putting the final touches on my Easter Sunday message after the Three Hours' Agony service which ended at 3:00. I locked up and walked past the Bingo hall on my way out to tell Veranell I was leaving. She was going to be in there for a while decorating eggs, and I wanted to let her know I was locking all the doors. I heard a retching sound, and when I stuck my head in the door, she was bent over the wastebasket vomiting. I asked if she needed help, but she said she was all right. She had some containers of broth in the freezer that she kept there in case of a flare up, and she was going to thaw some out."

"That happened a lot?"

"Not a lot, but sometimes. She knew how to manage her disease. She made the broths herself, so there was no chance of eating something she was allergic to."

"Was she drinking broth when you saw her?"

"No, come to think of it, there was a Styrofoam take-out box on the table. It must've been the food she told Bettina to deliver."

"Do you know where it came from?"

"She usually ordered in from The Lunch Pad. They had strict instructions on her take-outs of what she could and could not eat. I don't know for sure, but that's probably where the plate was from."

"I'll check it out. Did you see her on Saturday?"

"I stopped by my office for a bit. I passed Bettina coming out of the parking lot. Eva was with her. They rolled the window down and said they had dropped off some supplies for Veranell. When I went by the Bingo hall, Veranell was working on those eggs, painting, and sticking on shiny jewel things. She had a container of soup on the table and kept sipping from it. She looked pretty bad, though. Pale, clammy, her hair kind of mussed up. But she waved me away when I asked how she felt. Told me she was too busy to chat, so I left."

"You attended Tommie's luncheon on Sunday."

"I did, and it was wonderful. Food was great. Decorations delightful. Those themed teas and eggs were the best. Veranell didn't eat much, as you probably recall. She was already pretty ill, but she was a trouper about it. Next thing I knew, she collapsed in the gazebo and died, and I gave her the Last Rites on the spot. A tragic death."

Earl rose and patted the old priest on the shoulder.

"Thank you, Father. You've been immensely helpful with a truly horrific situation. One last thing you might be able to help me with. Has anybody else been ill these past few days that you've noticed?"

Father Duncan tilted his head back and pursed his lips. "Now that you mention it, Bettina didn't make it to Sunday mass, and it's not like her to miss. She didn't come to the brunch, either. I didn't see Louanne Weller at mass or at the luncheon. She came to the park for a little while, but she left before the grand prize raffle. I talked to Paul Weller at the egg hide, and he said his wife had complained of being sick after eating out Friday night. They had dinner reservations for Saturday night, but he had to cancel hers because she was still so sick."

"Hmm. Do you know where the Wellers ate dinner Friday night?"

"Sure, I do. Same place Bettina Taylor ate dinner. Caife Caife Holmes."

Chapter Thirteen

FINBAR AND TOMMIE passed right by Earl's squad car parked at St. Mary's, but they were too engrossed in conversation to notice it. They drove on to town and pulled in behind Caife Caife Holmes. They had solidified their game plan for the remainder of the day's investigation and were anxious to get to it.

Finbar planned to interview the Alvarez brothers while Tommie paid a visit to Jo Clay and Elly James at their shops. The detective duo had already arranged to meet their friends Henry, Don, Susan, and Elaine at The Lunch Pad at noon. They hoped they would be able to get Sid and Jeanette Spock to sit down with them, too.

After locking the car door, Finbar took a left and

crossed the cut-through street to the back of the brothers' shops while Tommie walked on to the right to conduct her interviews, first at Elly's store, and then across the lot at Jo's ceramic shop.

Leo Alvarez was working on a strip of softened leather when Finbar entered. His handsome face lit up when he saw his Irish friend.

"*Hola, el detective señor* Holmes. How are you, my friend?" Leo said.

"I am *muy bueno*, Leo," Finbar replied with an imaginary tip of the hat. "What're ye working on?"

"This is a fine calfskin I will make into a new belt. I am tooling some designs on it. Do you like it?"

"Ah, sure. That's a lovely piece of workmanship. Are ye making it for someone in particular?"

"No. This is one I am trying out a new pattern on."

Finbar ran his hand along the soft leather. "If ye can make it a size 30, I'll take it off yer hands."

"It is yours! I will have it ready at the day's end. What brings you to my shop today? Just a belt?"

"I am out and about on the town with Missus Watson. We're doing our errands separately and together since her shop is closed for the time being."

Leo's smile drooped. "It is sorrowful to me that she has been suspected of hurting that woman. I do not believe it, but there are others who talk unkindly about her."

"Yes, yer right. 'Tis a pity, sure. I'm glad you and yer brother are not like that."

"We are not. *Señora* Watson has been good to us since we've been living here. We care much for her."

"Who do we care for, *mi hermano?*" Santino asked from the connecting doorway.

"Haloo, Santino. *¿Que pasa?* What brings you over here?" Finbar asked, shaking the man's hand.

"I heard you talking, *señor* Holmes, and I wanted to see how you were liking your sandals or if you needed an adjustment on the buckles."

"Ah, they're grand, Santino. Most comfortable ones I have ever owned," Finbar said.

"And I am going to make this belt to match them," Leo said, holding the leather strip aloft.

"What were you saying, *hermano*, about who we care much for?" Santino asked.

"*La señora* Watson."

"*Sí.* She is a fine woman. A very good friend to us. I am so angry about the way she is being treated with the death of *la bruja.*"

Finbar cocked his head and lifted his eyebrows.

"That means a witch," Leo said. "The Collins woman was such a person."

"Did you and yer brother have a run in with her?" Finbar asked.

The two brothers looked at each other with identical grimacing expressions and nods.

"She did not like us. She tried to get us to leave our shops," Santino said.

"Every six months up and up goes the rent. We cannot pay so much," Leo said.

"We have thought we must give one shop up and combine into one business, but the spaces are each so small." Santino held his hands about a foot apart to demonstrate how cramped the shop would be.

"What did she have to do with rising up yer rents?" Finbar asked.

"She held the leases. She could do as she pleased. There was a ... what is that word that means an extra part added to something?" Leo asked.

"A clause?" Finbar suggested.

"*Sí.* She made a clause that we must sign a new lease every six months, and she can change the rent," Leo said.

"That would make ye rather angry, I suspect," Finbar said. "Did ye try to renegotiate with her?"

The brothers shook their heads solemnly.

"She would not. She did not want us here. We were the wrong color and religion for *la bruja.*" Santino said.

"She did not like our ladies, either. She told bad things around town about them," Leo said.

"That is right. She said that Jo was forced to divorce from her husband because she was unfaithful to him. It made her cry because it was not true. Elly says it was a big lie. Jo was not unfaithful. Sometimes people do not get along." Santino shrugged. "It cannot be helped."

"And she told all who listened that the jellies made by Elly were spoiled, but an inspector came to test them, and they were not. The man destroyed much of her jams and jellies in his testing, and people were afraid to buy them for a long time. *La bruja* said also that my *chica* was prejudiced against people who are not white, that she had a fight with the barber about some jellies his church did not pay for, and that Jo called *señora* Rush a bad name behind her back," Leo said, his fists clenched.

"Are ye talking about Amos Mosby? And Aubrey Rush?" Finbar asked.

The Alvarez brothers nodded.

"I don't believe it," Finbar said. "If Elly or Jo didn't like people of color, they certainly wouldn't take up with you two. Doesn't that make sense? Bah, don't listen to the likes of that kind of woman. No wonder she was killed."

The brothers stared at him.

"What do you mean she was killed?" Santino's brows furrowed as he shook his head from side to side. "That is a lie, *señor*. I do not believe *señora* Watson gave her bad medicine. I think she had a heart attack."

"No, no, Santino. You misunderstand. I wasn't referring to Thomasina. But I do believe someone meant Mrs. Collins to die. For that matter, I've always felt meanness can kill a person sure as a weapon." Finbar forced himself to grin.

"This is true, *el detective*. Perhaps it is best to put it in different words. You are much like us when it comes to saying things that Americans misunderstand," Leo said.

"Someone might think bad of you. *La bruja* told

many mean things about you, too," Santino said.

"About me? What?" Finbar asked.

"Oh, *señor* Holmes. She said in your café you cooked spoiled meals and tried to poison her. I hope people do not think *you* killed her ... and not with meanness ... but with food," Leo said.

Chapter Fourteen

TOMMIE WATSON filled her hand basket with various jars from the shelves of Elly's store as the two women walked along the aisles and chatted. She was delighted to find a wide variety of sugar-free items for Finbar, who was diabetic, but she was even more thrilled to sample the ones with exotic names like *Muscadine Marmalade*, *Prickly Pear Preserves*, and *Happy Jalapeño Jelly*.

"Leo Alvarez likes to pronounce that last one with all 'h' sounds. He says it's 'happy halapeenyo helly.' Makes me laugh," Elly said with a shy smile.

"They're nice guys, the Alvarez brothers," Tommie said with a knowing look. "I saw you sitting with Leo at the park yesterday."

"Yeah, I guess pretty much everybody saw us

together. We've been going out for a few months, but we were trying to keep it a secret."

"Why, Elly? What does it matter who you date?"

"Oh, come on, Tommie. You know how people are in this small town. Look at you and Earl. Yak, yak, yak. Talk of the town since February. In your case, most of the talking is other women who are jealous you made the catch and they didn't."

"Yes, I know." Tommie blushed. "All the same, though. I think Leo's truly fortunate ... and so are you."

"Thanks. Not everyone feels that way." She shook her head, and her light blond waves bounced. "Me and Jo took a big chance sitting with the guys on Sunday."

"Big dang deal! So what? Is there somebody else hot on their trail?"

Elly burst out in giggles. "No! But it's been a scandal already. We've had people from our church calling us, saying the Devil is tempting us to join a cult. My business has dropped off in just the past two days except for lookie-loos coming to stare me down through the window, to see the white girl who's going with a Mexican."

Tommie's jaw dropped. "Elly! That's awful. I don't think that. Finbar doesn't either."

Elly impulsively put her arms around Tommie's neck. "Thanks. You know, Me and Jo met the guys at the movies Saturday night, and then we sat in Jo's car in the Post Office parking lot afterward. I swear, we almost broke up, what with being scared of exactly what's going on now.

"I talked to you and Jo at Caife Caife Holmes on Friday night, and you both seemed really down in the dumps. Is that why?"

"Yeah. We parked at the Post Office afterward and talked about it … and cried. We were going to call the guys and explain things to them, but then we saw Aubrey Rush over at St. Mary's, and we decided to wait until Saturday."

"What was Aubrey Rush doing at St. Mary's? She's Jewish, isn't she?"

"She is. I don't know, but she was kind of sneaking around, it looked like. She'd crouch down, and then she'd stand up and walk around. And then she'd crouch down again, like she was hiding from somebody."

"Strange. Do you know her very well?"

"Not really, but she's always been nice to me. I got some really cool jars from her antique store. Those over on the display shelves. I'm not selling them, but I thought they'd make great decorations. She's bought jelly from me lots of times."

"Did you notice anyone else at the church?"

"Well, not with her on Friday night, but in the afternoon, before we went to dinner, we saw Amos Mosby go inside the building."

"Hmm! That's peculiar."

"Maybe not. I bet Amos was going to cut the priest's hair. He's such a nice man. Leo says Amos gives the best haircuts around."

"Finbar says the same. You've had a full weekend

of new and unusual happenings, haven't you, Elly?

"Well, that's not the half of it," Elly said in a conspiratorial whisper, looking around. "When we were in the car with Leo and Santino Saturday night, thinking about how to tell them we were breaking up ... and you can't tell anybody this ... not a soul, Tommie Watson."

"I promise. What happened?

"Leo and Santino proposed to us, right there in the car in the parking lot!"

Tommie sucked in air. "And what did y'all say?"

"We said 'yes!' We both did." Elly squealed and clapped her hands.

Tommie hugged the petite woman in earnest. "I am so excited for you. This was Saturday? How wonderful. I won't say a word until y'all make it public. Except Jo. Can I go tell her I know and hug her?"

"Yes, yes. Let me put your stuff in a bag ... no charge for you, Tommie ... and I'll give her a call while you walk over."

Elly packaged Tommie's items and sent her out the back door on her way to The Clay Pigeon. In less than two minutes, Tommie made it to the store and was greeted with a bear hug from Jo Clay. The two women made the obligatory squeals and coos reserved for engagement announcements before pulling apart.

"Are there any plans yet? Rings? Ceremony? A double ceremony, maybe?" Tommie gushed excitedly.

"They're going to get us rings, but they refuse to

give Bettina's Baubles their business. Bettina is so hateful and racist to them ... just like Veranell was."

"Veranell and Bettina are racist?"

"Oh, my Lord, yes! And Eva and Louanne, too. But Veranell was the worst. She spread so many rumors about people of color ... although that's not what *she* called them ... and Jews and Mormons and Mennonites and even Mr. Holmes because he's Irish. Yeow! She was a piece of work! I'm not sorry she's gone. No telling what she would have said about Elly and me engaged to Hispanic men. But I don't care. I love my Santino, and Elly loves her Leo. We couldn't be happier."

"Me too, Jo. I'm so thrilled for you. Hey, speaking of Veranell and the others in the mean girl club, have they been talking about me?"

"Are you kidding? Bettina still thinks she's got rights to Earl Petry. You're an interloper. That's the word she uses. She says she's getting him back if she has to wipe you off the face of the earth."

"Seriously? She's that jealous?"

"Honey, you don't know the half of it. She's even laid claim to Tom Beadwell, and him just divorced."

"Tom Beadwell? You mean Linda Beadwell's recent ex? I didn't know they had dated."

"Oh, they haven't. Bettina just wants him. Funny thing is, he's been seeing Eva Edgerton on the sly for at least six months now."

"Wait, what? He and Linda just split up in March

because of her affair with Charles Williams."

"Ain't that some stuff? Divorce your wife for having an affair when you're having one, too? Throwing stones in a glass house, as they say. But enough about them. How about you and Earl? Any future plans for y'all?"

Tommie blushed. "Oh, I don't know, Jo. We kind of like things the way they are. We'll just have to see, you know? Anyhow, I am so delighted for you and Elly. Please let me know what I can do for you. I can do a luncheon or a shower or whatever. You tell me."

"We will, we will."

"Well, I've got to meet Finbar at The Lunch Pad in a few minutes, but before I go, can you tell me about Aubrey Rush being over at St. Mary's? Elly said she was."

"I couldn't tell if she was at St. Mary's or at Trinity. They're right there together on that same block, and the backs of the buildings make like an L-shape. From my point of view, I'd say she was traipsing around the cemetery between the two ... popping up and down like playing 'Marco Polo' in the pool. Weirdest thing I ever saw, but hey, who am I to talk about strange behavior? Listen, wait right here just a minute. I've got something for you." She ran through the back door and came right back holding an object in her hand.

"What's this, Jo?"

"I made it for you after you and Mr. Holmes solved those murders last month. I've been meaning to give it to you. Hope you like it."

Tommie accepted the item and held it up. It was a large mug finished in a bright turquoise and yellow glaze. Bold black lettering on the side read *Thomasina Watson of Holmes & Watson, Investigators.*

"I love it, Jo! Thank you so much," Tommie said.

"It's just a little something. I know your favorite mug was broken when, um, when ... you know, that stuff with Sarah Beth Brewster. Anyway, if you need any custom mugs or teacups for your shop, I'd be glad to make some for you ... or you can come, and we'll make them together. Anytime. We'll support each other's businesses."

"That's a deal. We need all the help we can get!"

Chapter Fifteen

TOMMIE felt her phone buzzing in her scrubs pocket as she walked toward The Lunch Pad. She saw it was a text from Finbar: *"Change of lunch plans. Meet at my shop ASAP."*

Tommie did an about-face and strolled to the back of Caife Caife Holmes. As she stepped inside, she was surprised to see the "fab four" sitting at two tables. They waved when she entered. Finbar was in the kitchen area, preparing an assortment of lunch items, including toasted squares of brown Irish soda bread, cubes of Irish Dubliner cheese, *Quick Pickled Veggies, Slánte Slaw*, and a dip made with leftover minced smoked salmon, cod, and tuna.

"Halloo, Missus. Have a seat. Lunch will be right up," Finbar called.

Tommie pulled out a chair and sat at a table beside

the twin sisters, Susan Clay and Elaine Frank.

"Hi, Tommie. Have you heard the news yet?" Susan asked, her eyes wide.

"Of course, she hasn't," her brother Don said. "For cripes sake, she's just gotten here."

"What's going on?" Tommie asked.

"The Lunch Pad is closed down," Susan said.

"What?" Tommie did a double-take.

"Sister and I went down there early, and there was a sign on the door from the Health Inspector that said the premises were closed until further notice," Elaine said.

Tommie looked up at Finbar, who nodded in agreement as he set bowls and dishes on the tables.

"But why?" Tommie was wide-eyed.

"It didn't say on the notice, but we caught Sid outside the back door. He was so upset; he was pacing around puffing on a cigarette. Don't tell anyone. I don't think Jeanette knows he smokes. Sid said the Health Inspector was checking for salmonella contamination. Can you believe that?" Susan said.

"Rather puts ye off yer feed, doesn't it?" Finbar asked. "I don't believe it, though. I've been in their kitchen."

"That's true. Finbar was a professional food inspector in Ireland. He knows when something's not clean or up to par. Don't you, Holmes?" Henry Erving said.

"I do. They've a respectable clean place," Finbar agreed. "Here, let's eat. 'Tis not much but leftovers repurposed, but it should fill us up right well."

The guests served themselves and began eating, all the while speculating on what was happening at their favorite lunch spot. Half an hour later, they were joined by Sid and Jeanette Spock, the owners of The Lunch Pad.

Finbar rushed to bring them plates and beverages. Sid served himself a heaping portion of everything, but Jeanette just picked at her food, frequently wiping her eyes.

"I just don't know what could've happened," she lamented. "We're always so careful."

"Sure, sure. I know yer place is usually spic and span. I've a mind to believe it's a put up," Finbar said.

"Why would somebody do that?" Sid asked.

"I'm not an expert, but 'tis my opinion it has to do with Mrs. Veranell Collins and her death."

"I heard she drank ..." Sid clammed up abruptly.

Tommie sighed. "You heard she drank my tonic and died from it, right? Isn't that what everybody's heard?"

The group collectively looked embarrassed and ashamed as they continued to eat without making eye contact with Tommie.

"I don't think that, Tommie," Henry said. "I remember how you were there when Coral and Beverly died. You're not a killer. You're a healer."

Tommie was touched and hastened to blink away tears. "Thanks, Henry, but I don't heal; I offer suggestions to promote wellness and balance. Just so you all know, my tonic was cleared, and so were the foods I prepared for the luncheon. None of the rest of you have been nauseous, have you? Come to think of it, Jeanette, have any of your customers come down sick? Don't you think, if there was salmonella in your kitchen, the symptoms would surface, and other people would be terribly ill?

"Yer right, Missus," Finbar said. "And who's the only one who's gotten sick? Veranell Collins. No, lads. This is all about her."

There was silence as they each considered his statement. Don laid his fork down and looked around.

"Y'all realize we are sitting with two of the best detectives in Floral County. And we're not so bad on gathering dirt ourselves, are we Sisters? Maybe we need to share information to see what we can come up with."

"Excellent idea, Brother," Susan said. "Who knows anything important about Veranell Collins, other than she was a hideous shrew of a woman who did her best to make other people as miserable as she was?"

"Sister! What a thing to say," Don's eyes widened.

"Don't be so naïve, Donny. You know she was a viper, and so do you, Henry. Who do you think circulated the stories about you and Coral and Beverly? How did we know about Charles Williams and his affair with Linda Beadwell? Veranell Collins was a master at mixing truth with rumors all around town." Elaine was vehement. "Let me tell you what else she said. Jeanette, she said you were ignorant of the gluten-free requirements most reputable restaurants offered. She said she had to give you specific written instructions so you wouldn't screw up her meals."

Jeanette was aghast, and Sid just chewed harder.

"She … she did give us instructions, and we followed them religiously whenever she called in take-out orders. Like she did Friday morning. I made her orders up myself," Jeanette said.

"She didn't call 'em in, Jeanie. Bettina Taylor did, remember?" Sid said. "Picked 'em up, too. I even checked the ticket to make sure Veranell's was correct. Said right on the note *'No milk products. No wheat. Gluten-free.'* I showed Bettina when she got there."

"What did she order?" Finbar asked.

"Two salad plates. *Comet Chicken Salad, Constellation Coleslaw, Pluto Potato Salad,* and a *Crater Cookie.* Jeanie made one with skim milk yogurt and apple cider vinegar, just as Veranell had specified, and swapped out a gluten-free *Satellite Sugar Cookie.* The chicken came fresh from Winn Dixie that morning, and we used it all day with no problems," Sid said.

"We heard from Levi Muller that the eggs Veranell decorated were contaminated with salmonella, but Levi swears he sterilized them, and I believe him. He showed us his process," Tommie said.

"Oh, poor Levi. She was so horrible to him," Susan said. "She tried to ruin his business."

"How so?" Henry asked.

"Last year, Bettina bought herself two Border Collie puppies. She was dating Earl Petry at the time, and she thought, because Earl loves dogs, that she'd use the puppies to keep him interested. Well, they split up, and the dogs began to get really big, so she just up and dropped them at Levi's farm one day. He couldn't keep them because they weren't trained and kept trying to herd his birds. He gave them to The Doggie Dorm, and they were rehomed. Veranell said he had to surrender the dogs because he was cruel, and they were in such bad shape. They were mistreated, all right, but not by him. Bettina neglected them when they didn't work to keep Earl on the hook. Anyway, Veranell spread the rumor around, and the schools cancelled their field trips."

"She had a particular dislike for Levi, didn't she sister?" Elaine said.

"She sure did. About 25 years ago, Levi's wife Gayla gave birth to their second son. She had postpartum depression so bad she left Levi and took the boys with her to live with her mother in Alabama," Susan said.

"I remember that," Don said. "He was devastated until Melinda Fuller—now she's Melinda Layton—anyway, she came home for summer break from college and he had that fling going."

"With Melinda?" Tommie's eyebrows shot up.

"No, her roommate. They were quite an item until Veranell stuck her nose in it. Then suddenly, after months of no contact, Gayla shows up with the children and moves back in. Levi's new romance went up in flames. Veranell did that." Susan bobbed her head emphatically.

"That's right. So, I say, if there was something

wrong with Veranell's takeout order, it happened *after* it left your kitchen. I wouldn't worry about them finding any salmonella. The Lunch Pad will be cleared, and any scandal will blow over. We'll make sure of it," Elaine said with a decisive nod and a full mouth.

"What d'you know about the Alvarez brothers?" Finbar tried to sound casual.

"Oh, I like them," Susan said. "Did you know they're dating Elly James and Jo Clay? Jo Clay's like my ex-sister-in-law. She married my ex-husband's brother Jimmy Clay. Too bad she didn't ask me before she hooked up with him. I could've told her he and Larry both had a bad case of faulty zippers."

"Sister! There you go again!" Don was appalled.

"For cripes sake, Donny. You know good and well neither of those Clay boys could be faithful to one woman. Larry cheated on me. Jimmy cheated on Jo. That's a fact."

"You're right. You're right. It's just the way you say it that's shocking," Don said shaking his head.

"I heard it the other way around. Coral said she heard from Veranell that Jo was the one who got caught cheating, and that she lost her position as the Sunday School Secretary at the Baptist church because of it. I didn't believe it because …" Henry's voice trailed off.

"Because you used to date Jo. We know all about that, Henry. Don't worry. We don't care," Susan said.

Elaine and Susan gazed at Henry with doe eyes. Tommie suppressed a chuckle. Both sisters were obviously smitten with him. *Ah, the joys of elder love*, she thought, *and I'm right in there with them with Earl.*

"What d'you know about Veranell not liking people of color and other religions?" Finbar asked.

"That's the truth, Holmes. She was a raging racist. Used all the vulgar names for minorities, but she always stated things politely, as if that excused what she said ... you know what I mean ... like the 'bless her heart' our Southern women tack onto a statement," Don said.

"D'you mean like after a sneeze?" Finbar asked.

"No, Finbar. It's a euphemism that means the opposite," Tommie said.

Seeing his confused face, Elaine elaborated. "It's an insult covered up by a seemingly kind sentiment. Like if you saw a woman at church wearing a mismatched outfit, you'd say, 'she looks like she picked that out of the hamper after a three-day drunken spree,' and that would be the truth."

"But then, you'd end it with 'bless her heart' to soften it up a bit ... to make it sound like you're being sympathetic when you're really not," Susan elaborated.

Finbar grimaced. "You women are brutal."

Tommie pasted an exaggerated frown on her face. "Aw, he's beginning to understand us ... bless his heart."

Finbar's eyes widened, and he shook his head slowly. "Truly frightening, Thomasina." He looked around the table at the others. "So, if I understand ye correctly, Veranell Collins was notorious for spreading rumors about nearly everyone in town?"

"That's about it. Call out some names, and we can tell you a rumor she circulated about them."

Finbar and Tommie took the opportunity to ask about the people of interest on their list, all in one fell swoop. They alternated throwing out names, and Don and his sisters took turns providing the rumors.

Finbar started the exchange. "Amos Mosby," he said, recalling the names on the list.

"She called him the N-word. Said his shop was unsanitary and infested with head lice. Also, his church didn't pay their bills," Don said.

"Aubrey Rush," Tommie continued.

"Said she was a thieving Jew-girl who took antiques from properties without permission to sell in her shop. She attributed that rumor to Jo and Elly, but I don't believe they ever said such a thing," Susan said.

"The Alvarez brothers."

"Illegal wetbacks mingling with white women. I'm telling you, Veranell was harsh," Elaine said when Tommie gasped. "Ask us about some more."

"Elly James."

"She sold contaminated jelly and disliked Aubrey and Amos because of their religion and color, but Veranell said Elly 'loved them Mexican boys.' She said the same about Jo," Susan said.

"Tommie Watson." Finbar glanced at his friend.

"She called Tommie a fat outsider and a doctor-wannabe who sells ineffective remedies to ignorant people and can't keep a man." Elaine pushed food around on her plate to keep from looking at Tommie.

"Whoa! I've *never* claimed to be a doctor. I'm a certified herbalist, a natural wellness practitioner. Funny, isn't it, that she bought herbal tonics from me?" Tommie bristled at the comment.

"We don't agree with her, Tommie. We're just telling you what she passed around." Don's brows creased.

"I understand. I don't blame y'all. What did she say about Finbar?"

"I'll tell you that one, Holmes," Henry said. "She called you a 'low-life Mick' who couldn't cook his way out of a paper bag. She said you were an ignorant foreigner and had no consideration for anyone with a medical condition."

"Ach. She was a right git. She got angry because I wouldn't change the menu to suit her. Them words don't bother me one bit, Henry," Finbar responded.

"In case you're wondering, she even talked about her own circle of friends," Don said. "Sisters, why don't you just name them off."

The sisters alternated in a recitation of rumors and innuendos that had circulated around the town. Elaine began the litany.

"Bettina Taylor was an addle-brained simpleton who could barely follow instructions. She was hungry for any man in pants and would do anything to attract them."

"Eva Edgerton declared selected items in her store were 'damaged goods' and sold them at discounted prices to her friends while receiving credits from her suppliers for their damages," Susan said. "I noticed, however, that Veranell frequently wore clothing from her boutique, and I heard she conned Eva into giving them to her for free. Oh, and the news was Eva was having a fling with Tom Beadwell long before he divorced Linda. I've heard she'll be leaving Trinity soon to join Tom at St. Mary's."

"Louanne Weller wore a lot of Eva's 'heavily discounted' clothing and had her own 'damaged goods' scam. She got rebates from the suppliers for what she said were cracked liquor bottles, then she sold them at a discount to her friends. Veranell said Father Duncan was one of her biggest customers, because he loves to drink and even polishes off the sacramental wine after every service. Also—and I know this for a fact—Louanne is cheating on Paul with a man in Rivertown *and* a man in Cypress City. She used to be a patient of my first ex-husband Dr. Nelson Stone, the psychiatrist, until they got involved in some kind of sordid affair … so I was told," Elaine said with a snicker.

"Melinda Layton runs in their circle sometimes. She's president of the Trinity LCO and manages charities Veranell would have liked to run. Veranell said Melinda bought the discounted clothing from Eva and used the difference in the money her husband Carl gave her for a clothing allowance to buy discounted liquor from Weller's. Apparently, Melinda has a little drinking problem," Susan said, "but, at least, she's faithful to her hubby."

"Is that it, Sisters?" Don asked with a grimace.

"My gosh. Isn't that enough?" Tommie asked.

The sisters shrugged and went back to eating while the Spocks, Finbar, and Tommie sat in shocked silence. Henry just shook his head and shrugged in disbelief.

A knock on the front door caught their attention, and in walked Earl Petry with another man. Earl lifted his hand in a wave and motioned Finbar over. He introduced Holmes to the gentleman and walked toward the group seated at the tables.

"Hello, folks. Nice to see you. Sid, Jeanette. I'm sorry about your place, but I'm sure everything will get cleared up soon. Tommie, can I talk to you? Y'all excuse us for a minute," Earl said.

He helped Tommie stand and guided her over to a more private place near the back door.

"Hey, darlin'. You doing all right?" he said, giving her a peck on the cheek.

"I'm good, Earl. Haven't been inside my shop, just like you asked," she replied, a deep blush coloring her face.

"Oh, about that. It's clear. You can go in and clean it up and reopen whenever you want."

"Thanks. Can you tell me what's happening about Sid and Jeanette's place? I know about the salmonella."

"I figured. I don't look for anything to be wrong there. But, if there's a complaint, we have to have the health people investigate and close the place down until they're satisfied it's clean. Um, that's the County Health Inspector who came here with me." He cocked his head in the direction of Finbar and the man at the front, who seemed to be engaged in a tense conversation over a piece of paper.

"They're closing down Caife Caife Holmes? There was a complaint?" She searched Earl's inscrutable face for clues. Finding none, she pressed her lips together tightly. "That's ridiculous. Who made the complaint?"

"I can't tell you that, Tommie. Suffice to say, there are three people who've complained. Not to worry. It's just temporary. I know how fastidious Holmes is. It's just like your place. Has to be checked out. Please don't make a big issue of it, OK?" He smiled and put his large hand beneath her chin, tapping her lower lip with his thumb.

Tommie sighed and met his gaze, feeling a bit unsteady on her feet, as usual.

"All right. Is there anything else I need to know?"

Earl dropped his head, maintaining eye contact. He felt her tremble and gave her an encouraging smile.

"Yes. I'm afraid I'll have to cancel our date tomorrow night. There've been some developments that've come to light, and I'm going to have to work. I'll make it up to you."

"I understand. I've got some irons in the fire, too."

"Tommie ..."

"Earl ..."

"Lord, help me, woman. Will you please be careful? I'm not gonna tell you to stop investigating, but watch your back. There are pieces of this puzzle that just don't fit. I don't want you in danger like last time. Do your sleuthing on paper. It's safer. For me. All right?"

Tommie squinted her eyes and looked up at him. "All right. Am I still an official suspect?"

"Nope. But you're still *my* person of interest."

Chapter Sixteen

FINBAR AND TOMMIE went home instead of interviewing any more people for the afternoon. He was livid for the whole ride and spewed forth a steady stream of curses as he fumed. He continued when they entered his house, where his blathering was subsequently interspersed with great swallows of Guinness. Although Homes did his swearing in the Irish Gaelic language, Tommie was painfully aware of the subtext and easily recognized many people's names among the outbursts. She kept quiet and let him rant. The dogs, however, cowered and whined. As he drained the last of the large can of ale and took another cold one to his easy chair, Tommie dared to speak.

"Are you done now? The dogs are terrified."

Finbar looked surprised as though he were

emerging from a thick fog. "*Cad a dúirt tú faoi na madraí?* What did you say about the dogs?"

"You're scaring them. You need to calm down."

Finbar noticed Sherlock slinking away with his normally pert ears laid flat against his head.

"Ah, Jayze. *Tá brón orm, a lads.* I'm sorry, lads. Here, Sherlock. I'm not mad at ye. C'mon to me."

The little terrier jumped up onto his master's lap, his stubby tail wagging. Zed and Red emerged from behind the sofa and nuzzled Tommie's outstretched hand.

"Are you all right finally, or do you need yet another Guinness on standby to calm you down?"

Finbar sat back against the overstuffed chair and propped his feet on the round leather pouf, the little dog huddled against his belly.

"No, no. I'm sure this one will be plenty. I'm sorry to you, as well as the dogs, Thomasina. I've never in m'life been so undone. A former food inspector closed down by another health official. It's unthinkable. Who d'you think done it to me?"

"Veranell Collins, probably. The sisters just told us she complained that you didn't take her medical issues into consideration."

"And as a chef, I bloody well don't have to. If them that has issues don't want to eat at my place, they don't have to. According to what the health official told me, there were three complaints. Three people said I made them sick."

"I can pretty well figure who they are, can't you?

Think and connect the dots. Veranell got mad, and who did she use to spread her web of lies? Her little entourage. Bettina, Louanne, Eva, Melinda, those women from First Baptist. Could've been any one of them, if Veranell told them to. I would put my money on Bettina and Louanne. They're the ones who cancelled their Saturday night reservations, remember?"

"I think yer on to something, Missus. Mrs. Weller didn't come to yer luncheon, and she wasn't there to give out the grand prize. Her husband Paul did it. And I don't remember seeing Miss Taylor at Easter Sunday mass."

"I don't know about Eva and Melinda, but I can call and ask my friend Annie Lang. She goes to Trinity."

"That's a good idea, lad." He grabbed the legal pads off the end table. "Who've we not interviewed? Hmm. I need to speak with Father Duncan, and I should get a haircut from Amos Mosby. I think I might pick up a nice bottle of Jameson's Scotch from Weller's. You still need to see Bettina Taylor, Eva Edgerton, Melinda Layton, and Aubrey Rush."

Tommie stuck out her tongue. "Bleah. I don't know if I can manage them this afternoon. How about we just fill out our lists and stay in for the rest of the day. We can start fresh with face-to-face visits in the morning."

"Lovely. I'm afraid I may utter something indiscreet to Father Duncan and end up in confession."

He rolled his eyes dramatically, and Tommie laughed. "You won't do, Finbar Holmes. You won't do."

For the next hour, they worked on their list, filling in truths, lies, observations, and the valuable grapevine information provided by their gossipy friends.

One of the main tools Finbar used when trying to solve the crimes in the televised shows he so loved was to establish patterns and relationships between the suspects. The commonalities surrounding Veranell's death centered on her malignant personality and the dealings and ties to the people of the town. Finbar already knew, from his association as a member of St. Mary's Catholic Church, quite a lot about Veranell Collins, and he listed them out.

"Aside from her physical description and her considerable health problems, I have learned some critical bits about Mrs. Collins. One. She was an insulting and condescending socialite who came from money and delighted in managing others through fear and intimidation. Two. Our friends tell us she slandered and sullied the good names of the townsfolk she didn't like, which must've been nearly everyone, including her circle of chums. Three. I heard she appointed herself the *grand dame* of the annual Easter festivities and assigned all the churches in town 50 plastic eggs to fill—at their own expense—and hide for the egg hunt. Four. As you and I know, she bullied shop owners into providing prizes for the raffles."

"That's for sure. I would gladly have donated, but she harassed me and set the price for my participation. She did it to you, too." Tommie snapped to a more upright position on the sofa. "Finbar, do you remember when we talked to Levi what he said?"

"About her requiring him to provide the eggs and the rabbits free of charge? I do."

"Yeah, that. But something else. He told us she finagled free bunnies and eggs. I remember because the word 'finagled' stuck in my mind. But he also said she got grand prize money from him. That was $500 in cash, along with the eggs and rabbits!"

Finbar did some quick calculations on his paper. He whistled and held it up for Tommie to see.

"Yer right, Missus. Eleven eggs at $50 apiece. That's $550. Three rabbits at $20 a day each for four days. That's $240. Plus, the $500 prize money. Levi Muller was out of pocket for $1,290."

"Outrageous. You saw his place. It's simple and unassuming. He has no cash crops. His living is made from the sale of eggs, animals, money collected for school field trips, and byproducts like cheese, butter, and fiber from fleeces. Thirteen hundred dollars would've made a huge dent in his finances. She did damage to his livelihood with her accusations, and to keep her from doing more harm, he allowed her to take goods and money he didn't really have."

"It's called extortion, Missus. Common blackmail. D'you wonder how many others she forced into lining her pockets besides Levi?"

"Eva Edgerton, for one. The sisters told us Veranell was given free clothing, and she probably got free alcohol from Weller's."

"D'you see how her spiderweb grows?"

"I do indeed. What a horrible woman."

"Thomasina, I'd really like to fill in some more background information for our investigation. Can ye think about yerself as a suspect for a moment?"

"Oh, Earl said I'm no longer a suspect. I'm a person of interest." She grinned, a twinkle in her eyes.

Finbar smiled. "Ah, lad. That's grand. But just for good measure, let's profile ourselves to see where we fit in the black widow's web."

"All right, but can we skip over the embarrassing physical descriptions this time?"

"Sure, sure. Let's go straight to motive. Yers would be what?"

"Mmm. Probably revenge for the rumors about me being 'a fat outsider and a doctor-wannabe who sells ineffective remedies to ignorant people and can't keep a man.' I believe that's exactly what she said about me."

Finbar cringed. "Yer quite correct, Thomasina. Tell me something ye know you've done that might be of interest concerning her."

Tommie laid back against the cushion and stared at the honey-colored paneled ceiling. "Well, I had no reason to harm her, despite what she said. I've always believed what my Gramma told me. 'Sticks and stones can break your bones, but words can never harm you.' Not entirely comforting, but what Veranell spread around about me is untrue ... except the fat part."

"Think about the past week. Anything stand out?"

"Well, yeah. You know she came in Monday and bought a bottle of my 'ineffective' *Tender Tummy Tonic.* Didn't see her the rest of the week. I was working on my menu for the Easter brunch. I helped you on Friday until 9:30 that night. I did say something to Eva about Veranell complaining you wouldn't change the menu for her. Eva brought it up, though. She was being snide, and I guess I snapped at her because I was defensive already having to look at Bettina all gussied up in her new designer dress. Anyway, I know she texted Veranell and told her."

"How d'you know that?"

"I read her text as I was serving bread to her table."

"Did ye now? Cheeky girl."

"And I heard her say to the Laytons that she didn't really want to eat at the café on Saturday because you excluded Veranell."

"Rubbish. I can't cater to every person's whim."

"I know that. What else? Oh, yeah. I took the call on Saturday about 5:00 from Paul Weller to cancel Louanne's and Bettina's reservations. He came by himself, you remember, and sat with Tom Beadwell."

"I do remember. Quite a pleasant lad, all things considered, I might say."

"Yep. I worked with you until 9:00 Saturday night. Then I went home and finished up prep for my *Peter Rabbit* themed brunch. All the invited event participants came except Bettina and Louanne. Amos came late because of his church barbecue. Veranell was pretty green around the gills and went to the bathroom a lot. I made her a tea for the queasiness. After lunch, I packed the leftovers into the fridge, put the ribbons on the bunny rabbits over in your shop so you could take them outside to the park, and met you at the ticket table until the grand prize giveaway when I tried to help Veranell in the gazebo. That's it."

"Did you ever touch them eggs, Missus?"

Tommie shook her head. "Nope."

"Who might your testimony implicate?"

"Umm. Maybe Eva Edgerton because she was really mad I criticized her friend. Louanne Weller and Bettina Taylor for the strange last-minute cancellation of their dinner reservations and for missing the brunch due to some fake illness. Other than that, nobody."

"Well done, lad. Yer interview is complete."

"Yay. Toss the list over here so I can do yours."

Tommie adjusted her position and clicked the pen. "Ready," she said, righting the legal pad on her lap.

"My motive would be revenge for giving me derogatory reviews in the newspaper and about town, trying to disparage m' business."

"Oh, that's right. I forgot about that newspaper review. It was pretty brutal, but she kept coming to eat at the café. Kind of negates the review, huh? Tell me your goings on since Thursday."

"Thursday evening is when Father Duncan found the rabbits abandoned in the Bingo hall and asked me to take them into my charge. Friday night I cooked and served *Good Friday Fish Chowder, Individual Irish Soda Bread, Sláinte Slaw,* and *Barm Brack* to my guests. Caife Caife Holmes had a full house, as you recall."

"I remember how much people liked that speckled loaf for dessert. It was delicious and everybody had fun looking for the little items hidden inside the cake."

"D'you recall who discovered what?"

"My friend Annie Lang found the ring foretelling a marriage within the year. She called me all weekend speculating on her prospects." Tommie laughed. "And Bettina got the thimble, which meant a life of being single. Should've seen the look on her face. Priceless. Molly Bailey got the good fortune coin, and I didn't know the ones who got the other items. I forgot what they were."

"A dried bean for poverty, a pea for no marriage in the year, and a matchstick for an unhappy marriage. I believe them that got those were out-of-towners."

"Good. How about Saturday night?"

"I prepared and served my customers *Red Champ, Pan Fried Scamp, Quick Pickled Veggies,* and *Creamy Eggless Lemon Curd.*"

"Oh my gosh. That lemon curd was to die for. I left at 9:00, and you came home sometime around 10:30 according to Sherlock. What'd you do on Sunday?"

"I went to Easter Sunday Mass, then I came to yer shop after I checked the rabbits in the café. After luncheon, I met ye at the raffle ticket table at 2:00, as you stated."

"OK. So, did you have any significant interactions with Veranell or the others in her group?"

"I did. On Friday, as she was leaving, that Edgerton woman complained to me about not adapting my menu for Mrs. Collins and suggested it was because of the review in the paper. I told her that woman was a pompous arse, and I didn't care what she said or if she ever ate in my café again. I was surprised to see Ms. Edgerton again for the Saturday night dinner. I guess she didn't take too much offense to my comment. That's about the whole of it. I never talked to Mrs. Collins until Sunday, and that was just 'how d'you do' in passing at the luncheon."

"Finbar, who do you think your testimony would tend to implicate?

"Thomasina, I can only echo what you said. Ms. Edgerton, Mrs. Weller, and Miss Taylor."

"Did you ever touch the ostrich or emu eggs while you were picking up the rabbits?"

"I did not. I seen them on the table, but I was more concerned with the bunnies. The only person in the room at that time was Father Duncan, and I refuse to believe he had anything to do with contaminating them eggs."

"All right. So, what now?"

"How about a bit of food, a suppa tea, and we'll watch some telly? I see there's an Agatha Christie fil-um on for tonight that starts in just a few minutes."

Tommie smiled at his unusual pronunciation of film. "That sounds great. A movie should be just the thing.

Can I help in the kitchen?"

"Oh, no. 'Tis a simple meal we can eat on trays whilst we watch our fil-um. Sliced brown bread with Irish butter, Wexford cheese, fried egg, sliced red onion, and pickled beets, with potato crisps on the side."

"Sounds tasty, Finbar, only hold the onion for me or I'll be up all night making a reme-tea for heartburn."

Chapter Seventeen

TOMMIE drove her own car to interview her assigned persons of interest the next morning. Her first stop was at Aubrey's Antiques. When she arrived, Aubrey had just put out her OPEN sign. Tommie entered to the charming *ding-ding* of a hanging bell that bobbed when the door opened.

"Hi, Tommie. What brings you to my place so early? Not that I'm complaining, of course," Aubrey said.

"I was up and ready to get out of the house, and I thought the atmosphere of your shop would be just the thing I need to cheer me up," Tommie replied.

"Cheer you up? What's the matter?"

"Well, you know they had my business closed for a couple days as a potential crime scene again. Good news. I'm cleared. Bad news. Caife Caife Holmes got shut down yesterday because of food poisoning complaints. Finbar's so upset. We both are."

"No! I can't believe that. Not his place. He's so ... persnickety." Aubrey gave an almost imperceptible shrug.

"Don't worry. I'm not offended. He is quirky, to say the least. But he's incredibly careful with his food. I think the claims came from people who don't like him."

"I'd say that's a fair assessment, and I can guess who might have made those accusations."

"I have my suspicions, too. Want to see if they match up?" Tommie examined some small trinkets to keep from making direct eye contact.

Aubrey laughed, a musical sound that rivaled the bell over the door. "Tommie Watson! I do love you, but you're not as shrewd as you think. Here, come sit at this lovely Ethan Allen secretary, rest your ankle on this damask covered footstool, and let's trade tales. I'll tell you what I know, and you can fill me in on the investigation that I'm sure you're conducting behind Earl Petry's back."

Tommie blushed a deep crimson and limped to the chair. "Guilty as charged. I was told Veranell Collins died a suspicious death. Holmes and I believe it was murder, and we're trying to figure it out."

Aubrey pulled up a backless brocade dressing table bench and perched, smoothing a few loose tendrils back into the barrette that held her wavy dark brown hair. She regarded Tommie with heavy lashed chocolate brown eyes, a smile playing at the corners of her full lips. Tommie grinned, and deep dimples appeared in her cheeks.

"So, Holmes and Watson feel mischief is afoot? Tell me, am I a suspect or a resource?"

"At this point, anybody who was around Veranell for the past few days is a person of interest, including Finbar and myself." Tommie shrugged apologetically.

"That's cool. Ask away, Dr. Watson." She leaned forward in anticipation of the questions.

"Full disclosure, Aubrey. Veranell was sick to begin with, but somebody intentionally made her sicker. She had to eat a special diet, and somehow, her system was full of things she would have known *not* to eat."

"Was she forced to eat them?"

"I don't know. I think she probably didn't know her food was tampered with."

"Good assumption. Why put yourself in agony by deviating from your normal dietary regimen?"

"Exactly. To make matters worse, she had gotten hold of salmonella."

Aubrey sat up straighter on the stool. "Salmonella, huh? I seem to have heard that just yesterday. The Lunch Pad was closed to check for salmonella. News travels in a small town. Do you think Sid and Jeannette were careless in the kitchen?"

"No, I don't. I think they'll be cleared, but the last food Veranell ate, other than some homemade broths, came from The Lunch Pad."

Aubrey bit her lower lip and frowned. "Sounds like a setup to me. Sounds like a lot of setups. The Lunch Pad,

Caife Caife Holmes, a tried and true Watson's remedy. Yes, I know there's talk about you slipping a bad potion into her water. Everybody saw it. But you said you were cleared, so that seems like just an unfortunate 'wrong place at the wrong time' kind of thing. Salmonella. That comes from raw eggs and poultry, improper washing of raw food, reptiles. Stuff like that. I can't see where she would've been exposed to any of those. What's your take?"

"I, er, well ..." Tommie hemmed and hawed.

"You *know*, Tommie. Tell me," Aubrey insisted.

"Sandy found salmonella on the prize eggs."

Aubrey sat still as a stone. Her dark eyes widened, and the pupils became black beads. She pressed her lips into a tight line. "That's crap on a cracker! It's a stinking lie."

Tommie stared open mouthed. "What?"

Aubrey repeated her assertion, a little more calmly. "That's a lie. Someone's trying to put the blame on Levi."

"It would seem so, but I don't believe he's guilty."

"You'd *better not* believe it. There's not a more decent man in this whole town than Levi Muller. He's hardworking, eking out a living without doing harm to either animals or people. He's kind and generous and has been sorely taken advantage of. Levi Muller did not do it."

Aubrey was shaking and on the verge of tears. Tommie leaned forward and touched her on the knee.

"Aubrey, you're preaching to the choir, here. I didn't say I believe he's guilty of donating contaminated eggs. I even saw his sterilizing setup. Ingenious. And I got to feed the little critters. He's a wonderful man, and you obviously care deeply for him. I'm only telling you that salmonella was found on the eggshells Veranell decorated, beneath and on top of the paint. I don't know how."

"Aha! There's your proof that Levi didn't do it."

"What do you mean?"

"Think about it, Tommie. If the undyed shells were contaminated, that's one thing. But how did the salmonella get *on top of the paint?* It had to happen after the shells left Levi's possession."

The two women stared at one another for several beats before Tommie came to a decision. Holmes would probably not approve, but she felt she could trust Aubrey.

"Listen to me, Aubrey. I'm going to ask some questions, and I need for you to be absolutely truthful with me. Were you hiding outside St. Mary's on Friday night?"

"No."

"Seriously? I have two witnesses that saw you."

"No, Tommie. I wasn't hiding outside St. Mary's. I was in the Trinity Episcopal cemetery."

"Oh! Why?"

"Because, well, you realize I'm Jewish."

"I know that. So why traipse around a graveyard?"

"Friday was the first night of Passover, when Jews commemorate the Hebrews' escape from slavery in Egypt and the Angel of Death passed over houses whose lintels were marked with lamb's blood, sparing the firstborn children of the Israelites."

"OK. Why weren't you home celebrating it?"

"I was. I came out there later on. The first night we have a special meal called the Passover *Seder* where we do symbolic things like blessing the wine, ritual hand washing, and eating ceremonial foods on a special plate."

Aubrey rose from the stool and went behind the counter. She returned with a round plate with six depressions inside the outer rim, each decorated with a Hebrew symbol. She held it out for Tommie to examine.

"Each of these wells holds a specific food item. We put fresh parsley there, three pieces of matzah bread in this one, horseradish on romaine lettuce there, a mixture of nuts, apples, sweet spices, and wine in this one, a hard-boiled egg there, and a roasted shank bone there. Each food represents something from our early roots and is eaten in a particular order." She pointed to the different characters on the plate as she reverently related their significance.

"We dip the parsley in salt water to represent the tears of the Hebrew slaves. The matzah is broken and eaten at a couple different times. It represents the need to make haste, so no leavening is used. The bitter herbs are dipped into the sweet mixture, representing the bitterness of slavery and the brick mortar the slaves were forced to make. The egg symbolizes spring and the continuing cycle of our lives, and the shank bone stands for the sacrificial Paschal lamb."

Tommie's eyes welled with tears as she listened to Aubrey's account of the meal. "That's a beautiful story, but it doesn't explain why you were outside in the cemetery."

"I like to be authentic, Tommie, so I try not to use things from the grocery store if I can help it. I have friends with gardens or who can harvest things like apples when they're in season from other places. I make my own matzah. Levi gave me eggs from his chickens and a shank bone from a little lamb that had died in an accident on the farm. I needed fresh parsley for the rest of the weekend, and there was some growing wild in the cemetery. I had picked some earlier in the day, but I didn't think anyone would mind if I picked more. I left plenty."

"I think that answers the question for me. Did you see anybody else there when you were harvesting?"

"I did, actually. Jo Clay and Elly James were parked in Jo's car at the Post Office both nights. Friday, it was just the two of them, but Saturday, there was another car parked beside them. Two men got out, and they all sat together in Jo's car. I don't know who the men were. I couldn't see because the overhead light didn't come on. After a while, they got out, and both cars left."

"Anyone else?"

"I saw Amos Mosby go into St. Mary's when I was picking herbs Friday afternoon. I left before he came out."

"So, you never went inside the church, right?"

"Ha! Why would I? Oh, sure, I like Father Duncan. We get along great. But I have no business in a Catholic church, do I? People would have a fit if they saw me there."

"I get your point. What do you think of Jo and Elly, and Amos Mosby, for that matter?

"Personally, I like the two women, even though I was told they spread a rumor that I stole antiques from people's homes to sell in my store. I believe Veranell or Louanne or Bettina started that, though. Elly and Jo come in here all the time, and they're always nice to me. Amos is a sweet man. He has the cutest grandchildren. You should've seen them hunting those Easter eggs. The littlest girl—she's probably three—she was trying to keep up with the bigger kids, but they ran her over. I saw some eggs on the ground and in the shrubbery, so I stood in front of them until she came around. Then I kicked them out so she could pick them up. Melinda helped me. Cheating, I know, but who cares? We wanted her to be happy."

"You're friends with Melinda Layton?"

"Oh sure. We went to college together."

"Huh! Didn't know that. I like her, too, except when the rest of the mean girl club is around."

"Yeah, that's a pity she likes to run with them. You know, Veranell and her group tried to ruin me, but Melinda always came to my defense."

The bell over the door jangled, and Aubrey rose to greet her customer. Tommie pushed up from the chair with her cane and started to exit, but Aubrey stopped her.

"Tommie, I wanted you to know I really enjoyed your *Peter Rabbit* brunch and especially your *Peppermint Patchouli Passover Tea*. Thanks for including my Jewish heritage. Your friendship is so appreciated. Please take this *seder* plate as a gift. Maybe next year, you'll come celebrate a Passover meal with me?"

"Oh, Aubrey. You're so kind. Is that allowed? I'm not Jewish, you know."

Aubrey emitted that tinkling musical laugh again. "Of course, it's allowed. In fact, Father Duncan has Passover *Seder* with me every year on Saturday night."

Chapter Eighteen

FINBAR left The Barber Shop with a fresh haircut and important information at almost the same time Tommie left Aubrey. According to Amos, he was cutting hair until closing at 6:00 on Thursday night. By then, Holmes had already taken possession of the rabbits, and Father Duncan had locked up the church. After closing work early on Friday, Amos and his family attended a special Good Friday service at St. John Missionary Baptist Church—the oldest African American church in Floral County—where he had been a deacon for 25 years. Plenty of people saw and talked with him. He told Finbar he spent all day Saturday at the church with a group of other men barbequing a whole pig for the church's Easter supper the following day. All his claims were easily checked.

There were a couple of things that caught Finbar's

attention, however, during his conversation with the barber, and he brought them to mind as he drove through the parking lot toward Weller's Wine & Spirits.

"How late did ye work on Friday, Amos?" Finbar had asked as Amos carefully snipped stray hairs from around his ears.

"I usually close up at 6:00, but I shut the doors at 3:30. I had to cut the priest's hair at St. Mary's."

"D'you mean you went to the church to do it?"

"Yeah. He was trying to get a sermon ready, and he asked me to come out. I do that sometimes. He's a good fellow. Tips well, too."

"Did you see Mrs. Collins there?"

"Naw, I was only in the office. I saw some people around the church, though. Don't know who they were. My distance eyesight's not that great."

"Can you describe them?"

"Yeah, pretty much. There was a woman outside on the grounds between St. Mary's and Trinity. I think it might have been Joanne Clay. Best as I could tell, she was probably in her forties, well over five feet tall, and had long chestnut brown hair. But that morning, on my way to work, I saw a different woman going into the Bingo hall."

"Was it Mrs. Patterson, the church secretary?"

"No. I know Miz Patterson. Wasn't her. This lady had blond hair in a chin length wavy bob. Eva Edgerton or Louanne Weller or Elly James, I'm thinking. Maybe Melinda Layton Hard to tell from a distance. Lots of women in town have that same hairstyle. Does that help?"

"Sure, sure, Amos. Speaking of Miss James, there was talk about a problem with her. D'you mind telling me?"

"Oh, that old thing? It was a rumor went 'round that my church didn't pay her for some jelly we bought for our goodwill pantry. It wasn't true. She donated a case of jelly, right out of the goodness of her heart. Sweet lady. Don't know why that Veranell wanted to make her look bad, except that was a mean, hateful, wicked woman." His words were punctuated with forceful whisks of the hand broom as he swept errant hairs from Finbar's shoulders.

"Didn't like her, eh lad?"

Amos blew his breath out. "No sir! I did not care for Veranell Collins one little bit. She was a devious, evil-spirited blot on the face of this town who hated and conspired to divide all of God's children. Grand Pappy used to sing a song I liked a lot. Went something like, 'I be glad when you gone, you rascal you. Gone, gone.' And happy day for me, that rascal's gone."

Finbar was still thinking of the song when he parked and entered Weller's back door. Louanne was behind the counter reorganizing the cash register drawer. Her smile died when she realized who had come in.

"Halloo, Mrs. Weller," Finbar called.

"Good day, Mr. Holmes," she replied with tight lips. "What can I do for you? Need some liquor, I'm sure."

"That I do, Madame. Have ye some Jameson's, by chance? 'Tis a fine Irish whiskey. Triple distilled. Very smooth. I've visited the distillery in Dublin quite often."

"I'll bet you have," she said, arching her eyebrows. "You Irish are known for your drinking ... of fine whiskeys and ales, that is."

Finbar noted the condescension in her voice and manner and the double meaning of her statement but chose to resist taking the bait.

"Yes. And you have a fine understanding of yer alcohol, too, have ye not? I'd also like a case of Guinness, please. I'm sure ye have that."

"Of course. I'll have the stock boy get it for you. Is there anything else?" she asked with no trace of warmth.

"Tell me, d'you have anything that's discounted? Perhaps a bottle that's had the label scratched or defected in some way? I've never been one to quibble over a blemished package if the product is still sound."

Louanne looked shocked. "We don't sell damaged products, Mr. Holmes. That's illegal, and even if it weren't, it's certainly not up to our good standards."

"Ah, sure, sure. 'Twas just a passing query. Some places do that, y'know?"

"Well, maybe so, but we don't."

"Meant no disrespect for yer business practices, Mrs. Weller. My apologies. By the way, I heard ye had taken ill. Ye seem quite recovered now."

"You should know. It was something I ate at your restaurant that gave me food poisoning."

"Is that a fact? I'm curious that not anyone else who

ate there was afflicted ... outside of you and yer lady friend, Miss Taylor, that is."

"Really? It's a thousand miracles you didn't poison *everyone* who ate there. I don't know why you haven't been closed down sooner."

"Yer husband is all right? He ate at the café both nights, as I recall."

"He has a strong stomach. He could eat pig slop and not get sick. It's disgusting." She wrinkled her nose.

"Mrs. Weller, what have I done to offend ye so?"

"You killed my friend!" she shouted. "You and that Tommie Watson fed her bad food and fake medicine that made her sick and caused her to die. Why aren't you both in jail?"

"I assure ye, Madame, neither Missus Watson nor myself have done any harm to anyone in this town."

"Are you kidding me? She sells phony potions and passes herself off as someone with medical knowledge. She's a menace. And you couldn't cook your way out of a paper bag. What you pass off as food is horrendous, just like that overpriced tripe they serve at The Lunch Pad. Good thing they're closed down, too. I wish you'd just go back to your own Godforsaken country. Nobody wants a 'Mick' here in Floribunda. Billy, bring that booze and ring the man up. I've got to get away for some fresh air." She turned on her heel and marched out the back door, tossing her crimped blond hair and leaving Holmes at the counter.

Finbar paid his bill and loaded his purchases into

his trunk. As he pulled out of the parking spot and drove toward the cross street, he spotted Louanne, Bettina, and Eva at the back door of Eva's Divas Boutique. All three women stopped talking and glared as he drove by. Finbar could feel their animosity toward him, wishing him to leave America, and in his head, he could hear Amos singing, "I be glad when you gone, you rascal you. Gone, gone."

Chapter Nineteen

TOMMIE entered the front door of Eva's Divas just as Louanne and Bettina returned to their shops' back doors from their impromptu gathering in the parking lot. She noted the startled expression on Eva's face was quickly replaced with a simpering smile.

"Well, hello Ms. Tommie Watson. How nice of you to visit my boutique. I don't usually see you in anything other than those medical scrubs."

"That's true, Eva. I wear them for work because they have a bunch of pockets."

"Are you taking a foray into the fashionable side of clothing for a change?"

"Mmm. Maybe. I thought I might look around for something a little dressier to wear for a date, you know."

"Oooh, I'll do my best to help you, but we don't

carry many things in such large sizes. Have you considered Walmart or The Dollar Store? I hear they have big clothes."

Tommie's face burned, but she kept her cool. *Don't fall for it,* she told herself. *Smile and pretend you didn't hear her.*

"I was looking for a nice flowing tunic top to wear over black dress slacks."

"Let me think. I may have some loose-fitting tops on the sales rack, if you want to check over there."

"That would be great. I'm always in the market for a discounted item, even a factory second."

Eva's face froze. "We don't carry factory seconds."

"You don't? I heard differently. I guess I misunderstood. Must've been sales items I was told of."

"Yes. Must have. Well, look around, if you'd like. The dressing rooms are locked, so come to me for a key."

Tommie strolled to the sales rack and, with some searching, found a top she thought might work. After getting Eva to unlock the fitting room, she tried it on. Although she sucked in her stomach and held her breath, she was unable to fasten the front buttons. The blouse gaped open nearly three inches from neck to hem.

Not one to give up, Tommie examined the top and came up with a solution. She would buy the item, open the side seams, and insert panels of a coordinated fabric to make it fit. *I'll be darned if I'll let Eva Edgerton make fun of my weight anymore,* she decided. She looked at the price tag and nearly choked. On sale, the item was three times the cost of a good scrub top. *Guess I'll eat beans for a while,* she thought, *if it means I can preserve my dignity.*

She exited the room with the blouse held proudly over her arm as she approached the checkout counter.

"This top is a perfect fit, Eva. I'll take it." She gave Eva a self-satisfied smile.

Eva's eyebrows lifted as she checked the size, but she refrained from commenting, swiped Tommie's credit card, and placed the blouse in a tissue paper filled bag.

"How are you holding up after Sunday's tragedy?" Tommie asked, casually tucking the card back in her wallet.

"I'm fine. I heard your potion was not the cause," Eva said, "but Veranell's dead just the same."

"It's so awful. I knew she was sick, but I didn't think she was sick enough to die from her condition."

"Not many people knew how she suffered. She was in constant pain, and her bad health had a tendency to make her standoffish, even rude."

"What do you think happened?"

"I don't know. Maybe a heart attack."

"Do you believe someone could have tried to make her sicker? I heard she had salmonella or something."

Eva shrugged. "Really? I certainly wouldn't know. I didn't see her all weekend. She was decorating those prize eggs. I took Friday and Saturday off to be over at Melinda's. We were making chocolate eggs and preparing the basket for the raffle."

"I had one of the eggs y'all made. It was absolutely

delicious, and so pretty. You really did an outstanding job."

"Why, thank you, Tommie." Her smile fell short of her eyes.

"I bet they were pretty labor intensive with all that multicolored piping. Did they take a long time to make?"

"Oh, yes. Melinda molded the eggs all day Thursday, and I came that night and early the next morning to decorate them. We ran out of food coloring, there were so many. I had to run to Winn Dixie Friday and again Saturday to get more. They did look good, didn't they?"

"Did you come by St. Mary's and visit with Veranell on Friday or Saturday while she was decorating her eggs?"

"No, I was too busy to stop in, and she didn't like to be interrupted when she was being creative," she stated.

"Was there nobody else with her?" Tommie pretended to inspect a pair of drop earrings.

"No, not usually, although I did see a woman taking a Lunch Pad delivery into the kitchen Friday morning on my way to Melinda's. I swear it was Elly James, but I have no idea why she would be there instead of at her quaint little jelly store."

"What made you think it was Elly?"

"Her figure, for one. I'm usually rather good at judging a woman's size … except for today. And her blond hair, for another. She wears it like mine, only I started this style first, then everybody wanted to copy me." She shook her head dramatically, and the unbrushed waves bounced.

"Not me!" Tommie said.

"No, not you for sure." Eva gave a quiet snort, but Tommie ignored the slight.

"Anybody else there at the church?"

"You're mighty nosy, Tommie. Yes, I did see somebody else that afternoon. Jo Clay was skulking around, looking in the windows."

"Really? Are you sure it was Jo?"

"Well, of course I'm sure. I know her hair and figure, although she really can't afford to shop here. Why all the questions?"

"No reason, Eva. I'm just making conversation."

"I see. Here's your blouse, Tommie. I'm sure it will look stunning over your black sweatpants."

"Black dress pants."

"Oops. That's what I meant. Where are you planning on wearing it?"

"Oh, just out for a dinner date."

"But not tonight, right?"

"Um, no. Why do you ask?"

"Because Bettina was just in here buying a special outfit for *her* date tonight."

"I don't get your drift, Eva. What's that got to do with me?"

Eva pulled the corners of her mouth up into a tight smile. Her eyes glittered like a wolf regarding a lamb.

"I just meant that Bettina bought a new outfit for her dinner date tonight ... with Earl Petry."

Chapter Twenty

TOMMIE AND FINBAR happened to pull into their carports at nearly the same moment. As he carried his whiskey and the case of ale from the trunk to the front porch and fumbled with his key, she hastily entered her unit and slammed the door without so much as a word in greeting. By now, Finbar knew when Tommie was experiencing an emotional crisis. He hurried through the house to the back patio and waited with Sherlock for Tommie to let Zed and Red go outside. When the kitchen door opened, the dogs ran out, and Finbar stepped in.

"Thomasina, what's happened?" he asked.

"Nothing. I'm fine," she replied.

Finbar could see the red blotches on her face and the watery eyes she tried to hide. Taking her arm, he gently turned her to meet his gaze.

"Ach. D'you think I don't see ye lad? Tell me what's got ye upset."

Tommie could no longer hold out. She collapsed into his arms, sobbing heavily. Finbar awkwardly patted her on the back, thankful that she wiped her running nose with a paper towel from her pocket instead of using his shirt. When she was finally calm, she pulled away and sat down at the dining table. Finbar took the seat opposite her and waited for her explanation.

"Earl broke our date tonight," she said.

"I know that, lad. He's working the case," he said.

"He's not working. He's taking somebody else to dinner instead."

"What're ye saying? He's passed you over to have a date with another woman? I don't believe it."

"Believe it. I called The Fallen Oak to see if he canceled our reservation. He hasn't. Eva told me he's taking Bettina to dinner. She even bought a new outfit for their date. Eva was more than happy to throw it in my face."

Fresh tears erupted, and she let them fall onto the table like fat raindrops. Finbar sat back and folded his arms.

"I don't know what to say, lad. He gave ye no indication yesterday of any dissatisfaction with you. Did he not tell ye he had to work, that there were some leads he meant to follow?"

"That's what he said, but I can put it all together. He breaks our date. She's been hanging around having more contact with him. I mean, look at her. She's younger, prettier, half my size, and they have a history together."

"Not all men like young skinny women."

Tommie snorted. "Really? When given a choice, nine times out of ten a man will choose the newer, shinier sports car rather than the old beat-up jalopy."

Finbar pursed his lips, considering her rationale, hard-pressed to contradict the analogy. He struggled to think of a way to distract her.

"Shall we share our findings from the morning's interviews?" he suggested.

Tommie was grateful for his efforts to pull her mind away from thinking about Earl.

"How about we give the abbreviated versions and we can fill in our chart later?"

"Lovely. Would ye like to start?"

"Sure." She took a breath and continued in a monotone voice. "Aubrey Rush was picking parsley at Trinity cemetery for Passover Friday afternoon and evening and again on Saturday night. She saw Elly and Jo parked at the Post Office Friday night. Corroborates their stories. She saw them Saturday night, too, along with two men in another car. That's got to be the Alvarez brothers. She also confirmed that Veranell tried to put her out of business with nasty rumors. Your turn."

Finbar frowned at her lack of enthusiasm but refrained from commenting on it. Instead, he leaned in and raised his eyebrows as though he had a big secret to tell.

"Amos Mosby cut my hair."

Tommie narrowed her eyes. "I see that."

"Righto. He has alibis for Thursday through Sunday which can be easily verified. He was at St. Mary's Friday to cut Father Duncan's hair. He saw a petite blond woman that morning whom he thought was Elly."

"OK. What was he doing there that morning?"

"Driving to work."

"Oh. Hm. Elly never admitted to being there. We'll have to check on that."

"He also said he saw Jo in the garden between the churches on Friday after cutting Father Duncan's hair."

"Nah. I'm fairly sure Jo was working on those ceramic rabbits until early evening.

"Quite right. We now know the woman was Aubrey Rush because she admitted being there. I can understand the mistake. Both women are similar in appearance from a distance."

"That's true, Finbar. Evil Eva said she saw Jo peeking in the windows at St. Mary's, too." Tommie sniffed. "Yeah. I'm distraught. I can call her what I want."

Though she was peckish, Finbar was encouraged. The emergence of her acerbic wit indicated she had reengaged with the investigation.

"As ye wish, lad. Tell me about Eva's interview."

"She claims to be able to identify people based on their physical characteristics and figures, as if she's some great observationist. She claimed it was Jo on the grounds, but we know for sure it was Aubrey. She went to Melinda's

Friday to make chocolate eggs. She said it was Elly inside the building that morning, mostly because of her size and hair. But that could be a mistake or … or she's trying to cast attention away from herself and onto Elly."

"Hmm. Is it mistaken identity … or intentional misdirection? D'you know, Amos made a comment that many women in town have that same strange unbrushed wavy haircut?"

"Eva said she was the first, and everyone else copied her. You're right, though. A trend gets started and dozens follow. Eva, Elly, Louanne, Melinda, that one lady from First Baptist. They all have that cut, and they're all blond. They only differ in height and weight and skin tone."

"And eye color, but that can only be seen up close."

"Jo and Aubrey have similar hair color and length."

"Yes, they do. Bettina is the odd duck out with that black hair. D'you notice she frequently wears it in a low chignon like Mrs. Collins did? She certainly was a devotee of that woman … what you'd call a Veranell-wannabe."

At the mention of Bettina, Tommie grew morose. Finbar quickly switched topics.

"The Weller woman all but threw me out of her shop and suggested I leave Florida. She even called me a 'Mick' to m' face."

Tommie gasped. "That's what the sisters told us Veranell called you. I don't know what it means except it's a bad slur for the Irish, isn't it? How rude. Did she have any useful information to contribute?"

"Yes, she did. She bristled when I mentioned discounted merchandise."

"So did Eva when I asked about discounted clothing. She got real frosty."

"And Mrs. Weller accused the both of us of murdering Mrs. Collins. Said we needed to be imprisoned! I'm fairly certain she's the one who swore out the complaints of salmonella at The Lunch Pad and food poisoning in my café."

"Aubrey said the same thing. And, by the way, I think she's sweet on Levi Muller."

"D'you think so, Missus? That's grand."

"Yeah. This is what I think, Finbar. We have two sides of a coin here. Heads and tails. Good people and bad people, if you want to cast them in those roles. The good folks are the ones I'd call resources or material witnesses now. Amos, Levi, the Alvarez brothers, Elly, Jo, Aubrey, and maybe Melinda. Aubrey seems to think so, anyway."

"And the others are bad? Real suspects? Eva, Bettina, and Louanne? All in the group that idolized Veranell. What about Father Duncan and the Spocks?"

"Oh, the priest is heads. Sid and Jeanette are collateral damage. Good people in the wrong place at the wrong time. Or misdirection. Just like you and me."

Finbar considered her assessment. "I tend to agree, for the most part, but don't forget our experience with Sarah Beth Brewster. We thought she was an innocent, but she turned out to be a killer."

Tommie frowned. "I know, I know. I felt she deserved the benefit of the doubt all the way to the end."

"And what about Earl, Thomasina? Doesn't he deserve the benefit of the doubt?"

"I don't know. I really can't focus on that yet." She sighed, her entire body shuddering. "I'm done for now. I just want to lie down and take a nap."

"It's not yet half ten of the morning."

"I don't care. I am so, so exhausted. I need to have a *Zzzz-Tea* and let my mind rest. Will you wake me for lunch? I'll keep my phone by the chaise."

"Sure, sure. I'll go fill in our list whilst ye sleep. I'll close the flap, too. The boys can stay out in the garden with Sherlock. Rest well, dear. 'Twill be all right."

He made his way through the kitchen and out the door, herding the dogs as he went. Tommie decided she was too tired to even brew a cup of tea, so she curled up on the chaise lounge and instantly drifted to sleep.

Chapter Twenty-One

TOMMIE awoke to Red's tail thumping against the throw pillow beneath her head. When he saw her eyes open, he wagged harder and licked her nose.

"Bleah. I love you, little boy, but your kisses stink. All right. Go tell Finbar I'm coming."

The dog took off out the door flap as though he understood. Tommie washed her face to eliminate the tear tracks and drool crust before she made her way to her neighbor's open kitchen door. The table was set with a light lunch of brown soda bread fresh from the oven, Irish butter, Wexford cheese, quartered apples, pickled beets, fried eggs, sliced onions, and hot tea. Her chair was already pulled out, and her friends were waiting for her. She gratefully took her seat. Food was always a welcome balm for Tommie, as were her neighbor's smile and the happy faces of the three dogs watching from the floor.

Tommie and Finbar ate in silence, savoring the flavors of the meal. She ate her bread with cheese, butter, and egg; he ate his with all the ingredients piled on top. When they finished, Finbar put the plates in the sink to soak and refilled their teacups. He eyed Tommie with an appraising look.

"I'm fine. Stop staring at me," she grumbled.

"Lovely. Shall we get to work?"

"We've interviewed everyone except Melinda Layton. Oh, yeah ... and Bettina."

"We'll not be talking with her." He sat back in his chair, crossed his legs, and sipped his tea.

"Finbar! She has to be questioned. You don't expect *me* to talk to her, do you? That's cruel." She set her cup on the table with a *thud.*

"Of course, I don't, Thomasina. But neither must you expect me to interrogate her."

Tommie squinted her eyes and scowled.

"As far as I'm concerned, Bettina Taylor is our main suspect, and not because she's going out with Earl."

Getting no response from him, Tommie held up her hands and began to tick off the reasons for her opinion until she ran out of fingers.

"Bettina was Veranell's head honcho but Veranell humiliated her in public. She picked up the rabbits and what we're sure were sanitized eggs from Levi. The eggs were in her possession long before Veranell got them, and then they became contaminated. Veranell berated her because she got brown bunnies instead of white and for countless other things. She called in the order to The Lunch Pad and had access to Veranell's food. She attends St. Mary's, so she had the ability to do whatever she wanted without drawing suspicion. She wasn't sick Thursday after getting the eggs, but she was sick from Friday on. She cancelled her Saturday reservation at the café … because she was sick. She missed my brunch … because she was sick. She kept disappearing into the bathroom at the event on Sunday … because she was sick. What'd Levi say? 'Find out if anyone else in town has come down with salmonella.' I'd bet money that Bettina Taylor had salmonella!"

Finbar nodded, and Tommie started over with more fingers.

"Bettina wanted to reconnect with Earl. She said I stole him from her like she said Eva stole Tom Beadwell from her, so she probably perpetuated the rumor that my potion killed Veranell. You maligned Veranell, her supposed idol. Bettina was probably the one who phoned in the complaint against you and The Lunch Pad. So, with all those reasons, Finbar, why don't you think Bettina Taylor needs to be interviewed?"

He took a final swallow of tea and set his empty cup down gently on the table.

"Because, Thomasina, … Earl will interview her."

"What?" Tommie snapped her head back as though Finbar had slapped her in the face.

"Whilst ye slept, I spoke on the phone with the Detective … rather harshly, I'll admit."

"What did you say?"

He pursed his lips and raised his eyebrows. "I gave some very derogatory sentiments on his parentage and his ability to hold out a satisfactory relationship with a woman, and I questioned his motives regarding you. He was quite patient with me, under the circumstances, but he did say something that ye need to know, my dear."

"And, that is …?"

"He advised us to continue our current investigation, but under no circumstances are we to engage with Bettina Taylor."

Tears welled up in Tommie's eyes. "He still has a connection with her, then."

"No, no, Thomasina. Ye jump to the wrong conclusion. Let me finish. He said, and I quote, 'You two keep working the case to see if there are others involved. I will be interrogating the prime suspect at dinner tonight.' The prime suspect is Bettina. D'you understand, Missus?"

Tommie nodded her head slowly, but the tears continued to cascade down her cheeks.

"Why're ye still crying, lad?"

"Because … because he told me the truth. Some developments *have* come to light, and he has to work."

"So why the tears?"

"Because the last thing he said was, 'I'll make it up to you.' He *does* care for me after all."

Chapter Twenty-Two

EARL PETRY smiled at the woman sitting across from him at the dinner table. Her shiny black hair hung down her back, her heavily made up face was flawless, and her off-the-shoulder designer dress revealed more cleavage than he really cared to see. She babbled cheerily as she drank her Chardonnay and picked at her Waldorf salad.

Earl tilted his head to the side and wondered. *What did I see in you, Bettina ... beside the obvious endowments?*

In his opinion, Bettina Taylor was like a prettily wrapped package—all bows and ribbons, glitter, and fancy paper. But Thomasina Watson was the valuable gift inside the decorative box. He suddenly missed Tommie and hoped she would be forgiving of the method he chose to interrogate his old fling.

Though Holmes and Watson were quite apt in

their investigative sleuthing, Detective Earl Petry had his own ways of ferreting out criminal perpetrators. Rich food and alcohol were among his best tools.

He sliced off a chunk of filet mignon and savored its flavor, watching as Bettina continued to titter with her mouth filled with prime rib. Earl's mama taught him as a small boy not to talk with his mouth full. Evidently, Bettina's mother missed the mark on etiquette.

"... and now that Veranell's passed on, it will surely fall to me to organize the Easter event," she said.

"I'm sure you will handle it equally well."

"Equally well? I'll do a better job than she did, that's for sure. I'll appoint a committee to do the prize egg decorations under my supervision. Of course, we may have to get our eggs elsewhere. I don't trust that Levi Muller not one little bit."

"Why is that?"

"Are you kidding? Don't you remember how he mistreated those dogs you loved so much? He just gave them away without even asking my opinion. I only let him have them because I thought he needed guard dogs."

"I see. I'm surprised you didn't get ill handling those contaminated eggs, Bettina."

"You see, I'm very resilient and healthy. I take precautions, you know. I wash my hands all the time. I hardly ever catch diseases. I'm a super clean person." A morsel of food escaped her mouth, and she wiped it away with the back of her hand.

"But, didn't you come down with something last weekend? I was told you had to cancel your dinner reservation at Caife Caife Holmes."

"That's because that man gave me food poisoning. Louanne and Veranell, too. We all got sick from it."

"And you and Veranell both ate takeout from The Lunch Pad, didn't you?"

"We did, sugar. I forgot about that. I'll bet I got something from the diner first, and then the food at Caife Caife Holmes made it worse. That's a good point. I hope they both go out of business. They're unhealthy to the community. And so is that tea shop. I'm sorry. I know you dated the old woman, but I honestly don't know what you saw in her. She's not even a licensed medical professional. I hope you do an analysis on that potion of hers she forced Veranell to drink. No telling what's in it."

Earl inhaled slowly and focused on unclenching his fingers from around his knife. He forced himself to smile pleasantly at Bettina on the exhale.

"Aren't you worried about someone else taking over Veranell's charities? There were several women who worked with her."

"Well, Eva Edgerton and Melinda Layton don't go to St. Mary's, and neither do Katherine and Simone, so I'm not so much concerned about them. The other women at church don't pose a threat ... except Louanne Weller. She'd give me a run for my money." She glowered and held out her glass for a wine refill.

Earl obediently topped her off and signaled the waiter for another carafe.

"Bettina, why is it so important to be the charity head? What do you get out of it?"

"Seriously, honey? Besides the recognition … which I truly have deserved for years as Veranell's go-to girl … there are perks to heading the charities."

"Perks? Like what?"

"Well, for one thing, people give you money and other stuff all the time. Veranell got jewelry, clothing, antiques, liquor, tobacco goods, and things like that."

"For herself or for the charities?"

"What's the difference? She could do with them as she pleased. You think she lived on a widow's hefty insurance benefit only? Ha! I know for sure she put lots of the cash she collected in her own pockets and kept it off the books. There are expenses, after all, to running a charity. She didn't drink or smoke, but she could trade that merchandise out for other things she might want, like property or information. She acquired lots of gossip, and she used it to buy up people's store leases and whatnot. Being the head of a charity can be a very lucrative occupation. Don't look so shocked. It's done all the time."

"I never realized it. Is that what you want?"

"Lordy, sweetness. Your face is priceless. Of course, it's not. I'm just telling you what Veranell did. I was right there with her, so I knew about it."

"Did any of the others know?"

"Oh, sure. Eva, Louanne, Melinda, Linda, Simone, Katherine, Cynthia. We all knew. Of course, if one of them becomes the charities head instead of me, she'll get the perks and use them. That's simply how it works."

"Hm. Interesting. So, I guess it was a blessing in disguise that Veranell died so suddenly, huh?"

"That's an understatement!" Bettina laughed aloud and narrowly avoided spitting baked potato onto the table. She drained her wine glass and looked up in alarm. "I loved her dearly, of course, and I'm heartbroken that she has passed. Veranell was my mentor … like a mother to me. But I suppose it was God's will, what with her being in such a sickly state. She will be missed by one and all." She pressed her napkin to her eyes and sniffed conspicuously.

"Now, now, Tina. Don't cry. We'll discover who caused her untimely death."

Bettina reached out and grasped the hand he had casually laid on the table. He struggled not to pull away.

"You haven't called me that in a long, long time, dearest. It's so good to be with you again. I've missed you. We were so, so, so great together, don't you think?"

Earl's response was to pull his lips into a forced smile as Bettina stroked his hand.

She searched his face and took the smile as a sign to continue. "Do you think we can pick up where we left off? I'm ready if you are. How 'bout after dinner tonight?"

"I … don't know … maybe. Let's take it slow and see where it leads. Besides, I thought you had a boyfriend."

"Nah. Tom Beadwell means nothing to me. It's always been you, Earl Petry. Always you. How do you feel?"

"I feel ... like ... hey, how about some dessert?"

"I'll be your dessert, lover. I can be sweet and tasty and satisfying, as you well know." She batted her thickly mascaraed eyelashes and drew little circles on his hand with her manicured nails.

Earl's face grew flushed. "I ... think ... I'd like to have some strawberry cheesecake," he said. "How about you, Bettina? What would you like?"

"I'll just have more wine ... for now." She pushed her glass forward and licked her lips.

Earl's phone buzzed. He disengaged his hand and pulled the phone from his pocket. After a quick look at the screen and at his watch, he texted a response and gave his "date" a sympathetic shrug.

"I'm sorry, Bettina, but we'll have to cut this short. That's the Chief. I'm afraid I need to meet him in his office immediately." He signaled for the waiter.

Bettina poked her lips out and sighed heavily. By the time the waiter arrived with the check, she had poured herself another glass of wine and had already drunk it down. She finished the carafe before he brought back the receipt.

Earl worried she might be too intoxicated to walk on her own, but she clung to his arm as she shuffled out to the car. He was relieved to successfully get her home without incident, though she stretched the seatbelt to its maximum trying to lay her head on his shoulder.

At the front door, she threw her arms around his neck and pressed herself against him, lifting her face for a kiss. Earl tried to resist, but she grabbed the back of his head and pulled him toward her. Just as their lips were about to meet, his phone buzzed again. He cocked his neck, and her open mouth smacked wetly on his chin. He reached out, pushed her door open, and backed her into the house.

"Thanks for a real nice time. Gotta go, Bettina. Goodnight," he said as he slipped out of her grip and hurried to the car.

Earl drove to the end of the block and pulled out his phone to read the text message he had received, speaking aloud as he wrote his response, "Thanks, Finbar. Perfect timing. Saved me from disaster. Take good care of my girl."

Chapter Twenty-Three

TOMMIE got up early the next morning to clean and restock her shop. Finbar had left even earlier to drive to Sugar Sands Beach. Since Caife Caife Holmes was undergoing the health inspection, and there was no need for him to be present, he decided to bake himself in the sun on the white sands of the gulf coast and then meet Kevin Watson at his beachside restaurant for dinner. He had already told Tommie of Earl's successful interrogation of Bettina Taylor, and she was thrilled. She talked to him as she drove into town.

"I'm doing cleanup in my shop first and foremost. I've got to get it organized so I can reopen, maybe by tomorrow or Saturday at the latest. Tonight, I've been invited to attend a preview of the Historic Beadwell House's renovations that Tom Beadwell has completed so far. He's hoping to have a grand opening on May first, so he's invited several of us ladies to come give him our valued opinions. I'm really looking forward to it," she said.

"That's the big Colonial house where yer Ms. Coral Beadwell lived, isn't it?" Finbar asked.

"Yep. The one Tom's ex-wife Linda wanted to take away from her. I'm glad she moved away after the divorce, and she never got her hands on the family home."

"Oof. Nasty woman. Ugly hair." Finbar recalled the distinctive Prince Valiant hairstyle Linda Beadwell had worn. "I'm going to have supper with yer son, Missus. Want me to tell him anything for ye?"

"No thanks. I'll be over there Sunday. But, if you happen to have time, maybe check on Barry Brewster at the drug rehab center, and tell him I'll see him on Sunday, too."

"Ye really took a liking to the lad, despite the damage his mother did."

"He can't help it his parents were dysfunctional."

"Not to mention homicidal. Ach. Ye never know what's going on in people's minds. D'you mind being all alone today?"

"Not at all. I'm good. In fact, after what you told me about Earl's evening, I feel great. I wonder when he'll have Bettina arrested."

"Thomasina, don't get ahead of yerself. He's still got to assemble all the facts before that can happen. D'you think she'll be at the preview this evening?"

"Without a doubt, but don't worry. I'll stay away

from her ... just like Earl commanded."

Finbar snorted. "I know ye, lad. But sure, be careful. She's unhinged, and I'm charged with looking after ye. Yer man's too big for me to fight without climbing on a chair. Ringing off, now. I'll send ye a text when I'm on the way home. Take care. Have a lovely time."

Tommie stuffed her phone in the pocket of her scrub top and climbed out of her car. *A day fixing up my shop is just what I need to clear my head and calm me down,* she decided as she assembled her cleaning supplies; however, thoughts of Earl kept creeping into her mind, so calming down did not happen. Nevertheless, by lunchtime she was pleased with the progress she had made.

The forensic technicians had been much more careful than they were the last time they closed her shop, so the clean-up was minor. She waited until the last table was meticulously scrubbed and the floor was swept and mopped before she took a break to eat a sandwich of grilled brown bread and cheese.

Tommie did some mental calculations. In six days, it would be the month of May, and that meant she would need to change her window displays and introduce new herbal tea blends. She liked to design the windows and foods to match the month and feature a children's story, so she began to think of what she had read to her students when she was an elementary school teacher.

The first notable holiday in May was *Cinco de Mayo.* The next was Mother's Day. Tommie debated back and forth between two books featuring mothers: *The Runaway Bunny* by Margaret Wise Brown; and *Is Your Mama a Llama?* by Deborah Guarino. By the time she finished her sandwich, she had chosen *Is Your Mama a Llama?* Besides being about a child and his mother, it was multicultural. Perhaps she could hostess a Saturday or after-school snack time and get the Alvarez brothers to come in and read the book in both English and Spanish. She could also incorporate some *Cinco de Mayo* foods and Hispanic-themed tea blends for the mothers.

Much like her current window decorations, Tommie Watson disappeared down the rabbit hole as she started scribbling down her ideas. Before she realized it, the wall clock showed 6:12. The preview was set for 6:30.

She grabbed a pair of clean scrubs from her go-bag and ran into the bathroom to freshen up and change. Knowing Bettina and the other "mean girls" would be there, she even put on mascara, blusher, and lipstick. Leaving her cleaning supplies and display notes at the shop, she stuffed a handful of tiny, foil-wrapped chocolate Easter eggs into her pocket for a pick-me-up, rushed out to her car, and drove the few blocks to the Historic Beadwell House, arriving just in time.

Several cars lined the street in front of the house, and Tommie was glad to get a relatively close parking spot, so she didn't have to walk too far. The morning's cleaning spree had left her ankle swollen and painful. She limped up to the front door and was greeted with smiles from her friends Aubrey Rush, Jo Clay, and Elly James, as well as the twins, Susan Clay and Elaine Frank. She received scowls from Louanne Weller, Eva Edgerton, and Bettina Taylor, as expected. Melinda Layton remained aloof, not showing allegiance to either group.

Tom Beadwell appeared at the top of the double stairwell, dressed in navy slacks and a pale blue button-down shirt that accentuated his tan skin, tousled dark blond hair, and cobalt blue eyes. The women made various appreciative sounds as they took in his tall, fit frame. He was an attractive 52-year-old man, newly divorced and on the market. He held his arms out to his invited guests as he descended the stairs.

"Ladies, welcome to Historic Beadwell House. I am so glad you decided to come to my preview. I'm expecting great ideas from you. I want to tell you right now that I will consider everything you suggest, and I won't get upset if your opinion differs from mine. This house is to be a museum, of sorts, and a memorial to my sister Coral who passed away in February. You were among her dearest friends, and I know she'd be delighted for you to have some input into her home. Please, take your time and explore the house and grounds at your leisure. If you have any questions, I'll be around, and I'll be glad to answer them. Also, please grab a plate when you're in the kitchen, and take advantage of the dinner finger food in the dining room. It's all for you, so make yourselves at home!" He smiled broadly at the enthusiastic applause he received.

Right from the outset, Tommie noticed Bettina actively vying for his attention. She was wearing an outfit that was much too dressy for the occasion. Although it was decidedly *haute couture*, there was a small, but conspicuous, wine stain on the bodice. Tommie wondered idly if it was the new dress she bought from Eva's Divas for her "date" with Earl.

Not five feet away, Eva herself lurked, keeping a watchful eye on Tom, and tracking the movements of Bettina, who now emerged as her rival. *It's going to be an interesting evening,* Tommie thought.

The guests meandered through the rooms and made note of the antique furnishings and personal belongings that must have been passed down through the Beadwell family for many years. It was tastefully decorated, and Tommie felt no need to criticize or add her opinion.

She saw Tom go upstairs with Bettina at his elbow, followed closely by Eva. Determined to stay away from the drama of that situation and hungry for a suppertime meal, Tommie headed to the kitchen and fixed herself a plate of food. She engaged in pleasant conversation in the dining room with Elly and Jo, who were now sporting small but stylish engagement rings.

Aubrey and Melinda made an appearance in the doorway. Scanning the dining room and finding none of Veranell's friends there, Melinda ambled up to Tommie and gave her a hesitant smile.

"Tommie, um, I wanted you to know I don't

believe you had anything to do with what happened to Veranell. I'm sorry if I've been a little standoffish, but the sharks are circling, and I feel like I'm chum sometimes."

Shocked at her revelation, Tommie reached out and touched Melinda on the arm.

"I completely get it, Melinda. You're walking a fine line," she said, catching a meaningful look from Aubrey, "in a lot of ways. Just know I'm your friend ..."

"... until you cross the line and go after Tommie," Aubrey said, "and then you're on your own, because I can't tolerate that kind of behavior, Melly."

Tommie was equally shocked at the plainness with which Aubrey stood up for her.

"That goes for us, too," Jo said, as she and Elly rose to stand behind Tommie.

The five women looked from one to the other and appeared to forge a bond of mutual support in the middle of the Historic Beadwell House dining room. Tommie Watson was overcome with emotion and, while trying desperately to smile, excused herself to the restroom to wipe her eyes and salvage her makeup. When she came out, the group had dispersed to go their separate ways and explore the house rather than continue the awkward encounter.

The day was quickly becoming dusk, so Tommie decided to go upstairs and see what else the Historic Beadwell House offered. She passed Tom Beadwell on his way down the stairs. When she turned back, she saw he was in the front yard vaping an electronic cigarette. She continued up the stairwell and into the hall.

At the top of the stairs, Tommie heard raised voices coming from what Tom called "the Veranda Room," which featured a curved veranda directly over the front entry. She peeked into the room and recognized the speakers as Eva Edgerton and Bettina Taylor, so she lingered in the hallway just outside the doorway where she could eavesdrop without being seen.

"I told you once, Bettina, and I'll tell you again. Tom and I have been together for months. He's not interested in you. I don't know where you get that idea."

"That's because you up and snatched him from me, Eva. You probably twitched your little behind and bounced your bottle blond hair at him to get him in your bed, but it's me he wants to be with."

"What? You've lost your mind ... what little you had. Tom would never be with you. You're shared goods. Everybody knows it. Weren't you out with Earl Petry last night? That poor man. I hate to think of him getting mixed up with you again. I'd almost rather him be with that fat cow Tommie Watson."

"Earl cares for me. He never stopped caring. And so does Tom. He's mine, Eva."

Eva laughed shrilly. "You are delusional, Bettina. Really. You need help. Go home."

"You're the one who needs help, Eva. I know all about you. You just wait. You'll see."

Eva cried out in pain. "You clawed me! You

deranged feral cat! That's it. I know what you've done, Bettina Taylor, and I'll tell. You can forget about Tom."

Tommie heard the sounds of a struggle, followed by heavy breathing and the staccato of two sets of stumbling heels on the wood floor, quick steps, and a door closing. It was quiet for a moment, and then Tommie heard more walking. Bettina screeched a short squawky sound, followed by panting and more struggling. Tommie gripped her cane and flattened her ear up against the wall to hear more clearly.

"You're the one," Bettina said in a low, frightened voice. "You made Veranell sick. You dosed her food and put salmonella on those eggs. You killed her."

Eva's voice dropped to a guttural, more menacing tone. "So, what if I did it, you flat-backed floozie? You never know when to shut your stupid mouth."

Bettina gasped. "Stop! What are you doing? Get your hands off me. Eva! Eva! Somebody help me!"

Tommie heard the bumping and scraping of heels on the floor, but she stayed rooted to her spot in the hallway until a shrill scream pierced the air, followed by a loud wet *smack!* She was frozen in place trying to identify the sound, but she turned the corner and ran into the room when she heard Eva scream, "Bettina!"

Eva Edgerton was framed in the fading gold and red light of the approaching sunset, leaning over the edge of the curved balcony. Her left arm was scratched and bleeding as she clung to the heavy velvet drapes.

Tommie hobbled to the railing beyond the draperies and looked down. Below her, spotlighted on the bricked walkway beneath the balcony, lay Bettina Taylor. Her hair was splayed out in all directions from her head, which was laid over flat against her shoulder.

Tom Beadwell knelt beside Bettina's body and called her name. Getting no response, he raised his pasty white face and locked eyes with Eva.

Elaine and her sister Susan appeared at Tom's side, taking in the scene. Elaine calmly called 9-1-1 as Aubrey and Melinda ran out the front door and into the yard.

The Veranda Room was suddenly filled with other women. Louanne stood mutely at Tommie's right, and Eva still gripped the drapes at her left. Elly and Jo pressed against her back; their arms interlocked around each other.

Tommie Watson took a few shuffling steps backward to a safer position, reached into her scrub pocket, pulled out her cellphone, and called Earl Petry.

Chapter Twenty-Four

DETECTIVE EARL PETRY arrived with Sanderson Harper and several uniformed officers. Tommie and the other guests were sequestered in separate locations throughout the house for questioning, while Sandy pronounced Bettina dead and took her away to the morgue. Tommie was in the upstairs hallway, being guarded by Jenny Foran, the uniformed officer who was Earl's regular partner. Tommie saw the look in her eyes and could almost read her mind. *Yes, I'm involved in another murder case, Jenny,* she thought. *What's new?* Jenny, to her credit, remained silent and impassive.

Tommie was glad she had not seen Bettina zipped up in the body bag, but her mind could not stop replaying the argument she had overheard, nor could she keep Bettina's last panicked cries from surfacing over and over. *I should have done something,* she lamented. *But what?*

After a long while, Tommie heard Earl's heavy footfalls on the stairs. As his handsome, yet inscrutable face came into view, she knew he was going to be all business. He chose to question Tommie in the Veranda Room, which was the scene of the struggle and which had been crawling with crime scene technicians. Like her shop, there was fingerprint dust everywhere. Earl led her to a clean chair, while Jenny waited out on the balcony.

"Tommie ..." he began.

"I tried to do what you asked. I stayed away from her. I didn't engage, not even once. But if I had, maybe she wouldn't have been killed. I feel so responsible," she said.

Earl was quiet for a minute. "*Were* you responsible in any way?"

"No! I wasn't anywhere near her. Well, I was sorta near. I was in the hallway."

"What were you doing in the hallway?"

"I was ... uh ... listening." Her face blazed.

"Eavesdropping?"

"You could say that."

Earl snickered and flashed a knowing smile at Jenny. "I *would* say that, Tommie. Can you tell me *why* you were listening?

"Because you said for me not to engage. I was simply waiting for Eva and Bettina to finish up their business so I could view the room."

Earl surprised her by laughing aloud. "Lord, have

mercy! You're sending me to an early grave, Thomasina Watson. I swear you'll be the death of me sooner or later."

"It's not funny! Bettina was murdered ... and I was hearing it from the hallway. I should've stopped them ..."

"No, no, no, no, no. You did exactly the right thing. You did not need to be involved in the fracas. Thank goodness you *did* stay outside. Because of your *willingness* to *listen and follow* my advice, you are not a suspect ... not this time, anyway."

Tommie lifted her eyebrows and displayed her deep dimples momentarily. "I'm not a suspect? Wow! That's new. What am I now?"

"What is she, Jenny?"

Jenny tried to suppress a smile. "You're a material witness, Ms. Watson."

"Hey, I like that title better."

"Me, too," Earl said. "All right, Tommie. Use that detailed schoolteacher memory of yours and tell me exactly what you heard occurring inside the room. Don't speculate. Just tell me verbatim, as best you can, what the conversation was from the time you arrived until the time you called me. Jenny, you take notes. Jenny?"

The officer had disappeared. Then, she popped her head around from behind the draperies on the right.

"I'm here. I just saw something the techs left," Jenny held up a small oblong object with a reflective surface. "This candy egg was hiding behind the curtains."

"Oh! That was mine. It must've come from my

pocket when I pulled my phone out to call Earl," Tommie said with an embarrassed grin. "You can have it, Jenny."

The officer looked to Earl for permission. When he nodded, she stuck it in her shirt pocket for later, then she pulled out a small notepad and pen.

Tommie gave an extraordinarily detailed account of the altercation from her visually obstructed point of view, which consisted of hearing the conversation, the struggle, the sound of the footsteps on the wood floor, Eva's threats, Bettina's cries for help, and ending with the gruesome *smack* as Bettina's body landed on the pavement. All the while, Jenny took notes, and Earl concentrated on Tommie's expressions and body language.

"What about after you came into the room? What did you see, and who was where?" he asked.

Tommie described Eva holding the heavy drapes with her scratched and bloody arm. She named off the women in the room—Louanne, Elly, and Jo—and the women on the ground—Aubrey, Melinda, Susan, and Elaine, who called 9-1-1.

"Nobody came in or out before Bettina went over the railing. I was at the door the whole time," she said.

"Where was Tom Beadwell?"

"He had gone out onto the lawn to vape when I came upstairs. Afterward, he checked on Bettina, and then he … I don't know how to describe it exactly … but he and Eva intently held each other's eyes, like they were communicating telepathically or something. His face was really pale as he stared at her."

"Did Eva say anything at all?"

"No. Not after she screamed Bettina's name. She just stood there hanging onto that curtain while looking down at the body."

"And you're certain Bettina cried her name just before she went over the balcony."

"Yes. I'm positive. Eva admitted to killing Veranell and said, 'You need to know when to shut your stupid mouth.' Then Bettina said, 'Stop it. Take your hands off me, Eva. Somebody help!' The next sound I heard was when she hit the ground."

Earl nodded and patted Tommie's knee. "You did good, darlin'. I won't tell you not to confide in Finbar because I know good and darn well you will. But how about don't broadcast it to your four flappy-mouthed friends? You'll have to testify at Eva's trial." He helped her to her feet and planted a quick kiss on her lips. "It's all good with us, Tommie. Don't fret."

That was the best thing Tommie had heard in a long time. "I won't, Earl. I promise," she said, and this time, she meant it.

Chapter Twenty-Five

TOMMIE WATSON sat up in bed the next morning, awakened by the snoring of the brindle and white dog sharing her pillow. She petted Zed and extricated her feet from beneath Red. Leaving the dogs to their slumbers, she showered and dressed. Then, she limped into the kitchen, fixed herself a cup of *Easter Sunrise* tea, and settled herself comfortably onto her chaise to reflect on the previous day. Before she could even take a sip, there was a scratching at the kitchen door.

"I'm coming, Sherlock," she said with a sigh.

She opened the pet flap, and the little dog raced for her bedroom to wake his sleeping pals. Tommie followed them all next door for breakfast with Finbar.

Afterward, the duo decided to spend the rest of Friday cleaning up Caife Caife Holmes and restocking their shop pantries. Thankfully, the County Health Inspector had given Finbar the go-ahead to reopen, and he was anxious to get back on track.

"Sure, 'tis too late to book reservations for the weekend, Thomasina, but we can certainly relaunch tomorrow night with some complimentary snacks and drinks for whomever wishes to drop in. What d'you think?"

"I think that's a wonderful idea. What's your plan for the menu?"

"I was thinking of some good Irish favorites."

"No fish, I hope."

"No, Missus. No fish. I know yer partial to the fried potato *rissole*, so I'll cook plenty of it. And I can bake a batch or two of those individual *Irish brown soda breads* to eat with butter and strong cheese. Maybe you'd like to make some of yer deviled eggs."

"No way. I think we should steer clear of eggs. Don't want to remind people of salmonella, you know?"

"Good thinking, lad. I've got some of yer *Besame Bagel Bites* in my freezer. What about them?"

"Yeah. Let's rename them, though."

"Ha! I've got it. They're like little bread patties covered with poppyseed glaze, only I'll make them more Irish by changing the spelling with 'd' in place of 't' and call them *Poppyseed Paddies.*"

Tommie laughed. "Works for me. What other

kinds of snacks do y'all eat when you're entertaining?"

"We particularly likes *Tayto sandwiches.*"

"And that is ...?"

"Potato crisps between slices of buttered bread."

"Nah. Potato chips will get soggy. What else?"

"I enjoys *baps.*"

"Don't know what *baps* are."

"They're called *rollóg bhricfeasta* in Gaelic. They're like what you'd call biscuits, although biscuits are what we call cookies, but they're really a soft breakfast roll stuffed with pork links, bacon rashers, black and white pudding, and a runny egg."

"Your language is so convoluted. That sounds tasty, but let's nix the egg. Also, black and white puddings will definitely turn people off if they know they're pork blood. But, hey, we can make it with just sausages ... like bangers. Oh! Oh! I know! We'll call them *bangers 'n' baps* and *rashers 'n' rolls.*"

Finbar scowled. "Ach. 'Tis not quite the same things, but sure, we'll tame them down for you Americans."

After some more back and forth, they nailed down a tentative menu and began writing out ingredients for their grocery list. As the day progressed into the lunch hour, Finbar topped brown bread slices with butter and cheese and put them in the oven to toast. Tommie sliced onions and pickled beets, while Finbar rummaged in the storage room cooler for condiments, apples, and cold chicken breasts to round out the meal.

"Finbar, the bread is burning," Tommie called, shaking her head to clear the tears in her squinted eyes due to the irritating fumes of the strong onion.

Not hearing his reply, she called louder. "Finbar! The toast! Come get it out before it turns to charcoal."

Finbar rushed to the oven and opened the door. Reaching in, he grasped the tray with his dishtowel and set it on the counter.

"Yer nose is betraying ye, Missus. They could use a couple more minutes for melting the cheese."

Tommie pulled the neck of her scrub top up and wiped her eyes. "Then you've got something on the bottom of your oven. I still smell it burning."

Finbar coughed. "I smell it, too, but it's not in the cooker. D'you have something in yer cooker next door?"

"I don't have an oven in my shop. I have induction cooktops, but they don't even get hot without a pot or a pan on them. I smell it strong in here. Look around."

The two of them scanned the kitchen area, but there was nothing burning. The stovetops were off, and the oven was clean. Tommie's eyes itched and watered, and Finbar coughed. They frantically searched the shop for the source of the smoldering smell. As Finbar passed the bathroom, he noticed tendrils of smoke coming under the back door.

"Ah, I see, Thomasina. There's a fire outside somewhere. Go look out the front door."

Tommie hurried to the entry and pushed, but the

door remained closed. She turned the thumb latch, but the door wouldn't budge.

"Can't open it. Is it locked with a key?"

"No. It shouldn't be. Push it hard."

Tommie pushed harder; her vision still obscured by her stinging eyes. "It's stuck or something."

Finbar walked to the front and lifted the shade. Looking through the window, he saw a chain wrapped between the handle and a heavy wrought-iron bench that had been dragged up and wedged against the door.

"Ach. The health inspector must've chained it closed. Let's go out the back."

The two of them approached the back door. Finbar grabbed the handle and jumped back in alarm.

"Jaysus! Me hands! The door's hot as Hell. The fire must be close to us. Quick, Missus. Let's go out through yer shop."

Tommie pulled her keys from her pocket and unlocked the connecting door. When they stepped into Watson's Reme-Teas, they were engulfed in clouds of roiling grey smoke. She slammed the door shut, and they retreated into Caife Caife Holmes, which was quickly filling up with thick black smoke.

"Drop to the floor, Missus," Finbar shouted. "I'll call 9-9-9."

"No, it's 9-1-1 in America. Call 9-1-1," Tommie managed with a wheezing cough. She crawled to the front of the store and laid her head near the bottom of the door, hoping to get fresh air. Then, everything went dark.

*   *   *

The next thing either of them knew, they were outside on the front sidewalk sucking oxygen through plastic masks while firefighters stepped out through the shattered glass of the front display window.

Earl cradled Tommie's head in his lap. She looked up at his face and saw it was covered with black soot. A single clean line of pinkish skin streaked from his left eye down to his chin. When he noticed her looking at him, he took one large thumb and stroked it across her grimy forehead. She struggled to sit up, and he let her, keeping her circled within his arms.

"Finbar?" she managed with wild eyes and a raspy cough, craning her neck around. "Where's Finbar?"

"He's fine. His hands are burned and bandaged, but they're mostly bad first-degree burns," Earl replied.

"The shops?"

"Both damaged, but not irreparably."

"Bench chained to the door!"

"Both shops. Chairs against the back doors, too."

"Fingerprints?"

Earl shook his head. "Can't get any. Front benches were wiped. Back chairs were covered in flames."

"Eva did it?"

"Not possible. She's in custody and hasn't yet been

arraigned. Somebody else did this."

Tommie scanned her eyes side to side, blinking rapidly. "Who else would want to ...? Tom Beadwell?"

"No. He's at the courthouse waiting to post bail for Eva. I left him there when I got the call."

"Finbar called you instead of 9-1-1?"

"No, Tommie. He must've lost consciousness before he could dial it. I got a call from Dale about this after dispatch sent the truck, and that was after the store window was broken and the two of you were pulled to safety." He nodded in the direction of the street.

Sitting on the curb on either side of Finbar Holmes, with blankets wrapped around their shoulders, were Leo and Santino Alvarez. The EMTs were adjusting the bandages on the men's hands and arms.

"Apparently, the brothers saw the fire from their store and ran over. They knocked down the flames with their shirts and kicked the chairs away, but they couldn't get the doors open. They hurried to the front and saw you passed out on the floor near the chained-up door. They picked up the table and heaved it through the window. They carried you and Finbar out onto the sidewalk just as the firetruck arrived. Both brothers have some pretty severe cuts and burns, but those men saved your lives."

Tommie's eyes filled with clean, fresh tears of relief and thankfulness. Earl pulled her close to his chest.

"Now what?" she asked.

"Now, you rest up and heal before you try to repair

your shops."

"No, I mean what about who did this? I don't think there's anybody around who loves Eva Edgerton enough to avenge her for being arrested. We've made a mistake, Earl. I don't know how, but we've made a mistake."

Earl nodded slowly. "Maybe. Maybe. But until we get more evidence, Eva will be charged with Bettina's death. I'm sure it will be determined manslaughter instead of premeditated murder."

"But what about her admitting she killed Veranell?"

"Can't charge her for that just yet based on what you think you heard. Now don't get huffy, darlin'. I I believe you heard it, but we have to collect more evidence before we can build a strong case against her."

Tommie rolled her eyes. "If you say so."

"I do say so, Tommie. And I want you, my nosy little sleuth, to lay low and stay home. No investigating, no personal interviews, no phone calls, no getting the gossip group together to compare notes. None of that. You and Finbar both will rest in your own little houses, and I'll feed y'all with takeout food while you recuperate."

"But, Earl ..."

"But nothing, Thomasina Watson. For once, you are going to do as I advise."

Tommie pulled the mask off her face and gave him a squinty-eyed stare. "Make me," she challenged.

Earl didn't answer. He just pulled her close and

kissed her soundly on the lips.

"That'll work," Tommie said with a smile.

Chapter Twenty-Six

EARL dropped Tommie and Finbar off at their duplex with an admonition to stay put. They thanked him and departed to their separate units.

As soon as she got inside, Tommie brewed herself a cup of *Blues Reme-Tea* with *Honey-Honey* and laid on the chaise with her feet up and her dogs by her side. After her second cup, there was a knock at the front door. She opened it to see the smiling face of a teenager wearing a t-shirt from a local pizza place. He handed her a stack of food boxes and gratefully accepted a generous tip.

Tommie immediately took the boxes around the back to Finbar's kitchen door and knocked. Sherlock stuck his head out the flap and welcomed his canine buddies. Hearing nothing from her neighbor, Tommie opened the door and walked on in. The house was dark, so she flipped the light switch as she placed the boxes on the table.

"Finbar?" she called. "Finbar, where are you?"

"I'm here, Missus," he responded from the direction of his easy chair.

"Oh, hey. Why's it so dark in here? Earl sent us food. It's on the table."

"I'm not hungry, lad."

"You know, we never got lunch. It's fresh and ready. We don't even need plates. We can use the boxes."

"I don't want any."

"C'mon, Finbar. It's good and warm."

"So's me Guinness."

Seeing a bottle of the brew on his end table, Tommie went to the refrigerator and pulled out a cold one.

"OK. I've got you a fresh beer. Come to the table."

"Bugger off, Thomasina. Don't ye see I'm in no mood for company?"

Tommie stood still a moment, shocked at his tone of voice. Then she carefully approached his chair.

"Since when am I company? What's wrong with you, Finbar?"

"I don't feel like listening to yer yammerin', woman. I wants to be left alone."

Tommie went to the sofa and turned the table lamp on. She saw Finbar sitting in his chair staring at the wall morosely, an unopened bottle of Guinness beside him, his bandaged hands in his lap. He winced when the light came on.

"Oh, I see. Feeling sorry for yourself, huh? Me, too. I had a cup of *Blues Reme-Tea*, and I feel better. Maybe I should brew some for you."

"Will that repair the damage to m'shop? Will that save m'business? Did the bloody tea fix yers?" He glowered at her.

"Nope. Will you being a first-class jackass help? Will sitting in the dark moping help? I don't think so." Tommie's outrage matched her friend's.

"Shut yer yap, Thomasina. Don't ye see I can't even open m' bloody ale, for St. Brigid's sake?"

"Yep." She twisted the cap off the beer bottle she was holding and thrust the dark ale at him. "That's what friends are for. So, get over it, Finbar Holmes, and come to the table. We've gotta support one another. Besides, we have work to do ... despite what Earl commanded."

He waved away the bottle and reluctantly got up from the chair, muttering curses under his breath as he shuffled over to the dining room and sat down. Tommie set the beer on the table and began opening the take-out boxes. Immediately, the room filled with the scent of garlicky pizza, smoked chicken wings, and tangy vinegar-based sauce. Despite his foul mood, Finbar's mouth watered, and his stomach growled loudly.

"See, I knew you were hungry. Let's dispense with silverware and just eat." Tommie flattened out the boxes so they could be used as plates.

He grunted and held up his hands. Tommie

hopped up and rummaged through a kitchen drawer.

"Ta da," she said. To keep his bandages from getting soiled, she covered them in the cellophane she found in the drawer. When she finished wrapping, she looked over and caught a trace of a smile from her friend.

"First time I've ever eaten with cling film mittens, but I think I can manage. Pass me them chicken wings, lad, before m' stomach knocks on m' backbone."

They ate every morsel of the food—two dozen chicken wings, seasoned potato wedges, and a large meat-lover's pizza. Tommie refreshed Finbar's Guinness once more and refilled the iced sweet tea she made for herself. When they finished, she unwrapped the greasy plastic from his hands, set a cold beer on the end table by his chair, and bagged up the empty boxes, doling out the uneaten crusts to the dogs.

"That was a feast, lad. My compliments to yer man for sending it. Now, tell me about the work we've yet to do. And who d'you think set fire to us? If it wasn't Ms. Edgerton, and it wasn't her beau Mr. Beadwell, who could it have been?"

"I'm wondering if we need to figure out *who*, or if maybe we need to figure out *why*."

"Hmm. Tell me what yer thoughts are."

"Why do people commit murder?"

"Revenge, greed, power, passion, retaliation ..."

"... and coverup."

"And coverup. Another murderer besides Miss

Taylor or Ms. Edgerton, perhaps?"

"That's a possibility. How do we drill down to the perpetrator when we have lots of suspects?"

"Eliminations. Motives. Get yer list, lad."

"Got it. Let's start from the top. Levi Muller."

"Had motive for Veranell and Bettina. Eggs were sanitized, so he didn't cause the salmonella. But he was nowhere near the Beadwell House when Bettina died ..."

"Wait. Just so we don't get confused and do double work. Who do you think killed Veranell? I thought it was Bettina until Eva confessed."

"Did she?"

"Did she what?"

"Did Eva confess?"

"I heard Bettina say, 'You killed Veranell' and Eva said, 'So what if I did?' Isn't that a confession?"

"Are ye sure you got the speakers correct? Could it have been the other way around? What if it was that Eva accused Bettina, and Bettina admitted she did it?"

"I ... don't ... think so. But their voices *did* get very low pitched. I honestly can't say for sure which one was speaking. What if Bettina was trying to push Eva over the balcony and called her name out to make it seem like Eva was the aggressor? Oh, my gosh, Finbar. I could be testifying against an innocent woman!"

"Ye said Eva was injured."

"Yes, she accused Bettina of clawing her, and she did have a long bloody scratch on her arm, so that's true."

"What else? Earl seemed to be quite sure Bettina was Veranell's killer. Perhaps she was."

"Then what was Eva? The accomplice?"

"Perhaps. Or could she have been the mastermind trying to get rid of Bettina before she was exposed?"

"Then who the hell tried to get rid of us?"

"There's the rub. Perhaps it was a group of conspirators. Or …"

"Or what?"

"Or you were privy to something someone doesn't want you to recall. Your eyewitness account is incomplete. Somebody is afraid you will remember that important little detail and expose the true killer."

"That's why the fire … to eliminate me?"

"Exactly. And I am collateral damage, Missus."

"No, you're my partner. Whoever did this knows we talk and compare notes. Both of us are the threats."

"Righto. Read yer list off from the top and let's quickly eliminate all but those who are true possibilities."

"Levi Muller."

"No motive. Eliminate him."

"Amos Mosby."

"No motive. Eliminate him as well."

"Aubrey Rush. Absolutely not. She's good people. I'm crossing her off."

"I agree. Next?"

"Santino Alvarez. I'm eliminating him and his brother Leo. Why try to kill us and then save our lives?"

"Exactly. Who's next?"

"Jeanette and Sid Spock."

Finbar scoffed. "They were targets, just like m'self. I consider them allies. Next person?"

"Paul and Louanne Weller."

"Cross off Paul. But Louanne Weller. Hmm. She has motives, I believe."

"Me, too. She was in the gang, probably next in command under Veranell. Greed, jealousy, has that damaged merchandise scam going. She and Bettina were together a lot. Goes to the same church. I'm keeping her."

"I agree. Let's move on."

"Melinda Layton."

"Same gang, different church. She's a possibility."

"Maybe, but she's good friends with Aubrey. They were together the whole time we were at the Beadwell House. I have a hard time thinking she's involved."

"So, put a question mark on her name. Remember, ye thought Mrs. Brewster was innocent. Next?"

"Right. I sure did. Father Duncan. Nah. Not him for sure. The next two are Elly James and Jo Clay. I say no to them, as well. They're engaged to the Alvarez brothers, and they're my friends. I'm eliminating them."

"All right, lad. I trust yer instincts."

"They came up behind me after Bettina went over the balcony. There's no way they could have come out and in again without me seeing them."

"But wasn't Mrs. Weller there, too? Did ye see her

come out or in?"

"Hmm. Good point. I'll put a question mark on Louanne, then. That leaves Eva. She has motive and means for both murders. And Bettina would be the last one. She had motive for killing Veranell, and she might have been trying to kill Eva but fell off by accident."

"That leaves us with Miss Bettina Taylor and/or Ms. Eva Edgerton as Mrs. Veranell Collins' killer, with a possibility for Mrs. Melinda Layton and Mrs. Louanne Weller as accomplices. Peas in a pod. Miss Taylor's dead, and Ms. Edgerton's in custody. So, either Mrs. Layton or Mrs. Weller or both tried to do us in, Missus, and we're still in danger."

Chapter Twenty-Seven

EARL came by with their evening meal and stayed to help them eat. They dined in Tommie's unit for a change, and she was happy to play the hostess as she set out three place settings and even lit a candle on the table.

Dinner consisted of take out from The Lunch Pad, courtesy of Sid and Jeanette Spock. Having been deemed free from any traces of salmonella or other food-born contagions, they had outdone themselves with this meal.

Tommie cut and served heaping portions of *Lunar Landing Lasagna*, accompanied by a *Caesar Satellite Salad* and *Galactic Garlic Bread*. To help Finbar eat, she wrapped his hands in cellophane mittens again, but she added a knife in his right hand and a tines-down fork in his left. He managed well, eating in the European way of cutting and loading up the back of the fork without changing hands.

Dessert was furnished by their four outspoken friends—a quart of freshly churned vanilla bean and honeycomb ice cream from The Corner Creamery. Afterward, bellies full, the men retired to the living room while Tommie quickly washed the dinnerware and stacked it in the dish drain to dry.

Tommie took her place on the chaise, and Earl snugged up beside her on the adjacent seat with his hand laid on her leg. The dogs settled on the floor and fell asleep.

"Well?" Tommie said.

"Well?" Earl replied.

Tommie huffed. "Earl. Tell us something."

"Oh, you mean you want me to share information about the investigation?"

"Of course, I do. Don't keep us in suspense. You know you want to compare notes."

Earl grinned. "Yes, you're right. OK. Here's what I can tell you. Somebody figured you'd both be at your shops today. Whoever it was had to wait until you were inside before the fire was set in the back. The front doors had already been blocked. I believe that had to have been done late last night because moving those benches would've been noisy. The chairs at the back doors were not so much used as barricades as they were obstacles and a means to set the fires. The perpetrator had to move quickly to avoid detection. I believe the chairs were piled with branches, paper, and wood the night before and left sitting casually along the side of the building ... like trash. You didn't even notice them when you arrived. Then, once you went in, all the person had to do was move the chairs into the doorways, douse them with gasoline, and light the fires. Probably took just a matter of five minutes or less."

"D'you think it was more than one person that done it?" Finbar asked.

Earl shook his head. "No. I think it was a single individual. The chairs were considerably lighter than the front benches. A woman could easily have picked them up and piled more flammables in the seats."

"Then you suspect a woman," Tommie said.

Earl shrugged. "I do. There were no men at the premier. Just women. And Tom Beadwell was at Eva's arraignment this morning."

"We suspect a woman, as well," Finbar confirmed.

"We've narrowed it down to Louanne Weller ..." Tommie said.

"... and Melinda Layton," Finbar interjected.

"And Melinda Layton," Tommie muttered.

"Hmm. Interesting. I can't even conceive of how you came to those conclusions, but I don't necessarily disagree. What would their motives be?"

"We're thinking greed, jealousy, possibly power," Finbar said, "but most likely to coverup another crime."

"That crime being another murder? Veranell? Bettina?" Earl suggested.

"Exactly," Tommie said. "If Eva hadn't been in jail, I would have said it was her."

"That would've been a likely guess," Earl said. "But she was in custody."

"What happened at her arraignment?" Tommie asked. "Did she get released?"

"She did. Her bail was set at $200,000. Tom paid the bail bondsman and took her straight home. She's at his house. We've got a car out front keeping an eye on them."

"Them? Does that mean you suspect Tom of being involved in Bettina's death?" Tommie asked.

Earl shifted in his seat. "It does me no good to say this is off the record, and you shouldn't even know it, but it seems Tom may have witnessed the entire incident."

When he didn't elaborate, Finbar leaned in closer.

"Detective, if ye can, please share."

"On one condition. You both have to stay at home and keep out of it from here on out. Is that a deal?"

Finbar nodded. He and Earl looked at Tommie. She averted her eyes.

"Tommie ..."

"Earl ..."

"Dadgummitall, Tommie. I won't tell you if you don't promise you'll stay in this house and behave."

"OK, OK. I promise." She pooched out her lips.

"All right, then. I'm holding you to it. Tom confirmed he was in the yard smoking his electronic cigarette when he heard arguing from that Veranda Room. It was getting dark, but he could see the two women fighting in the setting sunlight. One was dark haired, and the other was blond. They seemed to settle down, but then they started again. He saw them struggling and moving out onto the porch. Then the blond pushed the brunette over the railing. He ran over, and Bettina was dead on the steps."

"Did he say it was Eva on the balcony?"

"No, he did not. I couldn't get him to admit to anything except 'it was a blond woman' in his statement."

"He was protecting Eva," Finbar said.

"Without a doubt," Earl said.

"I saw that look pass between them. He knew. He knew it was Eva," Tommie insisted.

"I'm sure, but I can't compel him to tell the truth. I can only continue my investigation and work towards finding some proof," Earl said.

"Detective, when we spoke on Wednesday last, you inferred that Miss Taylor had caused the death of Mrs. Collins. D'you still think that to be so?" Finbar said.

"I do, Finbar. I'm reasonably convinced Bettina had the motive and the best opportunity to taint her food with the contaminants. I just don't know if she had ..." He paused and pressed his lips together.

"You don't know if she had what?" Tommie asked.

"The intelligence, I suppose," he admitted.

"Really?" Tommie's eyes widened.

Earl nodded gravely. "Yep. Bettina had a lot going for her, but most of it was physical. She really wasn't all that bright, in my opinion."

So, that's why you dated her? Tommie thought,

sagely keeping her mouth shut.

As though reading her mind, Earl's face colored. Finbar broke the uncomfortable silence.

"Detective Petry, whilst ye were assembling yer investigation, did ye happen to uncover anything that might point to someone else killing Mrs. Collins?"

"I can tell you that her killer could be any of the women in her group of followers. She had amassed quite an arsenal of what Bettina called 'perks' from heading up various charities. She had dirt on just about everyone in town, and she targeted minorities in particular. Whoever profited from her death stood to have the means to hold the town of Floribunda a veritable hostage. No offense, Tommie. I hate to be so gender specific, but none of the men in our suspect pool have that ambition. None of them are remotely like Charles Williams."

At the mention of the name, Tommie shuddered, remembering the malevolent former realtor who had intimidated and threatened her and had been a suspect in Coral Beadwell's death.

"No offense taken. Finbar and I have already come to that conclusion. Earl, I have to ask. Do you think it could've happened that Bettina was the one trying to kill Eva and she accidently fell over the balcony?"

Earl squeezed her leg. "No, darlin'. I know where you're going with this. Sandy measured the angle of Bettina's body in relation to the railing. If she had just fallen, she would've ended up directly below the veranda.

She was a good three feet beyond it. Bettina was definitely pushed, and she was pushed with great force."

"I guess that makes it murder, all right. Thanks."

Finbar raised his arms and gave an exaggerated yawn. "I think I'm done in for the night. C'mon, Sherlock. Let's to bed with us. Good night, all, and thanks again for bringing us that meal." He followed the dog out the door.

Earl took the opportunity to gather Tommie in his arms. She relaxed against his barrel chest and felt herself peacefully drifting in his heady masculine smell. He lifted her chin and kissed her deeply. Rising to his feet, he pulled her from the chaise and stood with her in his embrace for a long while before reluctantly pulling away.

"Get some rest, darlin'. You've been through Hell and back, and I need you well and on your game. This thing ain't over, so I'd like you and Holmes to keep doing your armchair investigating. You notice that I said, 'armchair investigating.' Don't set foot outside this house until I tell you it's over and done with. Dale's gonna be cruising by periodically keeping an eye out. I've talked with your friends, and I've got your meals covered for the next few days, so y'all don't have to worry about cooking. Here's a list of who's bringing what and when. Don't open the door for anybody else that's not on this list, you hear me?"

"I hear ... and obey, master." She giggled.

"Seriously, Tommie. There's a dangerous person on the loose, and until we find out who it is, I want you protected inside this relatively fire-proof cinderblock house with your little barking watchdogs. You understand?"

"I do, Earl. I'll stay put. Thank you. I love ... uh," she stammered, "... uh, that you're concerned. I promise I'll only let in the people on the list. It's really sweet that you've done all this."

Earl's heart fluttered at the L-word because he had almost used it himself several times of late. "It's because I care about you, Tommie Watson, no matter how ornery you may be." He grinned and kissed her again before letting himself out the front door on shaky legs.

Chapter Twenty-Eight

FINBAR AND TOMMIE ate like a king and queen all day Saturday, so staying inside was not difficult for them.

Breakfast was delivered by Tommie's musical friends Annie Lang, Tina Brass, and Joan Carroll. After chit chat and catching up on the community chorus news for the week, the ladies left them alone to eat. Finbar was delighted with the individual ham and cheese quiches, which were made in oversized muffin tins. Portions of red pepper- and onion-laced hashed browns, which were also made in the large muffin tins, completed the meal. At six of each, there were plenty of leftovers to pop into the freezer and save for another day.

*   *   *

Lunch came in the form of cold cut submarine sandwiches and thick, kettle-cooked potato chips from their Riverton friends Maggie and Craig Kohl and Terry Jackson. Finbar and Craig took their lunches outside to the backyard while Tommie and the ladies ate inside. Maggie brought a couple of gifts besides the lunch: a white pillar candle for Finbar and a tiny glass jar covered in black wax for Tommie.

"The candle is for Mr. Holmes. He should light it and keep it on the table when he eats and sits in his living room, and he should put it on his bedside stand at night, but he must blow it out before he goes to sleep. It will promote healing of his hands," she told Tommie.

Tommie smiled. Her friend was a "free spirit" who felt a connection with nature and all the elements of the earth, and Tommie loved her dearly. "What about the jar?" she asked, turning it in her hand.

"Oh, that's to keep evil away from your home. You must bury it at night in front of your porch," Maggie said.

"Cool. What's in it?"

"Rusty nails, screws, thorns, bent needles, tacks."

"Okie dokie."

"Oh, and urine."

"What?" Tommie quickly put the jar down and wiped her hand on her pants while Maggie and Terry erupted in laughter.

"Not really, Tommie. I saw her make it. It's filled with vinegar and the other things," Terry said with a wink.

"You're so ... considerate, Mags. I'll bury it while the moon is out," Tommie said frowning.

After their guests left, Finbar pointed to the gifts.

"What're those, Missus?"

"Oh, the candle is for healing your hands. You're supposed to light it and keep it wherever you are in the house but blow it out before you fall asleep."

"And the black jar?"

"You don't want to know."

*　　*　　*

Just before dark, Aubrey Rush appeared at the door to bring them a special supper. She laid a white linen cloth on the table and placed a small lit oil lamp in the center.

"Finbar, I had invited Tommie to celebrate a Passover dinner with me, but since you two can't come to my house tonight, I've brought the dinner to you. We'll celebrate the eighth day of Passover called *Acharon shel Pesach*. This meal, called a *Se'udat Mashiach*—or meal of the Messiah—is devoted to *HaMashiach*, the Messiah."

Finbar and Tommie sat at her table and watched as Aubrey poured four small glasses of wine for Finbar and herself. She poured four glasses of grape juice for Tommie, who didn't drink alcohol.

"The wine and your juice symbolize the retribution that God will one day force upon the nations of the world and the comfort He will bestow upon the Jewish people."

She poured a fifth cup of wine and left it in the center of the table near the lamp. "The fifth cup is reserved for the prophet Elijah. It represents redemption and will remain undrunk."

Aubrey uncovered the dishes she had placed on the table. "All week, we Jews have eaten dry unleavened bread. Tonight, the matzah was leavened with water to make the matzah ball dumplings to go in this chicken soup. I've also baked a nice *mina*. It's a lamb pie made with fresh spinach, artichoke, peas, and layered matzah."

After offering up a prayer, she served the soup and lamb pie to each of them. The flavors were unlike anything Tommie had ever tasted, and she praised Aubrey robustly. Finbar was so enchanted with the meal he had seconds.

"Ms. Rush, would ye consider coming to Caife Caife Holmes one night and demonstrating the preparation of some of yer delicious ethnic dishes? I'm afraid I'm just a clumsy Irishman. I don't think I could replicate yer cooking to anyone's satisfaction," he said.

Aubrey blushed. "I'd love to do that, if you think people would be interested in eating them."

"Are you kidding? This is delicious. I'd like to bottle this soup and sell it in my shop as a healthy tonic," Tommie said.

"Hmm. Maybe we can work that out sometime. I'll barter with you. Matzah soup for herbal potions," Aubrey countered. "On another note, I've been thinking about Thursday. Detective Petry interviewed me first because I had to get home before the sun set, so I don't know what happened after I left. I heard Eva Edgerton was arrested."

"She was," Tommie said. "She's out on bail and staying with Tom Beadwell."

"Is that right? Well, at least they're out in the open now. Why do you think she pushed Bettina over?

"I'm not really sure except there was a feud going on over Tom. Eva had him; Bettina wanted him."

"Bettina wanted any man who showed her the least bit of encouragement, and even those who didn't. Tommie, you know your fella wasn't interested in her, don't you?"

"I do. Didn't stop her from trying, though. What has Melinda said about Eva? I know they're friends."

Aubrey snorted. "I put a stop to that relationship. I told you we went to college together. What I didn't say was that we were roommates. When I moved here to Floribunda, we reconnected. She married Carl, and they're happy, although the poor man can't hold his liquor, but neither can Melinda."

Finbar snickered. "I know that. He's in the poker club. Right nice fellow other than being silly after knocking back a few."

"He's harmless. I'm glad they found each other. They fit, you know? And lately, they've both committed to attending Alcoholics Anonymous. Anyway, this business with the snooty women has gone on long enough, so I gave her an ultimatum a few days ago. My true friendship or their toxic association. She chose me."

"I'm so glad. I really like her. She and the Trinity LCO have been excellent customers. They kept me in business when I first opened my shop," Tommie said.

Finbar leaned forward. "Ms. Rush, d'you think she had anything to do with Mrs. Collins getting sicker?"

"Why would you think that? Just because she ran with that group? She didn't have any reason that I know of. Melinda has her faults, but I don't think she's capable of deliberately hurting someone. Besides, I know for a fact she was making chocolate Easter eggs on Friday and Saturday, and Eva was with her both days decorating them. When would she have had time?"

"D'you think she'd have any reason to harm Thomasina or m'self?"

"Absolutely not. Are you telling me she's a viable suspect? Should I ask her about Veranell?"

"No, no! Aubrey, we're just fishing for clues to this mess. Trying to fit all the puzzle pieces together. I don't think Melinda would ever hurt anyone. Please don't get her upset. We don't suspect her. Really," Tommie said.

"Good. I want to help, but if Melinda's involved, I'll have to step away. I couldn't bear to incriminate her, but I won't excuse her if she's guilty. I can't condone that kind of criminal behavior at all," Aubrey said.

"I agree," Tommie said.

Aubrey smiled brightly and began clearing the table. Just before she left, she gave Tommie a quick hug, and then she drew back and looked her square in the eyes.

"If you want to know my opinion, Dr. Watson, my money's on Eva or Bettina. One or the other or both caused Veranell's death, and Eva killed Bettina to cover it up or keep her quiet."

Chapter Twenty-Nine

FINBAR AND TOMMIE dined like royalty again on Sunday, beginning with a delivery of fresh pastries from Jo Clay, along with an assortment of items from Elly's Jelly Jar. As soon as Elly entered, Tommie noticed her new look.

"Elly! Your hair!" she exclaimed.

The young woman blushed and shook her head full of blond ringlets. "Do you like it?"

"I love it! It's so cute. You look like a little pixie. Where did you get it done?"

"You're not going to believe this, but Amos Mosby did it." She put the food on the table and walked closer to Tommie, who immediately reached her hand out to touch the soft bouncy halo.

"The barber? I didn't know he does women's hair."

"He doesn't normally, but Leo had to get his cut

yesterday, and I went with him. When he got up from the chair, I was standing a little too close, and he knocked my arm. Well, I was holding a full cup of orange soda, and the drink went all in my face and hair. I was a mess! Amos got me wet towels to wipe my face, but my hair ... you wouldn't believe what that sticky drink did to it. Anyway, Amos sat me down in the shampoo chair and washed my hair. Then he noticed, when he took the towel off, all the ringlets. I have naturally curly hair."

Jo laughed. "That's for sure. She's spent so much time blow drying it, then flattening it with an iron, and cementing it with hairspray, I was afraid it would crack off one day."

Elly nodded, and the curls jiggled. "I thanked him and said I'd fix it when I got home, but he said he was an expert with curly hair and asked if he could trim it up for me. Leo agreed, so I let Amos cut and shape it. He didn't use product or anything and just let it airdry. Next thing I know, this is how I looked, and Leo can't keep his hands off of it." She giggled.

"I don't wonder," Tommie said. "It's like petting a lamb. So soft, so feminine. It's amazing."

"What's amazing?" Finbar asked as he entered the kitchen. Catching sight of Elly, he came forward with his hand extended to touch her hair. "Aw, lad, it's lovely. Ye look like a wee angel."

"Amos Mosby did it," Elly said.

"D'you mean the barber? I must say, he's got a right

good hand." He stared meaningfully at Tommie. "Ooh, do I see breakfast on the table? Will ye stay and join us?"

"No thanks. We've got to get to church. But you two enjoy everything," Jo said. "We've brought you bagels, croissants, buttermilk biscuits ..."

"... cream cheese and jellies and preserves. We even have sugar free ones for you, Mr. Holmes," Elly said.

"Thank ye, lads. I appreciate yer consideration for m'health conditions," he said.

After Elly and Jo left, Tommie and Finbar had a delicious breakfast of *Easter Sunrise* tea with their selection of pastries and sweets.

"Miss James looks like a completely different person altogether," Finbar said.

"She does, doesn't she? Amazing what a hairstyle can do for you," Tommie remarked. "Now she has her own personal style apart from the mean girls."

Finbar sat back against his chair and sipped his tea.

"Funny ye should say that, Thomasina. I was thinking the same thing. D'you remember us talking about how all them women copy one another and wear the same fashions, the same hairstyle?"

"Yeah. I see where you're going. Elly had the same hairstyle until yesterday. So do Eva, Louanne, Melinda, and half a dozen other women around town, including Earl's partner Jenny Foran and my friend Joan Carroll."

"True, but Ms. Carroll and Officer Foran are brunettes ..."

"... and our suspects are blond. I gotcha. So, what's your take on it?"

"I'm not sure yet, but something's forming in my head. I just have to think it through."

"OK. Let me know when you have something. Until then, it's another bagel for me with triple-berry jam."

*   *   *

Levi Muller met them for lunch at Finbar's unit. He brought fresh salad greens with raw garden vegetables and homemade goat cheese, along with gifts of huge washed and sanitized hollow ostrich eggs for each of them. Levi complimented Finbar on his house renovations, and the two men got involved in a game of chess, so Tommie took her egg and went to her own unit for a nap.

When she returned to Finbar's place before suppertime, she found him poring over the legal pads containing their case files. He had removed his bandages so he could hold a pen and write on the papers.

"Have you found something?" she asked.

"Halloo, Missus. Not yet, but there's a niggling thought I want yer opinion on."

"Ask away." She settled onto the couch.

"We know that four of our original suspects wore that wretched bent hairstyle."

"Right. Elly, Eva, Louanne, and Melinda."

"Yes. And yer Detective Petry said the woman

fighting with Miss Taylor wore it as well."

"And she was blond, like all four of our suspects."

"Correct. Suppose the woman who pushed Miss Taylor over the edge was not the one he thought. Suppose it was not Eva Edgerton."

"Mmmm. I see what you're saying, but don't forget that I was in the hallway listening. I heard them. In fact, I saw it was Eva with Bettina when I came up the stairs. That's why I hid in the hallway."

"Yer right. And yer certain nobody came past you before you ran into the room?"

"No way. I was right beside the door with my ear against the wall. I'd have seen another person enter or exit that room."

"And when you ran in, what exactly did you observe? Close yer eyes and visualize it."

Tommie closed her eyes and laid back against the cushion. "I heard Eva scream Bettina's name. I rushed in. Eva was clutching the drapes to the left of the French doors leading to the balcony. Bettina was nowhere to be seen. I looked over the edge and saw her body on the ground. Then Tom ran to her. Susan and Elaine came from the left side of the yard. Aubrey and Melinda appeared on the stoop. Elly and Jo bumped against my back. Louanne was standing on my right. It all happened very quickly."

"Did ye see Elly, Jo, or Louanne enter the room?"

"No, they were just there all of a sudden. They had to have come in after me. Right after me, because it was just a matter of seconds before I realized they were there."

"Ye said ye heard a door close. Were there any doors inside that room that led elsewhere? A closet? A bathroom? A sitting area?"

"Umm. No closet. There was a big wooden wardrobe on the right like they use in Europe instead of closets, but Jenny Foran said it was locked. I remember a little alcove room in the far left near the door. A toilet and sink. What do you call that? A boudoir?"

"I believe that would be a powder room *inside* a boudoir. Did ye see anyone come from there?"

"No, I could see it in my peripheral vision. There was no movement from that side of the room, and none from the other side either. It's possible they bumped the wardrobe, or the sound could have come from someone closing a door in another room on the same hall."

"And yer certain Ms. Edgerton was the woman struggling with Miss Taylor."

"Positive."

Finbar grunted and set the notebooks down. "Jayze. I thought I had it sorted out. It was Eva after all."

The ringing of the doorbell brought greetings from the dogs. When Tommie answered the door, Amos Mosby entered with a cardboard box of food. The dogs went into a whining frenzy at the aroma of fried chicken. Amos set the box on the table and grinned.

"Now, now, little fellas. Be good and you might get you some scraps, but no bones. Chicken bones ain't good for doggies. Finbar, Miz Watson! So good to see both of y'all. Hope you're healing well. I see your bandages are off."

Finbar held his hands up. "Ach, 'tis a nuisance with them mittens. Missus Thomasina will have me back in them soon enough, sure."

Amos laughed. "Good for you Miz Watson. Holmes is a stubborn ole cuss, I've found out. You make him mind you." He began taking food from the box. "My wife made you a feast. I hope you eat fried food. She fixed fried chicken ... her own secret recipe ... fried okra, fried green tomaters, and cornbread. Wish I could stay and break bread with you, but Sheela told me to get home quick for our own supper, and I always do what Sheela tells me to."

Tommie laughed, "You'd better, if you know what's good for you. By the way, I love what you did to Elly James's hair. It's so cute."

"That's a sweet little woman. She needed a natural hairstyle to reflect her personality ... so she's not associated with them other stuck up look-alikes. I declare, the only way you can tell 'em apart is by the shade of blond and their sizes. Good night, folks. Y'all enjoy yourselves."

Amos was out the door and Finbar was seated at the table waiting for his cellophane mittens. Tommie wrapped his hands with the bandages and topped them with the cling film. Then, they attacked the dinner with gusto.

Afterward, Tommie made tea for Finbar and heated some *Dreamer Creamer* for herself. She pulled a few foil-wrapped chocolate Easter eggs from her pocket and dropped them into her mug.

"What's that in yer cup, Missus?" Finbar asked.

Tommie chuckled. "It's just some chocolate candies. I had them in my pocket from when I last wore these scrubs, so I thought I'd make myself some cocoa to help me sleep."

"Yer a funny woman, Thomasina Watson. But, sure, I'm thankful for yer friendship, and I wouldn't have ye any other way."

Chapter Thirty

TOMMIE opened the door Monday morning to find two women clutching casserole carriers with both hands. Breakfast had been graciously prepared by some of the members of the Trinity Episcopal Ladies' Charity Organization. Tommie expected Melinda, but she was surprised to see Molly Bailey, the church organist. She invited the women inside.

As soon as Finbar heard people talking, he opened the kitchen door, and Molly—being of Irish descent— rushed to greet him outside to tell him of the Dublin kinsfolk she had discovered in her genealogy. This gave Tommie an opportunity to speak to Melinda by herself, so she drew her into the living room to sit and talk.

Melinda's smile was tentative, but genuine. "How are you doing, Tommie? I'm glad you let me provide your breakfast. Earl called and said it would be best if I brought another lady with me. I hope that's OK."

"Of course, it is, Melinda. I don't hold any hard feelings against you for wanting to be popular. I stopped caring about what other people thought of me long ago, but you're still young, and this is a ridiculously small town."

"I'm glad you feel that way. Aubrey thinks a lot of you, and I trust her with my life. Thanks for forgiving me."

"Don't give it another thought. But while we have a few minutes to ourselves, I really need your help trying to figure out who tried to kill Holmes and myself."

"My help? How can I help? I don't know much."

"I bet you know more than you think you do. First of all, no secrets. OK? That's how friends operate. Deal?"

"Deal. No secrets. What do you want to know?"

"Who stood to gain the most if Veranell died?"

"Wow, Tommie. You come straight to the point, don't you? Aubrey told me you were direct. My immediate choices would be Bettina Taylor, Louanne Weller, or Eva Edgerton. They were the main women in Veranell's pack. She was the majordomo, and they were the lieutenants."

"Why? How did they gain?"

"Ah, I'd have to say by being the head of the charities. I'm the president of the LCO, but we're small potatoes compared to the Catholic charities."

"How so?"

"We do modest fundraisers, support community- and minority-owned businesses like yours, contribute to thrift stores and consignment shops, have soup kitchens, stuff like that, you know."

"And the Catholic charities?"

"Most of them are not really sponsored by the Catholic church. It's just that a lot of the people in the charity group attend St. Mary's, so we call them that. I've heard the other women talking about the goods and money they receive. It's my opinion that Veranell kept those things rather than pass them on to the people and organizations they supported. Like the Easter Egg Hide and Charity Raffle. Not all the donations make their way to the homeless or whatever. I know Veranell made extra money that way, and so would whoever was the chair."

"Really? Let me ask you this, and don't get mad. Did you profit from Eva's and Louanne's defective merchandise scams?

Melinda wrung her hands. "Yes, I did. I bought some of the clothes, and I got liquor from Weller's at a discount. I'm ashamed to say it, but I ... I have a problem."

Tommie reached out and covered Melinda's hands with her own. "I know, Melinda. Aubrey told me. Nothing to be ashamed of. I'm glad you've taken steps on the road to recovery. My grandfather was the town drunk, and it made such an impression on my mother she went overboard and forced prohibition on my brother and me. Rebel as I was, I was well on my way to becoming an alcoholic as a young woman. Fortunately, fate and food allergies intervened, and I'm unable to consume alcohol at all."

"Carl and I both are going to AA. He's my rock ... like Earl Petry is yours. You know he and Bettina were never what you and he are, don't you?"

"Yes. I know." She overheard Finbar and Molly entering from the back yard. "Just a couple more quick questions while we still have time. Friday and Saturday before Easter, you were making chocolate eggs with Eva."

"Yes, it's one of our LCO charity projects."

"Were you together the entire time, or was there a time when either one of you left?"

"I was home the whole time, but Eva left on Friday and again on Saturday to get food coloring. She wasn't gone long, though, so she must've gotten it from the Trinity kitchen instead of the Winn Dixie."

"Was there any time that you can think of when Eva or Bettina or Louanne would have been able to sneak into St. Mary's and mess with the eggs or Veranell's food"

Melinda's eyes widened. "Yes. Any one of them could have done that. Bettina and Louanne had free access to St. Mary's, and you know Trinity and St. Mary's share a grassy play area for the kids. Eva could easily have grabbed the food coloring, then let herself into the other church."

"One last thing, Melinda. The night Bettina died, what do you remember?"

"Aubrey and I had been out on the front walkway. It was beginning to get dark, and Aubrey said she had to get home before sunset because of Passover. We heard shouting upstairs. Aubrey started back in, but I looked up at the Veranda. I could see the tops of two women's heads. One was dark, and one was blond. Then I stepped inside the door to the foyer where Aubrey was standing."

"Did you see the women's faces?"

Melinda frowned in concentration "No. They were exactly the same height, so I could only see from the forehead up. When Bettina fell over, and we rushed back outside, I looked up again, and I saw you at the balcony. Louanne was on one side of you, and Eva was on the other. Jo and Elly were behind you, but I could only see the tops of their heads."

Tommie leaned forward and hugged Melinda just as Finbar and Molly rounded the corner.

"Melinda, I've got to get back to the church to practice on the organ. Are you ready to go?" Molly asked.

"Sure thing, Molly. Let's go so Tommie and Finbar can have their breakfast," Melinda made her way to the front door.

"Don't worry about the dishes. We'll come back by another day to pick them up. There should be plenty for leftovers. Y'all enjoy!" Molly said. "Oh, by the way, you have a hole in your yard, just in front of your porch. Did you know?"

"Thanks, Molly. I'll check it out," Tommie said. She closed the door and laughed at Finbar's quizzical expression. "Maggie Kohl. She dug a hole for the black jar."

"Righto. Explains everything, Missus. Shall we get started? My belly's crying for some of this home cooked

American food."

"You're so spoiled, Finbar."

"No, Missus, I just smell that way."

Chapter Thirty-One

TOMMIE dozed on the chaise after breakfast. Her mind was filled with puzzling images of Easter eggs, balconies, brunettes, and blonds with all the same hairstyle. Unable to sleep, she opened her eyes and stared at the television.

Gunsmoke was playing in black and white, and there was a barfight going on. Two cowboys were taking turns throwing punches at each other. Then, Marshall Dillon entered and got into the mix. The three of them wailed and hammered on one another. Chester had been knocked behind the bar and onto the floor where he watched the fight. From his perspective, he could only see the hats of the first two fighters, but Matt Dillon was taller than everyone else. Chester could see his face and the tin star on his chest.

Tommie sat up quickly. *Suppose instead of their*

hats, he saw their hair and the tops of their heads, she thought. Her cellphone buzzed. It was a text from Earl saying he was ordering a takeout delivery for their lunch. Tommie replied with a smiley face emoji and put the phone back in her pocket.

In her mind, she visualized the women on the suspect list, lining them up side by side from shortest to tallest. She pulled a scrap of paper from her pocket and listed them with height, weight, and hair color: Bettina, Elly, Louanne—all 5'3" or less; Jo and Aubrey—5'6" and 5'7"; Eva and Melinda—both 5'8"; Jeannette—5'9." Tommie crossed off the brunettes and those she was sure were innocent: Elly, Jo, Aubrey, Melinda, and Jeannette. That left Bettina, Louanne, and Eva. She drew a stick picture from Melinda's perspective: *Two cowboy hats and a star.*

As Tommie got up to share her revelation with Finbar, the doorbell rang. Peeking through the window, she saw the back of a delivery girl wearing a baseball cap. She opened the door.

The delivery girl pivoted and pushed. Tommie fell backward into the room as the girl quietly shut the door. From the floor, Tommie looked up and saw her face.

"Louanne," she wheezed, the breath having been knocked out of her.

Louanne held a long, sharp knife in her hand. Her face was a contorted mask of hatred. Her eyes blazed.

"You fat, meddling mutt. Can't stay out of people's business, can you? No wetbacks or Irish Mick or big dumb policeman to save you now, huh? Time to die, Tommie Watson. Time to die."

Louanne drew the knife up over her head as she hovered atop the prostrate herbalist. Suddenly, there was a *flap, flap, flap,* followed by a cacophony of sound as three protective—but relatively harmless—dogs rushed into the kitchen and began to attack the intruder's legs as she kicked at them.

Seeing Louanne was distracted, Tommie scooted backward and grabbed onto the loveseat to pull herself up. Louanne advanced, still kicking at the dogs.

Just before she reached Tommie, there was movement behind her and a loud *thunk* as Finbar brought an ostrich egg down on her head. Louanne crumpled to the floor like a discarded ragdoll.

Finbar calmed the dogs and sat Tommie onto the loveseat. A police siren sounded down the street and got louder as the car pulled up in front of the house. Finbar opened the door to a frantic Earl Petry, who rushed inside.

Earl took in Louanne on the floor and Tommie on the loveseat. He gathered Tommie into his embrace, while Jenny and Dale cuffed Louanne and helped her stand, the dogs still milling around at her feet. They informed her of her Miranda rights, just as Zed lifted his leg on her. The two officers smirked and waited until he finished his business before escorting Louanne out.

"Took you long enough," Tommie said shakily.

"It didn't hit me until just a few minutes ago when

Jenny pulled that chocolate egg out of her pocket," he said. "I remember her finding it behind the drapes in the Veranda Room. Louanne was there all along, wasn't she?"

"Yeah. There was no way for anyone to come in or out, but there was a great place for a killer to hide."

"How did ye know, Thomasina?" Finbar asked.

"Chester told me," she said.

Earl and Finbar exchanged puzzled looks.

"Tom saw two women struggling who he knew to be Eva and Bettina from their voices. But Eva must've gone into the powder room. That's the door I heard closing. Then Louanne came from behind the curtain to finish Bettina off. When Eva heard Bettina call her name and opened the door, Louanne pushed Bettina over and slipped back behind the drapes before Eva could see her. Tom just assumed it was Eva when she appeared at the balcony because of the hairstyle and color ... just as we all did," Tommie said. "But Melinda said they were the same height. Eva is a good half foot taller than Bettina. Two cowboy hats and a star. That's what Chester told me."

"Did you hit your head, Tommie?" Earl asked.

"Nope. But my butt took a good whack."

"Missus, who's Chester?" Finbar asked.

"He's a hero, just like you two," she replied, "and I love him just as much."

"Well, if Chester saved your life, then I guess I love him, too," Earl said, squeezing her tighter.

Chapter Thirty-Two

TOMMIE, FINBAR, AND EARL sat together in Earl's car as he drove toward town. It was Tuesday and the last day of April, nine days since the death of Veranell Collins in the Confederate Memorial Park Gazebo. Earl planned to treat them to a meal at The Lunch Pad.

"It's good to get out finally," Finbar said.

"I agree. Earl, what's the latest on Louanne?" Tommie asked. "Did she confess or give any explanation?"

"Oddly enough, when presented with the overwhelming evidence and your ear-witness deposition, she not only admitted to killing Bettina, but she also seemed to brag about it. Not a trace of remorse, either" he said.

"Wow! Why'd she do it?"

Earl pulled to the side of the road and parked, so he could look at both of them. "Bettina was slipping out of her control. I told you she wasn't the brightest woman, and she had a tendency to blab without thinking. Louanne didn't think Bettina would put all the facts together, but she could easily let details slip which could point a sharp person to discover who actually killed Veranell Collins."

"Wait, I thought *Bettina* murdered Veranell," Tommie said. "Are you saying *Louanne* killed Veranell?"

"Yep. Bettina had plenty of motive, but she lacked the courage or ability to retaliate against her idol."

"Bless her heart," Finbar said under his breath.

"What's that?" Earl asked.

"I said that she had a heart." Finbar spoke quickly when Tommie snapped her head around to stare at him.

"That she did, but no common sense to go with it." Earl reached over and laid his hand on Tommie's leg. "I honestly didn't think she was capable of homicide, but I figured she had information on the murderer, even if she didn't realize it. Louanne was thinking the same thing, so Bettina had to be stopped. Simply telling her to shut up was not enough. Bettina couldn't control herself … especially if she got rattled … or drunk. That's why I had to take her out that night, darlin'. I needed her guard down, so she'd trip up and incriminate either herself or someone else."

"I understand," Tommie said. "Finbar explained it to me. You two were in cahoots."

"Right. She told me what I needed to know about the 'why.' I just didn't know the 'who' yet. Louanne figured the same thing. The only way she could truly keep Bettina quiet was to kill her, so when Eva, Bettina, and Tom went into the Veranda Room, Louanne followed and slipped behind the drapes."

"And she bided her time and hid there until Tom left the room?"

"Uh-huh. Louanne thought Eva would follow Tom out, and then she could be alone with Bettina. The argument presented another scenario for her where she could let Eva be the fall guy ... literally."

Tommie gasped. "Are you saying she planned to murder Eva, too?"

"Eva wasn't originally a target, but Louanne admitted she considered pushing both of them over the balcony while they were locked in their struggle. When Bettina scratched Eva, that set Eva up with a motive for revenge. All Louanne had to do was wait for Eva to go to the bathroom to tend to her arm. When the door closed, Louanne made her move and overpowered Bettina. She had the element of surprise on her side, too. She pushed her over, and then hid behind the curtains until the room filled up, leaving Eva as the perfect scape goat. None of you saw her step out."

"No. She was simply there," Tommie admitted.

"Detective, I believe I know her motive for killing Mrs. Collins, but exactly how was she able to accomplish it?" Finbar asked.

"That took some real planning. She framed Bettina for that murder, starting from the time Bettina picked up the eggs and the rabbits. That put Bettina as the last person in contact with the eggs. Veranell had actually asked Louanne to call in The Lunch Pad order, but Louanne passed the task off to Bettina. She then ordered the exact same food herself, but without the dietary modifications, and sent one of her employees to pick it up. She took it home and added more of the ingredients that would make Veranell sick, along with meltwater and blood from a frozen chicken she had thawed and left to sit in a container outside for several days ... to be sure it would be deadly."

"Earl! That's sick! That's devious," Tommie said.

"That it is. She was the woman Amos mistook for Elly James going into the church with the delivery on Friday. She substituted the dosed food for Veranell's plate while everyone was at mass. She also replaced Veranell's frozen broths with ones she had made that contained barley and the spoiled chicken blood and meltwater."

"My Lord, Earl! She had to have done that a good while in advance. How long had she been planning to kill Veranell?" Tommie said.

"Months, Tommie. It was months. Louanne had everything planned out to the most minute detail. She sent Bettina on the egg gathering errand, had her call in the order, switched the delivery food, substituted the frozen broths, and contaminated all the eggs by wiping the raw, putrid chicken all over them."

"And in the process, she dosed herself. That's why she cancelled her reservation for Saturday and was sick on

Sunday," Finbar said.

"Exactly. The unsuspecting Veranell ate the food while she worked oncoloring the eggs. Father Duncan never saw anyone but her with those eggs, remember? The next day, before Veranell came to the church, Louanne wiped them down again. That's why there was salmonella on the surface of the eggs and on top of the paint. And when Veranell began getting really ill, she ate the tainted broth and got even sicker."

"Just to head a charity? Who does that?" Tommie shook her head.

"A psychopath does that, darlin'. A criminally insane serial killer. An evil person with no empathy for other human beings." Earl put his hand on her head and smoothed her hair. "And she almost killed you and Holmes, too. She waited until late that night after the Beadwell House affair, and then she pulled those benches in front of your shop and Caife Caife Holmes and chained them to the doors."

"Them iron benches are so heavy, though, and her being just a wee woman," Finbar said.

"But strong, and fueled with an irrational affinity for homicide," Earl said. "She banked on the two of you going to your shops and entering in the back doors as you usually do. Then, it was simply a matter of placing the lightweight chairs full of flammables against the doors, squirting them with lighter fluid, and setting them afire. By the time you realized you were compromised, there'd be no way out, and she'd have eliminated the threat you posed."

Earl blinked rapidly, and Tommie was sure she saw his eyes water. She covered his hand with her own.

Finbar crossed himself. "Dear St. Brigid! Sure, sure. Another little while, and we'd both have been goners,"

"Luckily, the Alvarez brothers were also in their shops early. They smelled the smoke, saw the blazes, and came running. You owe your lives to them." He stared into Tommie's eyes. "And I owe them."

The three of them sat for a few moments until Finbar broke the silence.

"Thomasina, I thought yer man was going to feed us. M'belly's touching m'backbone."

Earl chuckled and put the car in gear. As they drove slowly down Bottlebrush Boulevard, Finbar anxiously looked over toward his shop.

"Look there. My shop window's been replaced!"

"Yeah," Earl said, "I didn't want anyone getting in there to vandalize it, so I had the plywood taken off and a new window installed."

"Yer man is a kind fellow, Thomasina. Thank you, Detective. Who knows how long it will take me to renovate after the fire, smoke, and water damage?"

"Yeah, mine, too." Tommie's voice was wistful. The next day was the first of May, and she had hoped to have her window displays up.

"Would y'all like to stop in and take a look at them?" Earl asked.

Tommie and Finbar both nodded enthusiastically, wanting to survey the damage but dreading it at the same time. Earl turned right on Oleander Street and made a square, coming out at the intersection of Nandina Street and Bottlebrush Boulevard. He took a sharp right and parked on the main street at the front door of Caife Caife Holmes. Finbar's hands had healed sufficiently to go without the bandages, and he gingerly opened the car door and stepped onto the sidewalk, letting Tommie out as well.

He unlocked the shop's front door, and the three of them entered. Tommie and Finbar were confused. The store was spotless. There was no water damage, no sooty walls, no trace of smoky smell.

"Detective Petry?" Finbar said.

"Well, I am just as puzzled as you are. I paid the Alvarez brothers to replace your window, but I don't know who did your repairs. It might have been them. They are fond of you, Holmes."

Tommie hugged Finbar and then hugged Earl.

"You're such a bad liar for a cop," she said.

Earl shrugged and feigned innocence. "Well, as long as we're here, let's take a look at your shop, Tommie. Maybe we can get them to help you, too."

Tommie approached the connecting door with apprehension. On the one hand, she was happy for Finbar, but on the other hand, she knew her shop was a wreck, so she was prepared to be devastated. She pushed the door open slowly. The natural light from the display windows illuminated very little, so she reached in and felt along the wall to flick on the overhead lights. When she touched human flesh, she screamed.

Suddenly, the lights came on to the sounds of cheers and applause. The trio stepped into a shop full of their friends. The herb preparation counter was laid out with finger foods, cans of cold soda, and cups of iced tea. A pair of Maggie's green candles (for wealth) flickered on the marble, and the entire shop was clean and sparkling.

"Who did this?" Tommie asked.

"We all did," Amos replied.

"Why?" Finbar asked.

"Because we love you and Tommie," Elly said.

"And Floribunda needs your businesses … and you." Melinda stood arm in arm with her husband.

"But how?" Tommie asked.

"Earl organized it …" Susan said with a smile.

Elaine handed Tommie an iced tea. "… and the rest of us pitched in and did the work."

"In three days?" Tommie asked.

"If a man can rise from the dead …" Levi said.

"And a phoenix can rise from the ashes …" Aubrey stepped forward to take his hand.

"A town can resurrect two shops." Earl cinched Tommie snugly around her waist and smiled. "A lot can happen in three days … my love."

Watson's Herbal Teas & Potions

Herbal information offered in the Holmes & Watson Culinary Whodunit series is for entertainment purposes only. Patent Print Books and Michelle Busby make no medical claims, nor do they intend to diagnose, treat, cure, or prevent any disease or medical condition. Teas, tonics, and potions prepared in the fictional Watson's Reme-teas have not been evaluated by the Food and Drug Administration. Readers must do their own research concerning the safety and usage of any herbs or supplements which appear in the books.

NOTE: PLEASE HEED THE WARNINGS IN [BRACKETS!] USED INCORRECTLY, HERBS CAN BE DEADLY AS POISONS!

TO MAKE TEA: Unless otherwise noted, measure equal amounts of each herb, and combine in a large bowl. Mix thoroughly. Fill one tea strainer or infuser ball with 1-2 TBS of herb mixture and put in cup or mug. Pour 6-8 ounces of boiled water over the herbs and allow to steep for 5-10 minutes. Remove herbs. Add sweeteners, cream, or lemon as desired. (TOMMIE'S TIP: Any herb may be omitted. For stronger tea, you may bruise or grind the herbs before adding. Store herbs in an airtight container away from heat and light. Tommie encourages the use of natural or organic sweeteners.)

Natural or Organic Sweeteners

100% grade A dark maple syrup
Agave - blue, red, or gold
Raw honey
Vanilla
Stevia
Molasses
Monk fruit
Coconut sugar

Raw turbinado sugar
Cinnamon/all-spice/nutmeg

Honey-Honey

Combine and let sit for 2-3 days. When ready to use,
pour into a cup and set in a pan of hot water.
Strain out blossoms before using in tea.
Honeysuckle blossoms, fresh or dried
Raw clover honey

Blues Reme-Tea

Spearmint leaves

Lemon balm

Basil leaves

Oregano
[AVOID if pregnant or breastfeeding]
Nettle leaves
[CAUTION: Fresh herb can sting skin; use dried herb for tea]
St. John's wort
[AVOID if pregnant or breastfeeding, or if taking antidepressants;
can cause photosensitivity]

Tender Tummy Tea

Thyme *(remove leaves from stems)*

Parsley leaves

Lemon balm

Meadowsweet

Peppermint leaves

Lavender flowers
[AVOID if pregnant or breastfeeding; omit if headache occurs]

Chamomile flowers

*[AVOID if pregnant or breastfeeding, if allergic to daisies or ragweed,
or with high blood pressure or cardiovascular disease;
can cause drowsiness, so avoid driving or operating machinery]*

Zzzzz-Tea

Lemon balm
Hibiscus flowers
Spearmint leaves (2)
Rose petals (½)

[AVOID if pregnant or breastfeeding; omit if headache occurs]

Chamomile flowers

*[AVOID if pregnant or breastfeeding, if allergic to daisies or ragweed,
or if high blood pressure or cardiovascular disease;
Can cause drowsiness, so avoid driving or operating machinery]*

Bouncing Bunny Blend

Lemon balm
Grated Ginger (¼)
Grated Cinnamon (¼)
Spearmint leaves (2)
Hawthorne leaves (2)

[NOTE: Check first with doctor if on heart medication.]

Nettle leaves (2)

[CAUTION: Fresh herb can sting skin; use dried herb for tea]

Easter Sunrise Tea

Lavender flowers
Elder flowers
Calendula flowers

Passionflower

Rose petals (½)

[AVOID if pregnant or breastfeeding; omit if headache occurs]

Chamomile flowers

[AVOID if pregnant or breastfeeding, if allergic to daisies or ragweed,
or if high blood pressure or cardiovascular disease;
Can cause drowsiness, so avoid driving or operating machinery]

Passover Peppermint Patchouli Tea

Peppermint leaves

Patchouli leaves

[NOTE: Can cause drowsiness, so avoid driving or operating machinery]

Holy Basil (Tulsi) leaves

Rosemary Rabbit-Tobacco Tootsie Soak

[NOTE: This is NOT a tea for drinking; it is an herbal foot soak.
AVOID touching eyes or other mucous membranes.]

Sage

Hops

Lavender (½)

Rosemary (2)

Lavender oil (3 drops)

PREPARATION: Combine herbs in a stewpot. Cover with water and simmer 5-10 minutes. Cool slightly and carefully pour into a deep container and soak feet, adding more hot tea as the foot bath cools. Try to keep it as warm as possible while feet soak. Can also be used for soaking hands. (See NOTE above)

Tommie's Easter Brunch Treats

Mr. MacGregor's Garden Veggie Salad
with Flopsy's Favorite Dressings

INGREDIENTS:

VEGETABLES (raw):

Bib lettuce

Yellow squash

Celery

Cucumbers

Carrots

Zucchini

French beans

Radishes

Cherry tomatoes

CREAMY DRESSING (makes 1 cup):

Yogurt, whole milk plain, ½ cup

Vinegar, white wine, ¼ cup

Mustard, Dijon, ¼ cup

Sugar, granulated, 1 tsp

Salt and pepper to taste

HONEY MUSTARD DRESSING (makes 1 cup):

Vinegar, apple cider, ¼ cup

Mustard, Dijon, ¼ cup

Olive Oil, ¼ cup

Honey, ¼ cup

Sea salt, ¾ tsp

Pepper, ¼ tsp

Lemon juice, I TBS
STRAWBERRY VINAIGRETTE DRESSING (makes I cup):
Strawberries, fresh or frozen, ¾ cup
Vinegar, red wine, ¼ cup
Olive oil, ¼ cup
Honey, to taste
Salt and pepper, to taste

PREPARATION - VEGETABLES: Wash and cut vegetables into I"-2" pieces. Wash, shake dry, and tear lettuce into 3" pieces. Arrange vegetables in individual dishes on a bed of crushed ice. (TOMMIE'S TIP: Don't cut lettuce with a knife; the edges will brown.)
PREPARATION — CREAMY DRESSING: Whisk together yogurt, mustard sugar, salt, and pepper until smooth. Add vinegar. Spoon over salad.
PREPARATION — HONEY MUSTARD DRESSING: Whisk together all ingredients until smooth. Spoon over salad.
PREPARATION — STRAWBERRY VINAIGRETTE DRESSING: Mash washed berries with a fork, then push through a fine sieve with the back of a spoon to remove seeds. Whisk together remaining ingredients until smooth. Add crushed berries and mix well. Spoon over salad.

Cotton-tail's Criss-Cross Buns

INGREDIENTS: (makes 32 servings)
Whole milk, 2 cups warm
Active dry yeast, 2 pkgs
All-purpose flour, 6 cups
(TOMMIE'S TIP: You can use whole wheat or almond flour, if desired.)
Butter, I/3 cup softened

Eggs, 2 + 1 yolk
Sugar, ¼ cup
Raisins, ½ cup
Cinnamon, 1 tsp
Allspice, ¼ tsp ground

PREPARATION: Heat oven to 375°. In a bowl, dissolve yeast in warm milk. In another bowl, combine eggs, butter, sugar, salt, spices, and 3 cups flour. Add yeast mixture. Beat until smooth. Stir in raisins and enough flour to make a soft, sticky dough. On a floured surface, knead 5-7 minutes until dough is smooth and stretchy. Place in a greased bowl and flip once to coat entire surface. Cover with tea towel and let rise for 1 hour until doubled in size. Remove towel and punch down dough. Place on a floured surface. Divide and shape dough into 32 plum sized balls. Set on greased baking sheets 2 inches apart and let rise in a warm place, covered with tea towels, for 40 minutes until doubled in size. Cut a cross-shape into top of each bun with a sharp knife. Whisk egg yolk and water, and brush over tops. Bake for 15-20 minutes until golden brown. Rest on baking sheets for 5 minutes. Cool on wire racks and serve with jam. (TOMMIE'S TIP: Freeze buns in a gallon-sized plastic bag for later!)

Mother Josephine's Jam

INGREDIENTS: (makes 2 cups)
Blackberries, 4 cups, fresh or frozen
Sugar, 2 cups (TOMMIE'S TIP: Honey or maple syrup may be substituted.)
Lemon juice, 2 TBS
Lemon zest, 2 tsp

PREPARATION: Thaw frozen berries; wash fresh berries. Add blackberries, sugar, and lemon juice to a deep saucepot or Dutch oven, allowing several inches headspace to allow for foam while cooking. Crush berries with potato masher or large spoon. Heat on medium low and simmer, stirring continually about 15 minutes until jam approaches gel stage, and no liquid is visible boiling to the surface. When bubbles cover the surface and foam appears, it is nearing the gel stage. Add lemon zest and continue stirring up to 5 minutes longer. To test for gel stage, dip spoon into jam and lift above the pot. The jam will come off the spoon slowly in a "sheet.". Drip a bit of mixture on a small plate which has been in the freezer. Place in freezer for 45 seconds and remove. Jam should wrinkle when pushed with fingertip. Chill in refrigerator until ready to serve.

Peter Rabbit's Eggstra Devilish Eggs

INGREDIENTS: (makes 12 halves)
Eggs, 6 whole
CLASSIC FILLING: (makes 12)
Mayonnaise, ¼ cup OR Yogurt, plain, ¼ cup
Mustard, yellow, 1 tsp
Vinegar, white, 1 tsp
Salt and pepper, to taste
Smoked paprika (garnish)
VARIATIONS, omit vinegar and/or mustard and add:
° Blue cheese, crumbled, 3 TBS (+ walnuts)
° Cheddar cheese, ¼ cup shredded (+ chives)
° Chicken, ¼ cup cooked, shredded (+ celery)
° Ham, ¼ cup cooked, minced (+ mustard)
° Cream cheese, ¼ cup (+ parsley)

- ° Sour cream, ¼ cup (+ dill)
- ° Cheese, ¼ cup sharp shredded (+ pimentos)
- ° Hummus – omit mayonnaise, substitute ¼ cup mashed chickpeas, 1 TBS olive oil, ½ tsp sweet pickle juice (+ sesame seeds)

PREPARATION - EGGS: Place eggs in single layer in deep saucepan and cover with water to 1 inch above eggs. Heat on high until boiling, then cover, decrease heat to low, and simmer for 10 minutes. Remove from heat and rinse under cold water for 1-2 minutes. Crack and carefully peel eggshells off under running water. Pat dry with paper towels. Slice in half lengthwise. Remove yolks.

PREPARATION – EGG FILLINGS: Place egg yolks in a bowl and mash with a fork Add filling mixture and combine well. Carefully pipe or spoon into egg halves and add finely chopped garnishes.

Mopsy's Marble Tea Eggs

INGREDIENTS: (makes 1 dozen eggs)
ORIGINAL BROWN COLOR: Eggs, 12 whole
Black tea, 2 cups
Cloves, whole, 2 TBS
Fennel seed, 2 TBS
Star anise, 2 TBS
Cinnamon, 2 sticks
Black peppercorns, 1 TBS
NATURAL COLOR VARIATIONS:
(makes 28 eggs—4 eggs of each color)
- ° Red Rooibos Tea, ¼ cup + beet juice, ¾ cup = dark red

- ° White Silver Needle Tea, I cup + pinch saffron = orange
- ° White Peony tea, ¼ cup + turmeric tea, ¾ cup = yellow
- ° Green tea, I cup + sprinkled matcha = green
- ° Oolong tea, ½ cup + butterfly pea flowers, ½ cup = blue
- ° "Blue" tea blend + 2 TBS lemon juice = purple
- ° Darjeeling White Tea, I cup = pale gold

(TOMMIE'S TIP: Add food coloring for stronger colors)

PREPARATION – ALL EGG COLORS: Place eggs in a deep saucepan and cover with water to I inch above eggs. Heat on high until boiling, then cover, decrease heat to low, and simmer for I0 minutes until hard-boiled. Remove eggs and crack shells all over, but do <u>not</u> remove shells. Allow to drain in a colander. Continue until all eggs have been boiled.

PREPARATION – ORIGINAL BROWN COLOR: Once all the water has seeped out, return I2 eggs to saucepan. Add ingredients for original brown color and enough water to cover eggs by I inch. Bring to a boil, then reduce heat to medium Simmer for 20 minutes. Remove pan and let eggs steep in liquid overnight in refrigerator. Discard liquid and carefully peel eggshells off under running water. Pat dry with paper towels. Chill to serve.

PREPARATION – RAINBOW COLORED EGGS: Once all the water has seeped out of the boiled eggs, return 4 eggs to saucepan. Add ingredients for color of choice and enough water to cover eggs by I inch. Bring to a boil, then reduce heat to medium Simmer for 20 minutes. Remove pan and let eggs steep in liquid overnight in refrigerator. Repeat process for each new color. Discard liquid and carefully peel eggshells off under running water. Pat dry with paper towels. Chill to serve.

(TOMMIE'S TIP These eggs are good with soy sauce, coconut aminos, sweet/sour sauce, in salads, or just with salt and pepper.)

Culinary Creations by Holmes

Even though Finbar Holmes is from Ireland, all ingredients listed are measured in standard United States customary units. Feel free to add, omit, or substitute ingredients.

Good Friday Fish Chowder

INGREDIENTS:
Irish Butter, 4 TBS
All-purpose flour, 1 TBS
Onions, 2 medium, diced
Carrots, 2 large, diced
Celery, 4 ribs, diced
Leek, 1, diced
Yellow potatoes, 2 large, peeled and diced
Smoked salmon, 2 fillets, cut in 2-inch cubes
White fish, 2 fillets, cut in 2-inch cubes
(FINBAR SUGGESTS: Fresh Cod is quite flavorful!)
Tuna, Mahi-Mahi, or other fish of choice,
1 lb, cut in 2-inch cubes
(FINBAR SUGGESTS: Fresh Florida Grouper is superb!)
Scallops, 1 lb (optional)
Chicken stock, 4 cups
Heavy cream or milk, 1 cup
Salt and pepper, to taste
Bay leaf
Thyme, 1 sprig
Rosemary, 1 sprig
Parsley, fresh (garnish)
Parmesan cheese, grated (optional)

PREPARATION: In a deep Dutch oven, sauté onion, carrots, celery, and leek with the thyme and rosemary until tender. Add the flour to make a roux, stirring continually so flour does not burn. Begin adding chicken stock little by little while continuing to stir to incorporate all the flour and make a smooth mixture. Add the potatoes and bay leaf and bring to a boil. Simmer for 15-20 minutes. Add cubed fish and continue stirring while bringing back to the boil. Reduce heat and add cream, salt, and pepper. Simmer until all the cubed fish is cooked through. Serve in deep bowls, garnished with fresh parsley and a small sprinkle of grated parmesan, if desired.

Individual Irish Soda Bread

INGREDIENTS: (makes 8 servings)
All-purpose wheat flour, 4 cups
Baking soda, 1 tsp
Salt, 1 tsp
Buttermilk, 1 ½ cups

PREPARATION: Preheat oven to 425°. Sift and whisk together flour, baking soda, and salt. Form a well in the center of the flour mixture and pour in buttermilk, Blend together using hands until the texture is crumbly but sticks together and pulls away from the bowl. Form into a large ball and cut like a cake to make eight wedges. Roll each wedge into a ball and cut in half. Roll each half into another ball. Place on a greased cast iron skillet or in a Dutch oven. Make an "X" across the top of each roll with a sharp knife, just about an inch or so deep. Bake for 40 minutes until outside is browned. To serve, break apart and top with an Irish butter (FINBAR SUGGESTS: *Kerrygold* is best.) and

strong firm cheese slices *(FINBAR SUGGESTS: Kerrygold Dubliner, Blarney Castle, Aged Cheddar, Ballyshannon, Wexford, or Skellig are lovely.)*

Sláinte (Good Health) Slaw

INGREDIENTS:
Lemon juice, 2 TBS
Apples, 3 medium tart, julienned
Red or green cabbage, 1 head
Fennel, 2 small bulbs, julienned
Onion, 1 small red, julienned
Carrot, 1 large, shredded
Apple cider vinegar, 1 tsp
English or Dijon mustard, 1 tsp
Yogurt, ½ cup
Salt and pepper, to taste

PREPARATION: Put lemon in bowl. Cut and julienne apples. Toss in lemon juice to keep them from browning. Finely slice cabbage. Julienne fennel and onion, and shred carrot. Add to bowl, along with yogurt, vinegar, mustard, salt, and pepper. Mix well. Keep cold in refrigerator until ready to serve.

Barm Brack (Speckled Loaf)

INGREDIENTS:
All-purpose flour, 2 ½ cups
Baking soda, ½ tsp
Sugar, 1 ½ cups
Egg, 1
Hot brewed tea, 1 ½ cups

(FINBAR SUGGESTS: *Barry's* is best, but any fine black or herbal tea will do.)
Dried fruit, 1 ½ cups chopped
Cinnamon, 1 tsp ground
Nutmeg, ½ tsp ground
Orange zest, 1 tsp grated
Orange or lemon marmalade, ¼ cup

PREPARATION: Soak the chopped, dried fruit in hot tea for 2 hours, then drain and squeeze out excess liquid. Preheat oven to 350°. Combine flour, baking soda, cinnamon, and nutmeg. In another bowl, beat egg, sugar, orange zest, marmalade, and fruit. Fold in flour until just combined. Pour into a greased Bundt pan or loaf pan. Bake for 1 hour or until the cake is springy when touched. Cool in the pan for 2 hours, then remove to a wire rack to cool until room temperature. Before serving, press clean items up into the bottom of the cake to represent the following: a coin for good fortune coming soon; a dried bean to foretell a time of poverty; a ring to indicate a marriage within the year; a pea to indicate no marriage within the year; a matchstick to warn of an unhappy marriage; a thimble for a life of being single.

Red Champ

INGREDIENTS: (makes 5 servings)
Red potatoes, 3 lbs
Green onions, 6, chopped
Irish butter, 6 TBS
(FINBAR SUGGESTS: *Kerrygold* is best.)
Salt and pepper, to taste
Cheese, shredded strong/sharp, 4 oz
(FINBAR SUGGESTS: *Dubliner, Blarney Castle, Aged Cheddar,*

Ballyshannon, Wexford, or *Skellig* are lovely.)

PREPARATION: Rinse and quarter potatoes. (FINBAR SUGGESTS: Leave skins on for a wonderful texture.) Cover potatoes, with water by at least an inch in a Dutch oven and bring to a boil. Add a pinch of salt and simmer covered until fork tender, about 20 minutes. Drain and replace in pot. Add remainder of ingredients to hot potatoes and mash until the mixture is chunky. Season with salt and pepper.

Pan Fried Scamp

INGREDIENTS: (per serving)
Scamp, 1 large filet
(FINBAR SUGGESTS: Fresh Florida Grouper is superb, too!)
Flour, 3 TBS
Breadcrumbs, 3 TBS
Eggs, 2, beaten
Oil, coconut or other high-heat oil, ¼ cup
Salt and pepper, to taste

PREPARATION: Rinse fish and pat dry with paper towels. Put the flour, breadcrumbs, and beaten eggs in 3 separate dishes. Place a cast iron or heavy-bottomed skillet over medium heat. When it radiates heat as your hand passes over, add oil. Dredge the fish in flour, then egg, then breadcrumbs, shaking off excess. As soon as the oil seems to shimmer, carefully lay the fish down in the center. Do not stir around. Cooking time will be 10 minutes per inch of filet thickness. For a 1-inch-thick filet, let the fish simmer for 5 minutes, then carefully turn with a spatula. Allow the fish to simmer for an additional 5 minutes.

It should be golden brown and crispy on the outside and opaque on the inside. Adjust cooking time accordingly for larger or smaller filets. To serve, lay the fish over a bed of champ or rice and serve with some *Quick Pickled Veggies*.

Quick Pickled Veggies

INGREDIENTS: (makes 4 cups)
Vinegar, white, 1 cup
Sugar, 2 TBS
Mustard seed, 2 tsp
Salt, 4 tsp
Garlic, 1 clove minced
Cucumbers, carrots, red onion, 1 cup each, very thinly sliced

PREPARATION: Heat saucepan over medium high heat. Add vinegar, sugar, mustard seed, garlic, and salt and whisk until sugar dissolves. Toss together remainder of ingredients in another bowl or a wide mouth lidded jar. Pour hot liquid over the vegetables and toss to evenly coat. Cover and chill before serving. (FINBAR SUGGESTS: Quickly chill by placing in freezer for 30 minutes to 1 hour.)

Creamy Eggless Lemon Curd

INGREDIENTS: (makes 8 servings)
Sugar, ½ cup
Cornstarch, 1 TBS
Cream or Milk, ½ cup
Lemon juice, ¼ cup
Lemon zest, 1 lemon
PREPARATION: Whisk together sugar and cornstarch in a

small saucepan. Mix in cream/milk, lemon juice, and lemon zest. Heat over medium, for 5 minutes or until the curd thickens. Whisk continuously to incorporate ingredients and get a smooth, creamy texture. Remove from heat and serve in glass custard cups. (FINBAR SUGGESTS This is delicious warm or chilled!)

Bangers & Mash with Onion Gravy

INGREDIENTS: (makes 2 servings)
Russet potatoes, 1 lb
Onion, 1 chopped
Irish butter, 4 tsp
(FINBAR SUGGESTS: *Kerrygold* is best.)
Milk, 1 TBS
Salt and pepper, to taste
Banger (Pork sausage) links, 2 in casings
Beef broth, 3 cups
Red wine (optional) 1 cup
Olive oil, 1 tsp

PREPARATION – MASH: Preheat oven to 200°. Rinse, peel, and cube potatoes. Cover potatoes with water by at least an inch in a Dutch oven and bring to a boil. Add a large pinch of salt and simmer covered until fork tender, about 15 minutes. Drain and allow to steam dry for 1-2 minutes. Add ¼ cup butter, milk, salt, and pepper to pot. Mash potatoes to desired lumpy or smooth consistency and set aside in warm oven.

PREPARATION – BANGERS: In a heavy skillet, heat olive oil. Separate sausages and cut a small opening in each to allow the steam to escape. Cook over medium-low heat, turning to brown all around. Keep warm in an oven-safe dish with the mash whilst preparing gravy.

PREPARATION – ONION GRAVY: In the same skillet in which the bangers were prepared, melt 1 TBS of the butter over medium-high heat. Sauté onions until translucent, about 7-8 minutes. Pour in beef broth and red wine (if desired) and boil for 10 minutes until mixture has reduced by half. Season with salt and pepper to taste. To serve, scoop a generous portion of the potato mash on a plate, top with sausages, and cover with the onion gravy.

Rissole

INGREDIENTS:

(FINBAR SUGGESTS: *Rissole* is excellent made from leftovers!)

Potatoes, boiled or fried

Fish, minced

(FINBAR SUGGESTS: Any minced meat will do.)

Onion, diced

Salt and pepper, to taste

Breadcrumbs or flour

Peanut or other high temperature oil for frying

PREPARATION: Heat oil in a Dutch oven to 375° or until a bit of flour sizzles when dropped in. Combine all ingredients except breadcrumbs/flour in a bowl and mash together. Scoop up with hands and fashion into golf ball sized portions. Either leave round or flatten slightly. Roll in breadcrumbs/flour. Drop into hot oil and fry until golden brown.

Poppyseed Paddies
(formerly Besame Bagel Bites)

INGREDIENTS:
Premade or refrigerated bagels
Milk, ½ cup
Sugar, ¼ cup
Butter, 1 TBS
Poppyseeds, 2 TBS

PREPARATION: Toast premade bagels or follow package directions on refrigerated bagels package. Cool on racks. DRIZZLING SYRUP: Simmer milk and poppyseeds on low heat. Whisk in sugar and butter until all ingredients melt and combined. Remove from heat. Drizzle over cooled bagels.

Bangers 'n' Beps/Rashers 'n' Rolls

INGREDIENTS: (Makes 12 servings)
Bread flour, 6 cups (+ additional for dusting)
Salt, 1 tsp
Sugar, 1 tsp
Water, 2 cups, warm
Active dry yeast, 2 TBS
Bangers (pork sausage links), 1 lb. in casings
Rashers (Irish bacon cut from the pork loin), 1 lb.
(FINBAR SUGGESTS: American bacon,
which is cut from the belly, may be substituted.)
Olive oil, 2 TBS

PREPARATION—BAPS/ROLLS: Combine 2/3 cup warm

water, sugar, and yeast in a large mixing bowl and stir to dissolve. Allow to sit and bubble 5 minutes. Add salt to flour and mix. Gradually add the flour mixture to the bowl and combine with a wooden spoon or hands. Add remaining water, but only enough until dough mixture pulls away from the bowl in a ball. Turn out onto a floured surface and knead about 5 minutes or until dough is smooth and elastic. Dough should be springy and stretch without breaking. Form into a rough ball and place in an oiled bowl. Cover with a tea towel and let rise (proof) in a warm place for 1 to 1 ½ hours until dough is doubled in size. Remove towel and punch down in the center. Remove dough and divide evenly into 12 pieces. Place on the flowered surface and roll each piece into a ball. Transfer all 12 balls to a baking sheet, keeping them fairly close together. Cover and proof again for 45 minutes to 1 hour. Dust tops with flour. Bake in a preheated 425° oven for 25-30 minutes. Set oven to broil and <u>watch carefully</u> for about 5 minutes as the tops brown. Cool rolls on a wire rack.

PREPARATION – BANGERS: In a heavy skillet, heat olive oil. Separate sausages and cut a small opening in each to allow the steam to escape. Cook over medium-low heat, turning to brown all around. Keep warm in an oven-safe dish. To serve, slice Bangers in half lengthwise and place in warm Baps.

PREPARATION – RASHERS: In a heavy skillet, lay individual slices of bacon rashers side by side and fry over medium heat until fat is rendered, and lean is firm/crispy. Flip each rasher over and fry the other side until firm/crispy. Drain on paper towels and keep warm in an oven-safe dish. (FINBAR SUGGESTs: Rashers may also be prepared by placing side by side in a single layer on a baking rack or broiler pan and baked at 350° until crispy.) To serve, break Rashers in half and place in warm buttered rolls.

HOLMES & WATSON

INVESTIGATIVE CASE FILES

EGG HIDE

HOMICIDE

Solved April 29, 2019

Finbar Holmes, Thomasina Watson

CRIME: DEATH IN CONFEDERATE
MEMORIAL PARK GAZEBO

VICTIM: MRS. VERANELL COLLINS

WEAPON: POISON BY FOOD TAMPERING (SALMONELLA)

METHOD: ADMINISTERED IN FOOD; ON HOLLOW EGGS)
WHICH EXACERBATED EXISTING MEDICAL CONDITION.

DATE/TIME: SUNDAY, APRIL 21, 2019 4:38 P.M.

DISCOVERED AT: CONFED. MEM. PARK GAZEBO

DISCOVERED BY: CROWD AT EGG HIDE/CHARITY RAFFLE

PRESENT: THOMASINA WATSON, FINBAR HOLMES

EARL PETRY, LEVI MULLER

AMOS MOSBY, FATHER HORACE DUNCAN

AUBREY RUSH, SANTINO ALVAREZ

PRIZEGIVERS: ELLY JAMES, JO CLAY

EVA EDGERTON, BETTINA TAYLOR

LEO ALVAREZ, PAUL WELLER (LOUANNE)

SID/JEANETTE SPOCK, MELINDA LAYTON

HENRY ERVING, DON LAREBY, ELAINE FRANK, SUSAN CLAY

DESCRIPTION OF VICTIM: VERANELL COLLINS

Age 70, 5'5", 126 lbs, Caucasian, pale papery skin,

wrinkled face, dark brown eyes, thin grey hair in

chignon, pink pantsuit w/matching pumps, pink hat,

St. Mary's Catholic Church, Charity Head

CRIME: DEATH IN CONFEDERATE
MEMORIAL PARK GAZEBO

VICTIM: MRS. VERANELL COLLINS

OFFICIAL CAUSE OF DEATH (BY SANDERSON
HARPER, FLORAL COUNTY CORONER): SUSPICIOUS
Dehydration, fluid/electrolyte imbalance, septic shock
from prolonged diarrhea/vomiting directly resulting
from exposure to salmonella bacterium, ingestion of
substances leading to complications of celiac disease.

NOTE: Mrs. Collins collapsed in the gazebo after
drinking water into which Ms. Thomasina Watson
added a tincture from Mrs. Collins's pocket. Tincture
was "Tender Tummy Tincture."

NOTE: Because of the number of people in direct contact
with Mrs. Collins, the SUSPECTS are listed as the
people inside the gazebo, and the others will be called
PERSONS OF INTEREST. They may or may not
become suspects at some point.

SUSPECT DESCRIPTIONS

1. LEVI MULLINS— OWNER, MULLER'S ANIMAL FARM

   Age early 50s, solid build, 6' tall , 185lbs, Caucasian,

   short brown curly hair, dk. Blue small eyes, ruddy

   complexion, widower, Mennonite, Floribunda Fellowship,

   2 grown sons (1 married) live w/him

2. AMOS MOSBY— OWNER, THE BARBER SHOP

   Age 60, 5'10", 175 lbs, African American, bald, lg. dk

   brown eyes, wide nose, pencil-thin mustache, white teeth,

   married (Sheela) 5 grown children, St. John's

   Missionary Baptist Church (Deacon)

3. AUBREY RUSH— OWNER AUBREY'S ANTIQUES

   Age mid 40s, 5'7", 135-140 lbs, Caucasian, sturdy

   build, wavy dk brown hair to shoulders or ponytail, med.

   Brown eyes, full lips, olive complexion, attractive,

   divorced, no children, Jewish, Beth-el Jewish Synagogue

4. SANTINO ALVAREZ— CO-OWNER SANTINO'S SHOE
   SHOP, LEO'S LEATHER GOODS (W/BROTHER LEO)

   Age 40, 5'8", 175 lbs, Mexican (legal immigrant

   gaining citizenship), muscular build, strong hands,

   brown skin, dk. Brown eyes, wavy black hair above ears,

   handsome, single, The Church of Jesus Christ of Latter-

   day Saints (Mormon), speaks fluent Spanish/English

PERSONS OF INTEREST DESCRIPTIONS

POI 1. LEO ALVAREZ— CO-OWNER SANTINO'S SHOE
SHOP, LEO'S LEATHER GOODS (W/BROTHER LEO)

Age 38, 5'8", 155 lbs, Mexican (legal immigrant

gaining citizenship), muscular build, strong hands,

brown skin, dk. Brown eyes, straight black hair above

ears, handsome, single, The Church of Jesus Christ of

Latter-day Saints (Mormon), speaks fluent

Spanish/English

POI 2. JEANETTE SPOCK— CO-OWNER, THE LUNCH PAD

Age 50, 5'9", 180 lbs, Caucasian, stocky build, med.

Brown hair in straight square bob, lt. blue eyes, thin lips,

large teeth, pale complexion, First United Methodist Church

POI 3. SIDNEY SPOCK— CO-OWNER, THE LUNCH PAD

Age 54, <6', 200 lbs, Caucasian, stocky build, dk hazel

eyes, thin, lt. brown hair, crew cut, ruddy complexion, wide

mouth, small teeth, First United Methodist Church

POI 4. LOUANNE WELLER— CO-OWNER WELLER'S WINE &
SPIRITS

Age 45, 5'3", 110 lbs, Caucasian, petite, thin, lt. blond

hair, trendy curly/wavy "bent" bob, med. Blue cat eyes,

snooty, 2 grown sons/daughter in college, Veranell's

group, St. Mary's Catholic Church

PERSONS OF INTEREST DESCRIPTIONS

POI 5. PAUL WELLER— CO-OWNER WELLER'S WINE &
        SPIRITS

Age 50, 5'11", 180 lbs, fit, Caucasian, med/dk

complexion, lt brown eyes, dk. Blond hair, crew cut,

pleasant, 2 grown sons/daughter in college, St. Mary's

Catholic Church

POI 6 MELINDA LAYTON— PRESIDENT, TRINITY EPISCOPAL
        CHURCH LADIES' CHARITY ORGANIZATION

Age 47, 5'8", 140 lbs, Caucasian, pretty, mid-length

strawberry blond hair, zig zag waves, fair complected, jade

green eyes, married, 2 adult married daughters, ~~$$~~,

friendly, Veranell's group, Trinity Episcopal Church

POI 7 FATHER HORACE DUNCAY— PRIEST, ST. MARY'S
        CATHOLIC CHURCH

Age 61, 6', 210 lbs, Caucasian, (Scottish?) ruddy

complexion, full wavy grey hair, blue-grey eyes

POI 8 ELLY JAMES— OWNER, ELLY'S JELLY JAR

Age early/mid thirties, 5'3", 120 lbs, lt blond "bent" hair

to chin, med. Blue eyes, fair skin, single (dating Leo

Alvarez), First Baptist Church

PERSONS OF INTEREST DESCRIPTIONS

POI 9. JO (ANNE) CLAY— OWNER, THE CLAY PIGEON

Age 40, 5'5", 145 lbs, full-figured, pretty, Caucasian, long dk auburn hair behind ears, divorced (Jimmy Clay), made ceramics for emu eggs, dating Santino Alvarez, First Baptist Church

POI 10 EVA EDGERTON— OWNER, EVA'S DIVAS BOUTIQUE

Age 41/42, 5'8", 125 lbs, Caucasian, slender, shapely, honey blond hair in wavy "bent" bob, brown eyes, pretty (makeup!), divorced, daughter in 20s, Trinity LCO, stuck up, Veranell's group, Trinity Episcopal Church

POI 11. BETTINA TAYLOR— OWNER, BETINNA'S BAUBLES

Age 40, 5'2", 110 lbs, Caucasian, slender, long dk black hair to shoulders or in bun, lg dk brown eyes, (makeup!), Veranell's group, [dated Earl Petry!], St. Mary's Catholic Church

OUTSIDE RESOURCES

1. SANDERSON HARPER

   County Coroner, Tommie Watson's cousin, sold Finbar

   the space for Watson's Reme-teas and Caife Caife

   Holmes, First Presbyterian Church ams

   Description: 63, 5'10", 210 lbs., dark salt/pepper hair, dk. Brown
   eyes, black frame glasses, middle-age spread, sallow complexion

2. EARL PETRY

   Detective, Floribunda Police Department, Floribunda

   native, dates Tommie Watson

   Description: 58, 6'2", 200 lbs., silver crew cut, blue/grey eyes, white
   beard, muscular, olive complexion (tanned)

3-5. DON LAREBY, ELAINE FRANK, SUSAN CLAY—

   CO-OWNERS, FLORIBUNDA REAL PROPERTIES

   (Don Works First Floribunda Bank), town gossips,

   know all the dirt on everybody, like Finbar and Tommie,

   regular customers both shops

   Description: Don- 41, 6', slender, brown hair/eyes; Sisters- (twins)
   45, 5'7", 200 lbs, brown hair/eyes

6. HENRY ERVING— MANAGER, UPS STORE

   4th member of the town gossip group, friends w/Don, has

   a "platanic courtship" going with both the sisters

   Description: 61, 6'1", 185 lbs, lt hair/ lt blue eys, ruddy skin

INTERVIEW   (TOLD TO Holmes by Earl Petry)

POI 7 : FATHER HORACE DUNCAN, MONDAY, 4/22

INTERVIEWED AT: ST. MARY'S CATHOLIC CHURCH

MOTIVE(S):

1. NONE(Veranell was a sick parishioner; he had no reason to suspect her of any untoward behavior

ALIBI: Preparing sermon for Three Hours' Agony service on Thursday; preparing sermons on Friday & Saturday; preached sermons Thursday, Friday, Saturday, Sunday

LIES:

None

TRUTHS:

1. Veranell was a very sick woman and could be unkind to others
2. Overheard her cursing at Bettina about the color of the rabbits on Thursday, then he called Finbar to come take them
3. Heard/saw Veranell vomiting on Friday; noticed Lunch Pad delivery container
4. Veranell missed Sunday mass; Louanne & Bettina missed Sunday mass & Tommie's luncheon

IMPLICATES: Bettina Taylor - she was being browbeaten by
Veranell Thursday

GOSSIP & HEARSAY:
1. He likes to drink the sacramental wine with his dinner

QUESTIONS:
1. Did he have any access to Veranell's food or the eggs? Yes, but
   he had no reason to bother them.
2. Did he know what kind of "investments" Veranell had to earn
   her extra money?
3. *Was he anywhere near the Beadwell House when
   Bettina was killed? No*

OBSERVATIONS:
1. Refuses to divulge confidential information
2. Called her friends "groupies"
3. Said Veranell used the F-word with Bettina on Friday
4. Noticed Veranell got progressively sicker from Friday on
5. Veranell had made up and frozen special broths for when her
   illness flared up
6. The Wellers and Bettina all ate at Caife Caife Holmes on Friday
   night

INTERVIEW (by Holmes & Watson)

SUSPECT 1: LEVI MULLER, TUESDAY, 4/23

INTERVIEWED AT: MULLER'S ANIMAL FARM, 7:30 A.M.

MOTIVE(S):

1. REVENGE FOR BLACKMAIL (Veranell spread a rumor he

mistreated animals, caused schools to cancel field trips

to his animal farm; she bullied him into donating

eggs. Rabbits, & prize money)

ALIBI: Washed shells in bleach on Thursday; ate brunch at

Watsons's Sunday; worked at farm every other day

He was nowhere near Beadwell House when Bettina

was killed; had no relationship w/Eva

LIES:

He had no problems with Veranell; it was Bettina he

had issue with because she dumped dogs at his farm.

TRUTHS:

1. Sanitized the egg shells in bleach

2. Gave Bettina eggs & brown bunnies (free)

3. Gave Veranell $500 cash for grand prizes

IMPLICATES: Bettina Taylor - she picked up the eggs &
The rabbits.

GOSSIP & HEARSAY:
1. He mistreated his animals
2. Mistreated Bettina's dogs before giving them away

QUESTIONS:
1. Why did he agree to fund the prize $$?
2. What hold did Veranell have over him?
3. Did he have any access to Veranell's food?
4. Levi's Q: "Who else in town has come down with salmonella poisoning?"
5. "Was he anywhere near the Beadwell House when Bettina was killed? No

OBSERVATIONS:
1. Makes his living off rental/sale of animals & field trips
2. Mennonites are generally viewed as honest, hardworking people
3. Sanitization set up allows for completely sterilising of eggs
4. Genuinely loves animals (evidenced by his home & farm)

INTERVIEWS   (by Holmes)

SUSPECT 4: SANTINO ALVAREZ, TUESDAY, 4/23
POI 1: LEO ALVAREZ, TUESDAY, 4/23

INTERVIEWED AT: LEO'S LEATHER GOODS

MOTIVE(S):

1. REVENGE, DESPERATION (Veranell held the lease to the
    shops; raised their rent every 6 months; tried to evict them to
    take shops; spread rumors.)

ALIBI: Had no access to St. Mary's or eggs; worked in shops
getting items ready for prize raffles; were with Jo Clay & Elly
James Saturday night
*Nowhere near Beadwell House when Bettina was killed;
had no relationship w/Eva*

LIES:

None.

TRUTHS:

1. Alibis check out – all conversations truthful
2. Met Jo & Elly Saturday and attended film in cinema; talked
   w/them in car Saturday night

IMPLICATES: Jo Clay & Elly James - they were parked at the Post Office near St. Mary's Friday/Saturday nights

GOSSIP & HEARSAY:

1. Couldn't pay their rent

QUESTIONS:

1. What were they doing in the P.O. parking lot?
2. What hold did Veranell have over them?
3. Did they have any access to Veranell's food or eggs?
4. *Were they anywhere near the Beadwell House when Bettina was killed? No*

OBSERVATIONS:

1. Mormons are known to be truthful, honorable, hard-working
2. Working legally toward citizenship
3. Seem to genuinely care for Jo Clay & Elly James

INTERVIEW   (by Watson)

POI 8: ELLY JAMES, Tuesday, 4/23

INTERVIEWED AT: ELLY'S JELLYS

MOTIVE(S):

1. REVENGE FOR SLANDER (Veranell spread rumors her jellies were contaminated. Health inspector destroyed much of her product; Veranell spread nasty rumors of her relationship with Leo Alvarez.

ALIBI: Thursday - none; Friday - ate at Caife Caife Holmes that night, parked at P.O. w/Jo afterwards; Saturday - went to movie w/Jo Clay & met Alvarez brothers there; came back & sat in car w/them afterward in Post Office parking lot

LIES:
 none evident; forthcoming about relationship w/Leo

TRUTHS:

1. Sat in car in P.O. parking lot Friday & Saturday nights
2. Saw Amos Mosby enter St. Mary's Friday afternoon
3. Saw Aubrey Rush around St. Mary's Friday night

IMPLICATES: Amos Mosby - at church Friday afternoon;

Aubrey Rush - at St. Mary's church late Friday night

GOSSIP & HEARSAY:

1. She dates Leo Alvarez (true - engaged!)
2. Sold contaminated jelly
3. Run-in w/Amos Mosby - nonpayment for church's jellies
4. Rumor - made racist comments about Aubrey Rush

QUESTIONS:

1. What was the run-in w/Amos Mosby about?
2. What hold did Veranell have over her?
3. Did she have any access to Veranell's food or eggs?
4. * Could she have gotten into Veranda Room w/out Tommie
   seeing her?

OBSERVATIONS:

1. Had a legitimate issue with Veranell
2. In love w/Leo Alvarez (engaged to be married)
3. Defends best friend Jo Clay's innocence

INTERVIEW   (by Watson)

POI 9: JO(ANNE) CLAY, Tuesday, 4/23

INTERVIEWED AT: THE CLAY PIGEON

MOTIVE(S):

1. REVENGE FOR SLANDER (Veranell spread rumors she was
cheating on husband Jimmy Clay; Veranell spread nasty
rumors of her relationship with Santino Alvarez.

ALIBI: Thursday - none; Friday - ate at Caife Caife
Holmes that night, parked at P.O. w/Elly afterwards;
Saturday - went to movie w/Elly James & met Alvarez
brothers there; came back & sat in car w/them afterward
in Post Office parking lot

LIES:
none evident; forthcoming about relationship w/Santino

TRUTHS:

1. Sat in car in P.O. parking lot Friday & Saturday nights
2. Saw Amos Mosby enter St. Mary's Friday afternoon
3. Saw Aubrey Rush around Trinity Episcopal Friday night

IMPLICATES: Amos Mosby - at church Friday afternoon;

Aubrey Rush - at Trinity church late Friday night

GOSSIP & HEARSAY:

1. She dates Santino Alvarez (true -- engaged!)

2. Lost position as Sunday School Secretary because of affair

   that led to her divorce

3. She and Elly gossiped about Aubrey stealing antiques

QUESTIONS:

1. What was the nature of her divorce from Jimmy Clay?

2. What hold did Veranell have over her?

3. Did she spread rumor about Aubrey? Or did Veranell?

4. Did she have any access to Veranell's food or eggs?

5. * Could she have gotten into Veranda Room w/out Tommie

   seeing her?

OBSERVATIONS:

1. Had a legitimate issue with Veranell

2. In love w/Santino Alvarez (engaged to be married)

3. Defends best friend Elly James's innocence

INTERVIEWS (by Holmes & Watson)
POI 2: JEANETTE SPOCK, TUESDAY, 4/23
POI 3: SID SPOCK, TUESDAY, 4/23
INTERVIEWED AT: CAIFE CAIFE HOLMES, 12:30 P.M.

MOTIVE(S):

1. REVENGE FOR SLANDER (Veranell spread a rumor they
got food orders wrong; didn't understand gluten-free
requirements; food was bad.)

ALIBI: CALL-IN ORDER FROM BETTINA FRIDAY PREPARED PER
VERANELL'S INSTRUCTIONS; SID SHOWED TICKET TO BETTINA;
WORKED AT LUNCH PAD ALL DAY SATURDAY
*They were nowhere near Beadwell House when Bettina
was killed; had no relationship w/Eva*

LIES:
They had no problems with Veranell; they knew how to
prepare food for her condition without her telling them

TRUTHS:
1. They prepared Veranell's order correctly & marked it clearly
before giving it to Bettina to deliver

IMPLICATES: Bettina Taylor — she called in the order AND picked it up for delivery; Sid showed her the ticket.

GOSSIP & HEARSAY:

1. They were ignorant of gluten-free requirements & proper food preparation

1. Their kitchen was unsanitary

QUESTIONS:

1. Who supervised Veranell's order preparation?

2. *Were either of them anywhere near the Beadwell House when Bettina was killed?*

3. *Who reported salmonella contamination in the kitchen?*

OBSERVATIONS:

1. Veranell ate the order not prepared to her specifications. Why?

2. Someone (not Veranell) tried to shut their business down by implying they were the source of the salmonella poisoning!

3. *Misdirection by real killer!!!*

INTERVIEW *(by Watson)*

SUSPECT 3: AUBREY RUSH, Wednesday, 4/24

INTERVIEWED AT: AUBREY'S ANTIQUES

MOTIVE(S):

1. REVENGE FOR RACIST SLANDER *(Veranell spread a rumor she stole furniture from people & attributed it to Elly/Jo; encouraged people to boycott Aubrey's business)*
2. SELF-PRESERVATION *(Veranell was trying to take control of her business with the slander)*

ALIBI: *Friday - first night of Passover. She was home, but picked parsley at Trinity cemetery afterward; Saturday - worked all day & was home for Passover w/Fr. Duncan*
She was with Melinda at Beadwell House the whole time

LIES:
 None detected

TRUTHS:

1. Alibis check out as truthful
2. Saw Amos Mosby at St. Mary's Friday afternoon
3. Saw Elly & Jo sitting in car w/two men Saturday night

IMPLICATES: Elly James/Jo Clay - they were at Post Office, near St. Mary's Saturday night

GOSSIP & HEARSAY:

1. Aubrey's antiques were taken w/out permission (stolen); attributed to Elly/Jo, but spread by Veranell

QUESTIONS:

1. What was her feud with Veranell?
2. Did Veranell have any other hold over her?
3. *Did she have access to Bettina at the Beadwell House without Tommie knowing?

OBSERVATIONS:

1. College roommates w/Melinda Layton (best friends)
2. Helped Amos Mosby's grandchild at Egg Hunt (
3. Has Father Duncan over for Passover dinner Saturday
4. *With Melinda at Beadwell House the whole time & heard Bettina & Eva fighting rom the foyer

INTERVIEW   (by Holmes)

SUSPECT 2: AMOS MOSBY, WEDNESDAY, 4/24

INTERVIEWED AT: THE BARBER SHOP

MOTIVE(S):

1. REVENGE FOR BLACKMAIL & LOSS OF BUSINESS

    (Veranell spread a rumor his shop was lice infested; lost

    business from St. Mary's; she bought his lease out &

    raised rent, tried to evict him.)

ALIBI: Worked in shop Monday - Saturday; closed up

early Friday to cut Father Duncan's hair at St. Mary's

*He was nowhere near Beadwell House when Bettina

was killed; had no relationship w/Eva

LIES:

None detected

TRUTHS:

1. Admitted extreme dislike of Veranell (she was racist)

2. Came late to Tommie's brunch because of church BBQ

3. Entered St. Mary's Friday p.m. to cut Fr. Duncan's hair;

    Saw small blond woman exit Bingo hall as he arrived

IMPLICATES: Elly James or Louanne Weller (both small blond women with identical hairstyles)

GOSSIP & HEARSAY:

1. His shop was unsanitary and had lice outbreak.
2. His church didn't pay for jellies supplied by Elly James
3. He didn't like Aubrey Rush because she was Jewish

QUESTIONS:

1. Why did he go to St. Mary's? to cut priest's hair
2. What hold did Veranell have over him?
3. Did he have any access to Veranell's food?
4. *Was he anywhere near the Beadwell House when Bettina was killed? NO

OBSERVATIONS:

1. Frequently cuts Father Duncan's hair at the church
2. Amos praised Elly & said she donated jelly.
3. Aubrey helped his granddaughter find eggs at the Egg Hide
4. *Amos said, Lots of women in this town have that same hairstyle!*

INTERVIEW   (by Watson)

POI 10: EVA EDGERTON, Wednesday, 4/24

INTERVIEWED AT: EVA'S DIVAS BOUTIQUE

MOTIVE(S):

1. REVENGE FOR BLACKMAIL (Veranell knew of her "damaged goods" scam & got merchandise free of charge)

2. *JEALOUSY - BETTINA laid claim to Tom Beadwell & fought w/Eva at Beadwell House

ALIBI: Off work Friday to decorate chocolate eggs at Melinda Layton's house; helped decorate eggs Saturday

* Said she was not in room when Bettina fell over balcony.

Where was she? I did not see her come out!

LIES:

1. Only left Melinda's on Friday to get food coloring from Winn Dixie & was nowhere near St. Mary's

2. Did not sell discounted clothing on the side

3. Elly James was at St. Mary's w/food Friday

4. Jo Clay was hiding on St. Mary's grounds Saturday

→ Melinda said she left on Saturday, too.

NOTE: Trinity & St. Mary's share playground areas!!!

TRUTHS:

1. Decorated eggs w/Melinda BUT got food coloring Friday AND Saturday from Trinity Episcopal kitchen!

2. Had a "damaged goods" scam on store clothing

IMPLICATES: Elly James - seen going into St. Mary's w/food on Friday; Jo Clay - seen hiding outside St. Marys on Saturday afternoon

GOSSIP & HEARSAY:

1. Claimed shop items were damaged, then got rebates; sold at discounts to her friends

2. Affair w/Tom Beadwell while he was married to Linda

QUESTIONS:

1. What was relationship w/Tom Beadwell? How long?

2. What hold did Veranell have over her?

3. Did she have any access to Veranell's food? Or eggs

4. *Did she push Bettina over the balcony??

OBSERVATIONS:

Logical choice for Charity Head???

1. Same hair color and style: Eva, Elly, Louanne, Melinda

2. As Tom's wife, will attend St. Mary's again

INTERVIEW   (by Holmes)

POI 4: LOUANNE WELLER, WEDNESDAY, 4/24

INTERVIEWED AT: WELLER'S WINE & SPIRITS

MOTIVE(S):

1. GREED (has ambitions of being the Charity Head)

ALIBI: Did not see Veranell all weekend; Bettina called in
food order and delivered it; wasn't at luncheon or Raffle due
to food poisoning from Caife Caife Holmes

LIES:

1. Did not see Veranell all weekend
2. Food from Caife Caife Holmes made her sick
3. Does not sell discounted merchandise

TRUTHS:

1. Ate at Caife Caife Holmes Friday; cancelled Saturday (by Paul)
2. Missed luncheon & part of Easter Egg event (sick)
3. Saw Veranell at Mass of the Lord's Supper Thursday
4. *Was at Beadwell House; stood on Tommie's right near
railing on veranda after Bettina was pushed over.

IMPLICATES: Bettina Taylor - she picked up the eggs & the food

order from The Lunch Pad and delivered to Veranell Friday.

GOSSIP & HEARSAY:

1. Racist, follower of Veranell

2. Discounted liquor scam

3. Wore Eva's discounted clothing

4. Cheating on husband w/two men in neighboring towns

QUESTIONS:

1. Did Veranell have any kind of hold over her? Discounted liquor scam?

2. Did she have access to food or eggs?

3. How did she stand to gain from Veranell's death?

4. *Where was she when Bettina was killed??*

OBSERVATIONS:

1. She has same hairstyle/color as Elly, Eva, Melinda

2. Same height as Elly & Bettina

3. Most likely candidate for Charity Head because she attends

   St. Mary's & was in Veranell's circle of cronies

Had motive to kill Bettina, Tommie, Finbar!!

INTERVIEW (as told to Holmes by Officer Earl Petry)

POI 11 BETTINA TAYLOR, WEDNESDAY, 4/24

INTERVIEWED AT: THE FALLEN OAK, 8:15 P.M.

MOTIVE(S):

1. ANGER, HUMILIATION (Veranell often berated her in public)
2. GREED (wanted to be Charity Head to get "perks")

ALIBI: Picked up shells and rabbits, dropped them off at the Bingo Hall; attended Thursday night service at St. Mary's; called in food order and delivered to Bingo Hall, but did not attend service; said she was sick Saturday and Sunday from eating at Caife Caife Holmes; unwell at Easter event

LIES:

1. She was next in line to become the charity head.
2. She gave her dogs to Levi Muller because he needed guard dogs
3. Food from Caife Caife Holmes Friday gave her food poisoning
4. She didn't think Levi sterilized eggs

TRUTHS:

1. Left eggs & rabbits at St. Mary's Thursday
2. Veranell got numerous "perks" from being Charity Head.

IMPLICATES: Levi Muller – he didn't clean eggs properly and gave Veranell Salmonella; self – revealed motive for herself!

GOSSIP & HEARSAY:

1. She was a pants-chaser (including Earl Petry & Tom Beadwell)
2. She was not very bright.
3. Got puppies to keep Earl on the hook; dumped them at Levi's farm when Earl broke up with her

QUESTIONS:

1. What was the order she called in to The Lunch Pad?
2. What access did she have to Veranell's food & the eggs?
3. Was she capable of murder?

OBSERVATIONS:

1. Friends w/Eva Edgerton, Louanne Weller
2. Cancelled Saturday reservation at Caife Caife Holmes
3. Missed the luncheon; sick at the Easter event
4. Levi's Q: "Who else in town has come down with salmonella poisoning?

___INTERVIEW___ (by Watson)

POI 6: MELINDA LAYTON, Monday, 4-29

INTERVIEWED AT: TOMMIE WATSON'S HOME

MOTIVE(S):

1. REVENGE FOR SLANDER (Veranell spread around that Melinda and husband had drinking problems)

ALIBI: Friday & Saturday - at home all day making and decorating chocolate Easter eggs w/Eva Edgerton
*She was with Aubrey Rush at Beadwell House the whole time

LIES:

None detected. She was forthcoming, even about her drinking problem

TRUTHS:

1. Alibis check out as truthful
2. Profited from Eva's & Louanne's "damaged merchandise" scams (got clothes & liquor)
3. College roommates w/Aubrey Rush
4. Not interested in being Catholic Charities Head

IMPLICATES: Eva Edgerton - she left Friday & Saturday
to get food coloring; but was only gone long enough to
have gotten them from Trinity Episcopal kitchen

GOSSIP & HEARSAY:
1. Drinking problem (both she and husband)
2. Bought discounted clothes from Eva; liquor from Louanne

QUESTIONS:
1. What hold did Veranell have over her?
2. Did she have access to Veranell's food or the eggs?
3. *Did she have access to Bettina at the Beadwell House without Tommie knowing?

OBSERVATIONS:
1. College roommates w/ Aubrey Rush (best friends)
2. Helped Amos Mosby's grandchild at Egg Hunt
3. Confirmed Eva, Bettina, Louanne all had access to food & eggs in St. Mary's Bingo Hall!
4. *With Aubrey at Beadwell House the whole time & saw the fight between Bettina & Eva from the front stoop
5. *Could only see tops of heads - both women same height.

Death #2 in <u>same case</u>!

CRIME: <u>DEATH AT HISTORIC BEADWELL HOUSE</u>

VICTIM: MISS BETTINA TAYLOR

WEAPON: BROKEN NECK

METHOD: FALL/PUSHED FROM BALCONY ONTO CONCRETE

DATE/TIME: THURSDAY, APRIL 25, 2019 7:40 P.M.

DISCOVERED AT: HISTORIC BEADWELL HOUSE

DISCOVERED BY: TOM BEADWELL/GUESTS AT PREMIER

PRESENT DOWNSTAIRS:

      AUBREY RUSH

      MELINDA LAYTON

      ELAINE FRANK

      SUSAN CLAY

PRESENT UPSTAIRS:

      TOMMIE WATSON

      EVA EDGERTON

      LOUANNE WELLER

      ELLY JAMES

      JO CLAY

DESCRIPTION OF VICTIM: BETTINA TAYLOR

Age 40, 5'2", 110 lbs, Caucasian, slender, long dk black

hair to shoulders or in bun, lg dk brown eyes, St. Mary's

Catholic Church

<u>SUSPECT DESCRIPTIONS</u>

Prime suspect per Tommie Watson's eye/ear witness

testimony from hallway outside Veranda Room.

1. EVA EDGERTON— OWNER, EVA'S DIVAS BOUTIQUE

Age 41/42, 5'8", 125 lbs, Caucasian, slender, shapely,

honey blond hair in wavy "bent" bob, brown eyes, pretty

(makeup!), divorced, daughter in 20s, Trinity LCO,

stuck up, Veranell's group, Trinity Episcopal Church

<u>MOTIVE</u>: Greed, Coverup of Veranell's murder!

NOTE: <u>I personally heard</u> 1) Bettina and Eva

argued; 2) Bettina accused Eva of killing Veranell;

3) Eva admitted it; 4) they struggled; 5) Bettina

screamed as she went over the balcony. T.W.

NOTE: Because of Ms. Watson's proximity outside the

room, and there being observance of other persons leaving

or entering the room, Eva Edgerton is – for now – the

prime suspect (barring circumstances or testimony to

prove otherwise); however, we continue to research all

possibilities pertinent to the case. F.H.

SOLUTION 4/29/2019

NOTE: *Louanne Weller was evaluated & determined a sociopathic serial killer!*

KILLER: LOUANNE WELLER

MOTIVE:

FOR KILLING VERANELL – GREED – SHE WANTED TO BE
THE CHARITY HEAD TO "CASH IN" ON THE PERKS

METHOD – VERANELL'S MURDER:

1. Switched Veranell's order from Lunch Pad with foods
   that would trigger her illness
2. Covered hollowed prize eggs with raw chicken and
   chicken meltwater before Veranell began decorating them
   and after she had dyed them to ensure there were two
   doses of salmonella
3. Replaced Veranell's healthy frozen broths with duplicates
   containing barley and chicken meltwater (salmonella)

MEANS – VERANELL'S MURDER:

1. Had Keys & access to St. Mary's Church
2. Knew when food was delivered, when services were
   attended, & when Veranell would be out of the Bingo room
3. Made toxic food substitutions in her own kitchen (which is
   why she got sick, too!!)

MOTIVE:

FOR KILLING BETTINA - COVERUP- SHE WAS AFRAID

BETTINA WOULD REVEAL LOUANNE KILLED VERANELL

METHOD - BETTINA'S MURDER:

1. Hid behind heavy draperies in room where Eva & Bettina were fighting.

2. When Eva went into the powder room, she stepped out & pushed Bettina over the railing.

3. Stepped back behind curtains until others entered room

MEANS - BETTINA'S MURDER:

1. Followed Eva, Tom, & Bettina upstairs and hid behind curtains, waiting for Tom to exit room

2. Could see by peeking out when Eva left for the power room

3. After pushing Bettina over the edge, waited until Tommie looked over the railing to step out, just before Elly/Jo entered room

MOTIVE:

FOR TRYING TO KILL TOMMIE & FINBAR - COVERUP - afraid Tommie had figured she killed Bettina, afraid Holmes & Watson had deduced she killed Veranell

METHOD – HOLMES/WATSON ATTEMPTED MURDER:

1. Thursday night: Barricaded front doors with chains through heavy benches wedged against doorway.
2. Piled wrought iron chairs in back with flammables
3. After Holmes & Watson entered, placed chairs at back doors, doused with gasoline, lit fires, ran to own store.

MEANS – HOLMES/WATSON ATTEMPTED MURDER:

1. Barricaded front doors of shops and set chairs beside wall for the next day
2. Parked at own store & walked to corner of building, watched for Holmes/Watson to come
3. Set fires and walked to own store via front sidewalk

TURNING POINT (s):

1. Tommie's conversation w/Melinda pointed to Bettina's killer being the same height
2. When Earl saw Jenny eat the chocolate egg, he realized someone had been hiding behind the draperies
3. Finbar heard the dogs barking in alarm

DISPENSATION: LOUANNE WELLER IN MAXIMUM SECURITY PRISON FOR CRIMINALLY INSANE FOR LIFE!

Height - Weight - Hair

		Height	Weight	Hair
Dead	Bettina	5'2"	110	long black, straight
??	Louanne	5'3"	110	lt blond, bent waves
NO	Elly	5'3"	125	lt blond, bent waves
NO	Jo	5'6"	145	dk auburn, long
NO	Aubrey	5'7"	145	dk brown, wavy, long
??	Eva	5'8"	125	honey blond, bent waves
??NO	Melinda	5'8"	140	s'berry blond, bent waves
NO	Jeanette	5'9"	180	md. Brown, blunt bob

Heights - Bettina to "Bent" Blond Hair

Bettina - 5'2" **HAT**

Louanne - 5'3" **HAT**

Eva - 5'8" **STAR**

NOT EVA!!!

Melinda

Hat Hat Star

About the Author

MICHELLE BUSBY is a Florida transplant who lived for a time in California where she was an actress, singer, and writer and a member of the American Federation of Television and Radio Artists (AFTRA). A life-long thespian and former teacher, she has performed on stage since her teens and has written plays, musicals, and novels for all ages under the pen names of Mickey MorningGlory, Mickey Middleton, and M.M. Busby. An avid puzzle solver, mystery buff, and self-proclaimed foodie, she combines her talents into one large pot where she stews up her Holmes and Watson Culinary Whodunits. She is a member of *Sisters in Crime (SinC), Women's Fiction Writers Association (WFWA), National Association of Independent Writers and Editors (NAIWE), American Copy Editors Society (ACES), and Society of Children's Book Writers and Illustrators (SCBWI).* Michelle lives in Florida with her family.

Readers can visit Michelle at patentprintbooks.com.

Printed in Great Britain
by Amazon